SPEED METAL BLUES

DAVE STANTON

LaSalle Davis Books

ISBN: 0989603121
ISBN 13: 9780989603126

ALSO BY DAVE STANTON

Stateline

Dying for the Highlife

Dark Ice

Hard Prejudice

FOR MORE INFORMATION, VISIT DAVE STANTON'S WEBSITE:

DanRenoNovels.com

Cover art by *Steve Whan*

LaSalle Davis Books

For Heidi

1

WHEN I FINALLY TRACKED down Billy Morrison, he was in the middle of the mosh pit at Zeke's Bar off Highway 50. There must have been thirty sweat-drenched men in there with him, stomping and flailing to the music, their violent energy like a rebellion against humanity. I assumed they considered this dancing, but it looked more like a gang brawl. The death metal band on the small stage pounded out a relentless assault on the ears, the singer's guttural growls imploring the wild-eyed participants to maim and kill the weak. My initial instinct told me to retreat to my truck and wait for Morrison to leave. Instead, I waded into the churning melee of knees and fists. That was my first mistake.

I caught Morrison from behind and jerked his arm into a police lock. "You're under arrest," I shouted in his ear, and started pushing him toward the exit. When he resisted, I cranked his wrist hard into his back, while he yelled something I couldn't hear over the deafening wall of sound blasting from the band's stacked cabinets. I'd almost steered him out of the ruckus when some dude jumped on my back. The man wasn't heavy, and I probably could have carried him and still walked Morrison outside, but he got his arm tight around my neck. "I'm gonna kill you, bitch," he screamed, his breath reeking of rotting meat and liquor. I drove an elbow into his ribs, but his grip only grew tighter. Cursing, I let Morrison go and peeled the man's arm from my throat. Then I turned and busted his nose with a straight right. That was my second mistake.

Within a second I was on the ground, trying to defend against a storm of boots and fists. I rolled into a ball and covered up the best I could, but Morrison was intent on kicking me in the face. I dodged a few shots, then he connected with a glancing blow, his heel gouging my forehead. "All right, then," I said, and yanked my Beretta .40 caliber pistol from beneath my coat. When Morrison tried to kick me again, I shot him in the ankle. The Beretta's report was barely audible over the band.

I scrambled to my feet and waved the gun, but the musicians wouldn't quit playing until I shot the guitar player's amp.

"That was uncool, asshole," the lead singer said.

"Too bad," I said, and put a bullet in the mixing board behind him. A loud buzz came from the speakers, then the board sparked and went dead, a wisp of smoke rising from the expired circuitry. The place became quiet, except for Morrison's cries of pain.

"This man is coming with me," I said, grabbing Morrison's good ankle and dragging him toward the door.

"Bullshit he is," another man said. He was a good six feet and two hundred pounds, nearly my size. A loose-fitting white T-shirt hung off his torso, and the black shorts he wore went well past his knees. His arms were a blur of tattoos, as were all the men's surrounding me.

I ignored him and continued lugging Morrison toward the exit. The man followed, trying to get in my face, but I raised my gun and he slowed. A different man tried to rush me from the side, but stopped in his tracks when he found himself staring into the large bore of the Beretta.

"Next man that comes at me is gonna get shot," I said.

"You're messing with HCU, motherfucker," the first man said, displaying an assortment of misshapen and crooked teeth.

I backed out the saloon-style doors and pulled Morrison down the four wooden stairs to the parking lot, holding the moshers at bay with the automatic. They followed as I dragged Morrison toward my truck, and I thought I'd likely have to shoot at least one in the leg to discourage the rest. Then I saw flashing lights, and Sheriff Marcus Grier's squad car bounced into the lot. The gangbangers slowly retreated.

"What the hell is going on here?" Grier said, stepping from his car, his hand on his holstered revolver.

"Good timing, Sheriff," I said. "This here is Billy Morrison. He's got warrants in New Jersey for rape, robbery, and assault."

"You got paper on him?"

"Yes, sir. He skipped two month ago."

"What happened to his leg?" Grier said, his black skin shining in the moonlight.

"He fuckin' shot me," Morrison hissed through gritted teeth. His white sock was soaked through and dripping with blood.

"Mr. Reno?" Grier said.

"His buddies jumped me." I gestured to a group of about ten men standing in front of Zeke's. They glared back, arms crossed, feet planted wide. One shot his arm straight out, middle finger extended.

"Did you have to shoot him?"

"I could have just curled up and let them kick the shit out of me, I suppose."

Grier let the remark slide. "That gash over your eye is bleeding pretty bad," he said. "It probably needs a couple stitches." He reached in his car and handed me a wad of paper towels.

"Do you know any of them?" I asked.

"The big guy with the bad teeth is Joe Norton. He's their ringleader."

I eyed Norton as he walked toward us. "He is, huh?"

"That's right. They call themselves HCU. Stands for Hard Core United."

Grier went to his cruiser and began talking on the radio. Joe Norton knelt down to Billy Morrison, who lay holding his ankle. He whispered in his ear and they clasped hands. Then Norton locked his eyes on me.

"You screwed over my friend pretty good. You know that, right?"

"Your friend raped a woman. He's got to pay for it."

"You don't know shit, understand? Billy was framed. Try that on for size. What's your name?"

"My name?" I looked over at the sheriff, who was still occupied with his radio. "Chuck U. Farley."

"Hey, I get it. You're a funny guy. You live around here?"

"Do you?" I said. Despite his oversized T-shirt, I could see that Norton had spent some serious hours in a weight room. His biceps stretched his cotton sleeves tight when he bent his arms, and his forearms rippled with veins underneath his tats.

"As a matter of fact, I do. I'm what you would call a permanent resident. Me and all my friends there," he said.

"You must be new in town."

"That's right. I love it up here, man. The mountains, Lake Tahoe—freakin' beautiful, man. The only problem I see is a lack of poontang."

"Try the whorehouses in Nevada."

He narrowed his eyes and spat. "Is that supposed to be funny?"

"Take it anyway you want," I said.

One of his group walked behind my pickup truck and began writing my license plate number on a matchbook. I started toward him.

"You don't like it we got your license plate?" Norton said, right behind me. I spun around and he cupped a match and lit a cigarette. His eyes were a pale brown, and each was shaped differently, as if they belonged to separate faces. He smirked and patted me on the shoulder. When he spoke, his breath was rife with beer and testosterone.

"Your life is about to get real interesting, pal," he said. Then he blew a stream of smoke in my face.

I could feel the cords in my arms straining against the skin as the beginnings of an old and familiar refrain began playing in my head. *Walk away. Don't empower your adversary by playing into his threat.* But my hands squeezed into fists, and in my mind I saw myself punch Joe Norton so hard he left his feet and rotated in the air.

At that moment an ambulance bounced up the curb, and Sheriff Grier walked to where I stood face to face with Norton. Grier told Norton to back away from the scene so the paramedics could attend to Morrison.

"Making new friends, I see," Grier said, smiling, his sheriffs cap too small for his jumbo-sized head.

"Have these guys caused you much trouble yet?" I said.

"Nothing major, so far. Why, what did Norton say to you?"

"Not much. But I don't think we'll ever be best buddies."

"Imagine that."

• • •

By the time Grier took my statement and determined my actions were in self-defense, it was nearly midnight. I drove the two miles to my house, checking my rear view mirror when I turned from the highway onto my street. The last of the season's snowpack lining the pavement had melted away, leaving the neighborhood pitch black except for a porch light or two. It was late April, and though the ski resorts surrounding Lake Tahoe had closed, the evenings still felt like winter. I parked in my garage, went inside, and threw a log on the embers in the stove. The black coat I favored while working was ripped and streaked with dirt. I threw it in my laundry basket, but it would probably need to be replaced.

I drenched the scrapes on my face with alcohol and applied a butterfly bandage to the wound over my eye. Then I made a whiskey-seven and drank it while I sat on the couch icing a bruise on my elbow. When the drink was gone I moved to the desk below the large window in my living room, and wrote an e-mail to the bail bondsman in New Jersey who hired me to bring in Billy Morrison and a known associate of Morrison's, a man of mixed Asian and white blood named Jason Loohan. It was the first job I'd taken since renewing my bounty-hunting license a couple months back, and posting my name on an Internet site frequented by bondsmen.

Billy Morrison had plainly surfaced in South Lake Tahoe, but this was not the case with Jason Loohan. There was no evidence he'd ever left New Jersey. The only rationale for Loohan being in the area was his history with Morrison. The two were reportedly close friends and had been arrested together on three separate occasions, the most recent being the New York home invasion for which Morrison was accused of rape. For his role, Loohan was charged with rape and sodomy, as well as armed robbery.

I still had no clue as to the whereabouts of Loohan. As for Morrison, he'd been an easy man to find, but a difficult one to catch. First, he gave me the slip in a crowded casino in Stateline, Nevada. I caught up with him the next day after following his car into a residential area, only to lose him when he pulled over and sprinted into the woods. His trail went cold for a week, and when I found him again, he outran me in a 1970 Chevy Chevelle I thought was probably supercharged. I was beginning to think I'd lost my touch, which might have been part of the reason for my recklessness at Zeke's. Pulling Morrison out of the mosh pit was plain stupid, and my injuries were probably well deserved. Regardless, Morrison would soon be on a plane back east, likely to face twenty years at Sing Sing.

I eased out of my chair and mixed another highball, promising myself it would be my last of the night. When I came back to my PC, I logged on to a site requiring multiple passwords. As a licensed private investigator and bounty hunter, I subscribed to a service providing access to information typically only available to law enforcement agencies. I typed in Jason Loohan's name, hoping there might be an update, something to suggest he'd come out west with Morrison. I came up empty, then ran a search for Joe Norton.

Soon I was staring at his weirdly disconnected eyes, choppy brown hair, and a set of teeth that grew from his gums at every angle.

Norton had spent most of his twenty-eight years in New Jersey. He was a high school dropout whose record began with a shoplifting arrest at age fourteen. His activities escalated from there—burglary at sixteen, a pot dealing bust at seventeen, drunk driving and assault at eighteen, and then he did three years in Trenton State Prison for a purse snatching that left an elderly woman seriously injured. After that he stayed clean for a few years, until he was arrested and charged with manslaughter for his role in a gang brawl that left a man dead. He was acquitted due to lack of evidence.

Before I retired for the night, I sprinkled a couple handfuls of two-inch nails on the street in front of my home. Then I tied a length of fishing line to the pine tree next to my driveway, stretched it ten feet into the street, and nailed it to the asphalt. After checking the locks on my doors and windows, I set the Beretta in my nightstand drawer and went to sleep.

• • •

I woke later than usual the next morning. After starting a pot of coffee, I fried three strips of bacon, then grabbed a granola bar and went out to my back deck for breakfast. The sun was already bright in the blue sky, warming the redwood table where I often sat to eat or read. I looked out over the meadow beyond the low fence separating my lot from miles of federally protected forestland. A family of beavers was building a dam in the creek that ran a hundred feet from my property. I kept an eye on their progress, hoping no flooding would result. The stream was high with snowmelt, and sections easily crossed by foot in the summer were now four feet deep and running hard and fast.

When I finished eating, I took my coffee cup and walked out to the street. The fishing line I'd strung was broken. I looked up and down the avenue. My neighbor's homes were quiet and still. A large black dog came trotting down the street. I called him over and scratched his head for a minute. Then I backed my truck out from my garage and drove toward Highway 50.

It only took ten minutes to find what I was looking for. Behind a gas station, a few miles from where I lived, sat a car with two flat tires folded under its rims. I can't say I was surprised at the car's make and model—it was a 1970 Chevy Chevelle. I had run the car's plates before, after Morrison outran me. It belonged to Joe Norton.

2

MARCUS GRIER RETURNED TO the station from his lunch break to find two plainclothes cops waiting for him in the lobby. They were men Grier had met before, perhaps six months ago. He couldn't remember their names, but vaguely recalled they were recently hired transplants from out of town, and worked for Douglas County PD, a few miles up the road in Nevada.

"Got a minute, Sheriff?" one asked.

"Not really, but come on back." They followed Grier through the card-activated door, and down a hallway to his office.

"What can I do for you fellows?" Grier said, sitting at his desk and frowning at the stack of paperwork left from the morning.

"Not a lot, Marcus," said the larger man, sitting without invitation. His eyes were bulbous under meaty lids, the skin heavily freckled. Grier stared at him, thinking he bore an uncanny resemblance to a large fish. The man picked up a framed photo on Grier's desk, studied it for a moment, then smiled and put it back down. "You got a good-looking wife," he said.

"Excuse me?"

"I'm just paying you a compliment." The man stood, walked over to the window, and stared out at the sunny afternoon. He was tall, but despite his large frame he moved with a casual grace, as if he'd be equally comfortable on a football field or a dance floor.

"God, nothing like Tahoe in the spring," he said to his partner, a slim man of uncertain race with a pockmarked complexion and eyes that didn't blink.

Grier shook his head, an incredulous expression taking hold on his face. He placed his hands on his desk, his thick neck threatening to burst the buttons on his collar. "I've got a busy day, men. You mind getting to the point?"

"Now, slow down there, champ," fish face said.

"I'm not sure what you yahoos think you're doing here," Grier said, his words coming from deep in his throat. "State your business. And you can start with your names."

"Why, of course, Sheriff. I'm Pete Saxton, and my partner there, that's Dave Boyce."

"What do you want here in California?"

"You had a shooting in a bar last night," Dave Boyce said. His skin was coarse, and the crow's feet around his eyes flared when he squinted at Grier. "A man was shot in the ankle, and from what I hear, the perp admitted his guilt and is still on the street."

Grier straightened the pile of papers on his desk. "You want to read my incident report?"

"Yeah," Saxton said.

"Sorry, you can't. I don't know what you think you're doing here, but I've got work to do. If that doesn't sit well with you, tell Don Cunningham to call me."

"Old man Cunningham? I don't think so. He had a heart attack last weekend. Looks like he gonna retire." Saxton smiled and made a popping sound with his lips.

"If that's true, it's news to me," Grier said.

Boyce stepped forward, a pungent aroma wafting from his clothes. Apparently he believed an overdose of cologne was the solution for his body odor.

"What's your deal with Dan Reno, Grier? You two queer for each other?"

"Get out of here, you jackasses," Grier said.

"Come on, Dave," Saxton said. "We're wasting our time."

After they left Grier checked his blood pressure with a portable device he strapped to his wrist. Then he opened the window and turned on his fan, trying to blow the stink out of his office.

• • •

Not far from the Nevada border and the casinos, a collection of apartment buildings occupied a cul-de-sac off Pioneer Trail. Originally built to house the low wage laborers who serviced the tourism industry in South Lake Tahoe, the structures had been there as long as anyone could remember. The apartments were typically inhabited by hotel maids, casino janitors, and welfare recipients. Over time, the tenants had become almost entirely Mexican.

The Pine Mountain apartment complex was configured in a square, its four rows of units surrounding a large common area. In better days there had been a swimming pool in the common, but it had long been cemented over. Still, the residents liked to gather there; it was a favorite place for children to build snowmen in the winter, and in the warmer months there would be barbeque parties, lively events with mariachi bands, colorful balloons, and piñatas.

But in the last year, the common area had become the turf of the Diablos Sierra gang. To many, it seemed the gang had sprung from the streets of South Lake Tahoe. Few knew that the dozen *cholos* had actually been sent from Juarez, El Paso's notoriously violent sister city. Their mission was to establish control of the drug trade in the communities around Lake Tahoe, and then to expand their presence to Reno, a larger market controlled by a rival Mexican gang.

Sixteen-year-old Juan Perez looked out from the sliding glass door of his small apartment. A handful of gang members sat at the table in the square, drinking forties and throwing knives at a target they had spray painted on a huge pine tree. The leader of the gang, a man Juan knew only as Rodrigo, flashed his knife and threw a bull's eye from twenty paces, the silver blade quivering in the bark.

Juan watched them, knowing he couldn't be seen from behind the glass. The *cholos* were never without red bandanas covering their heads, stuffed in their belt loops, or sometimes tied around their upper arms. Within a few minutes, two white teenagers walked into the common. Cash was exchanged, and one of the teenagers shoved something in his pocket. Probably weed, or maybe crank. It didn't matter to Juan. He never touched the stuff.

After lunch, Juan went out to the small patio outside his unit to repair a flat tire on his bicycle. His eyes carefully avoided the gangbangers milling around the table in the common. They were behaving as they usually did, flashing signs, their beer bottles prominently displayed. The sun shined warmly, promising a fine day, one that might have been perfect for a gathering. But no residents congregated in the square, save for the men with their bandanas.

Beyond the roofline of the apartment building, the Sierra Nevada rose five thousand feet, the whitebark pines and red fir standing against a spring sky so blue and clear it seemed magical. Juan had the day off and decided to test himself by seeing how high he could ride into the mountains. He'd patched the tube and was pumping up the tire when he saw a man enter the common.

The man was slender and of average height, and he wore loose-fitting jeans low on his hips, the way some of the boys did at Juan's high school. His upper body was huddled in a cotton jacket, his face obscured by a hood. Juan watched him walk toward the gangsters. Though he dressed like a teenager, something about his gait made him seem older.

From his patio Juan could make out bits of the murmured conversation taking place at the picnic table. He didn't pay much attention—he assumed it was a drug buy. But then the quiet morning erupted in loud curses and activity. The hooded man held a gun and a badge and shouted at one *cholo* that he was under arrest. The other gangbangers, except for one, ran off in different directions. A scuffle ensued, but soon the cop had his suspect cuffed and lying on the ground. Rodrigo, the *Mero Mero* of the Diablos Sierra, stood beside his prone comrade, his brow creased deeply over his black eyes.

"You know what would happen to you in my town?" he said to the cop. "You would be found headless in the gutter. Dogs would eat your guts."

"Yeah? Well this ain't your town, bean boy, it's mine," the man said. His head no longer covered by the hood, Juan could see his grayish, pockmarked face. "Step aside," he said. "I need to read your *amigo* his rights."

A moment later a tall white man strode into the common. Juan watched him approach the picnic table, thinking the casual bounce to his step seemed somehow incongruous with the situation.

"Everything under control here?" he said.

"Yeah. Let's go." Pock Face began leading the handcuffed suspect away.

The tall white man, his eyes protruding from under the mottled flesh on his forehead, pointed two fingers at Rodrigo. "What's your problem? You look like someone stole your chimichanga."

Rodrigo didn't reply for a long moment. Then he sat on the table and leaned back on his elbows. "No, everything is fine, homes," he said, his face transformed into that of a man at peace with himself and his world. "I'm just enjoying the beautiful weather."

"Let me see your ID."

"No problem, man." He flipped open his wallet and handed a card to the big man with the fish eyes.

"Are you working, Rodrigo?"

"No, man, not yet. I'm still looking for a job, see?"

"You need to find one soon. Otherwise, immigration will put you on a bus and send you back to Mexico."

"I don't think so. My green card means I'm a lawful, permanent resident."

Fish Eyes stared off toward the mountains. A hawk glided out of the sky, floating on the current until it was lost in the shadows.

"That's an interesting interpretation." The big cop smiled and joined his partner.

Juan watched the two policemen escort their prisoner out of the common. At first he was gratified to see the drug dealer arrested, then his stomach roiled with a sense of apprehension and foreboding so severe he had to sit down. He closed his eyes, remembering how his family lived in fear of the local *policia*. The Mexican officers wielded their power like a club, extorting and raping at will. The manner of the American cops brought the memories flooding back—the callous abuse of authority, the casual destroying of innocent lives, and the hunger for power and money that fueled it all. Juan had been told American police were honest, trustworthy servants of the people. When he looked at the two cops leaving the square, he knew he'd been lied to.

3

IT WAS MY HABIT to jog to the local gym and pump iron on Sunday afternoons, but the bumps and bruises I'd suffered the night before were ailing me to the point that exercise was improbable. Instead I headed over to Whiskey Dick's for a dose of old fashioned pain medication. I'd just finished my second bourbon-seven when my cell rang.

"Hey, Dirt," the voice said. My old buddy, Cody Gibbons.

"I'm heading your direction," he said. "I've got to file some paper work at the state clerk's office in Carson City. Some bullshit about a tax lien from that job I did in Vegas."

"You mean the one when you slept with the mayor's daughter and ran into his car when you dropped her off?"

"Yeah, yeah. They're claiming my insurance was lapsed. It's all a big misunderstanding."

"How, if you don't mind me asking, did you end up seducing the daughter of Las Vegas's top public official?"

"Me seducing her? Christ, it was the other way around. And you make it sound like I defiled some young, innocent schoolgirl. This broad was a thirty-year-old nymphomaniac."

"Where are you now?" I said.

"A few miles outside Sacramento. I should be in South Lake by seven or so. What are you doing for the next few days?"

"You between jobs?"

"Something like that."

"Call me when you get into town."

I shook my head and hit off my drink. Then, out of the corner of my eye, I saw two men take a seat at the far end of the bar. They both wore T-shirts and baggy shorts hanging to mid-shin, leaving only a narrow strip of exposed skin above their white socks. I swiveled away from them and focused my attention on the TV in the opposite corner of the room.

The middle-aged lady bartender asked me if I was ready for a refill. I declined, and listened as she approached her new customers.

"Gimme a Bud and a shot of brown water," one said loudly.

"Same here," said the second man. His voice was abrupt, the syllables merged and almost indecipherable.

"Brown water? You mean whiskey?"

"Goddamn right I do."

"Any particular brand?"

"Yeah, the eighty proof kind."

I looked out the window, watching the occasional car pass by. Sunlight filtered into the bar and cast a pattern across the wooden floorboards. A newly divorced man who worked as a plumber shot pool, alone with his thoughts.

"Hey, lady, bring us another round over here!"

"Yeah, like pronto!" said the second man. He had a speech impediment of some kind.

I turned toward them. From where I sat, I could see the man with the odd voice was of average height and had sandy-colored hair. He looked back at me and I noticed his shoulders seemed deformed. I stared at him, more out of curiosity than anything else.

"You got some problem?" he said, his words slapping at the air between us. The bar went quiet.

"Not really. Do you?"

He pushed himself off his barstool and walked to where I sat, his arms swinging at an unnatural angle. His friend, slightly taller, his hair buzz cut and a ring in his nostril, followed behind him. I sat facing out from the bar.

"What you looking at?" the sandy-haired man said. His shoulder joints were turned inward, causing his hands to hang with the palms facing to his rear, like an ape's. It wasn't something that could have been the result of an accident—it must have been a genetic deformity.

"This is a quiet, neighborhood lounge," I said. "Especially on Sundays. You want to get drunk and loud, take it somewhere else."

"What are you, a wannabe cop?" said the one with the ring hanging from his nose. His arms were crisscrossed with tattoos, and I recognized him as one of the pack from Zeke's mosh pit.

I looked at the two men and decided this was not what I wanted for my afternoon. I threw some cash on the bar and stood to leave. "Knock yourselves out, fellas," I said.

"Hold on a second," the taller man said. "I want you to see something." He grabbed my empty cocktail glass, a short, thick-bodied variety many bars no longer used. "Rabbit," he said, addressing his friend. He turned the tumbler upside down on the bar and backed away.

Rabbit stepped forward. He looked at me with an expression I think was meant to be intimidating, but one of his eyes wandered, ruining the effect. I shrugged and suppressed a smile. But then he whirled his arm overhead, the elbow locked, and slammed his palm down on the glass. The impact sounded like two cars colliding at high speed. Shards of glass flew like shrapnel, and the handful of patrons at the bar jumped from their stools.

"What the ever livin' hell?" the bartender shrieked, hurrying to where Rabbit was picking slivers of glass from his blood-flecked palm. The pulverized remains of the tumbler were imbedded in the lacquered surface of the bar.

"That was pretty impressive," I said. "I'd shake hands with you, but I think I'll pass."

Rabbit barked out a short laugh. "Pretty impressive," he repeated. "Right, Tom?"

"Nice job," the man said, patting Rabbit on the shoulder. Then he looked at me, a crooked grin beginning on his mug.

"Hey, buddy," he said, "me and my pals think you're a yump-chugging queer bait, and we invite you to join us at Zeke's for the show next week. But we don't expect to see you, because we think you're probably too much of a pussy to leave home without your gun."

"Your pals? You mean HCU?"

He peeled back his sleeve to show the words "Hard Core United" tattooed on his shoulder. The capital letters were inked dark and bold.

"I'm calling 911," the bartender said.

"Good for you, hag," Tom said. He turned and headed for the exit. Rabbit looked confused for a second, then straightened and followed him out of the bar, but first he gave me a short wave, as if we were friends.

I walked outside and watched them climb into a black Buick sedan with faded paint and a long key scratch down one side. As they drove away in a cloud of dirt and smoke, I jotted down the license number. The bartender came out front, and I asked her for a cigarette.

"Do you know those jerks?" she asked.

"No, not really."

"I swear I'm gonna start keeping my .38 underneath the bar. If those losers ever come back I'll straighten their shit out."

"Now, take it easy, Pam."

"What? Screw that."

A minute later Marcus Grier pulled up. He turned off his bubble lights when he saw me leaning against the building. The citizenry of South Lake Tahoe generally regarded Grier as a polite and friendly public servant. For the most part, it was an accurate assessment. But if pushed, or perhaps caught at the wrong moment, there was a side to Grier that could be both unexpected and alarming. Grier had been raised in the Deep South, and once, after we'd met over stiff drinks to discuss a case, he spoke to me of his past. It left no doubt in my mind that beneath his outwardly benign personality, hot coals of rage smoldered in corners of his psyche he preferred not to visit.

He walked toward where the bartender and I stood, his down-turned lips creasing his heavy jowls, his eyes dark beneath the shadow of his cap. His body, resembling an overfilled inner tube, rendered him the butt of occasional jokes. Anyone who ever saw him in a physical altercation knew better.

His eyes flashed at me and he shook his head. "What's going on here?" he asked the bartender.

"A couple white trash a-holes came in and tried to pick a fight. One broke a glass on the bar. Come see the mark it made. It will probably need to be sanded and re-stained."

We went into the bar, and Grier studied the damage to the bar top.

"These guys were real weirdos," she said. "The one who broke the glass looked like some kind of circus freak. I think maybe he was a mental retard."

Grier finished taking her statement, and I went with him to his cruiser.

"It was a couple of the HCU boys. Here's their license number," I said, handing him a cocktail napkin. He tossed it on his dashboard, then crossed his arms and leaned on the car. We both stared out over Lake Tahoe. The sky was cloudless, the stone faces on the far side of the lake streaked with snow. The sun burned white against the blue of the sky, the heat pleasant after the long winter.

"I never thought it would be like this when I moved here," he said.

"Like what?"

He didn't respond, then he shook his head, and when he looked at me, something about his expression made me remember that Grier was a man with a wife and children, considerations I might never have.

"Listen," he said, getting into his squad car and starting the engine, "if any of those gangbangers mess with you, call me—no one else, got it? And another thing. Don't provoke them. I've got enough problems."

"Why would *I* provoke *them*?" I said, but he was already pulling away, his tires crunching on the gravel, the sun reflecting off his windshield in silver bursts.

• • •

A few minutes later I returned to my home, an updated three-bedroom A-frame a mile off the lake and within staggering distance of Whiskey Dick's. I was at my desk, idly browsing the Internet and contemplating whether to have another drink and resume my earlier buzz, when my cell rang with a number I didn't recognize.

"Is this Mr. Reno?"

"Yes."

"Hi, this is Juan Perez. Remember me?"

"Of course, Juan. How are you?"

"I'm fine," he said, then hesitated.

"Well, what's up, my man?"

"They assigned us a project at school for career day," he blurted. "We need to bring an adult to talk to the class about their job. Most kids are bringing their mom or dad."

"Oh," I said. Juan was a teenager who worked at The Redwood Tavern, a place I sometimes went for a steak or drinks. I'd hired him a month ago to help me build a fence. He was a small kid, and I'd been hesitant since it was heavy, physical work, but he'd busted his ass, damn near outworked me.

"Do you think you could talk to my class?"

"Hell, Juan, I don't know what I'd say to a bunch of high school kids. Are you sure I'm who you want for this?"

"I think they'd think it was cool hearing from a private eye."

"Ahh," I said. I almost asked him about his parents before I remembered they were back in Mexico. He was living here with his older sister, relying on their combined income to survive.

"Okay, I guess so," I said. "When is it?"

"Two weeks from now."

"All right. What do I need to do to be ready?"

"I have a bunch of papers for you to read."

"How about if you drop them off at my house?"

"Will you be there tomorrow morning?"

"Yeah, I should be around."

We hung up, and I stared at my blank computer screen, wondering how I might whitewash my career to pass it off as respectable to a room full of sixteen-year-olds. The reality was I worked sporadically—my ability to drum up business was questionable, on a good day. If not for the good fortune of pulling a bag stuffed with cash out of a burning house last fall, I'd probably have been forced to pursue other career options, most likely in San Jose, where I used to live.

Playing the role of the responsible adult, I would probably discourage the kids from my profession, or at least tell them to definitely seek a firm that offered full health benefits. As an independent contractor, I paid my own health insurance, and I made damn sure to stay current on the payments. In the course of my work, I'd nearly lost two fingers to frostbite, my life had been saved by body armor at least twice, and I'd been involved in more physical altercations than I could remember. In the process, I'd killed six men. Seven, if I included a bail skip who ran in front of a bus while I was chasing him.

I left my desk and washed the few dishes in my sink. Besides health and financial risks, the profession was also hell on relationships. Or maybe that was just an excuse. My first and only wife left me when I was drinking heavily after first killing a man. My longest relationship after that was with an ex-prostitute fifteen years my junior, who lived with me here in Tahoe for six months before running off. I kept the plates and glasses she bought neatly arranged in my kitchen cupboard, the sole reminder my home had once enjoyed a woman's touch.

The best romantic prospect I had now was a curvy brunette named Candi who lived six hours down the road in Elko. She stayed with me for a week during the winter, and we hit the local ski resort every day. I thought we made a hell of a team, her on a snowboard and me skiing on the new Rossignols I'd bought with my windfall. We had talked of her moving to Tahoe permanently, but that was when we lay naked on my crushed sheets, aglow with booze and sexual chemistry. The conversation didn't continue once we were sober and dressed. But she still took my calls, so I hadn't lost hope we could work something out. Hope's cheap, so I indulge myself.

· · ·

I swept the nails from the street and mowed my lawn, which had grown in nicely in the few weeks since the snowpack melted. After watering the flowers lining the walkway, I opened an energy drink and began working out on the bench press in my garage. I had just finished the sixth set of ten when my cell rang.

"I'm just coming over Spooner Pass," Cody Gibbons said. "You have dinner yet?"

"Nope."

"Why don't you meet me at Zeke's Pit? I haven't had real Texas brisket since I was there last. No one knows how to make it in San Jose."

"I got bad news, Cody. Zeke's restaurant is closed down."

"What?"

"Zeke Papas passed away a few months back and left the joint to his son. The prick shut down the dining room and gutted the bar. The place now hosts death-rock concerts."

"You're kidding, right?"

"I wish I was. Why don't you stop at Armadillo Willy's in Stateline and bring some grub over to my place?"

"Aw, shit," he sighed. "All right, I'll see you in half an hour."

I set the phone down and removed a five-pound iron plate from each side of my weight bar. Despite being old and rusty, the weights were reliable and unchanging, unlike California's restaurants and bars. Having lived in northern California most of my life, I'd witnessed almost all my favorite hangouts close down. Apparently there wasn't much market left for dark, ramshackle joints. They'd been replaced by strip-mall eateries offering Asian-fusion cuisine, sushi, and obscure varieties of ethnic food I had no interest in trying.

But business is business, and what's the point in complaining about a society that gives the public what it wants? In the case of Zeke's, though, their barbequed fare was popular and considered top notch. Even on weeknights the joint was packed. The shuttering of the restaurant seemed not only unnecessary, but abrupt and pointless.

I lay on my bench and pumped out another ten reps, then checked my refrigerator and drove out to the local convenience store for a case of beer. Cody could make six-packs vanish in minutes.

When I returned home, he had just pulled up and was climbing out of his red, dual-cab Dodge truck. He wore tennis shoes, faded blue jeans, and a gray Utah State sweatshirt stretched tight around his shoulders. He waved at me with his free hand, the other clutching a plastic bag heavy with take-out food. At six-five and around three hundred, Cody's physical presence reminded me of the abominable snowman, but he'd trimmed and neatened his red beard since I'd last seen him, lessening the effect. He hadn't changed his hairstyle, though—the blond mop covering his head was still straw-like and unruly.

"Dirty Double Crossin' Dan," he greeted me, the nickname resulting from a drunken episode at a pickup bar at least fifteen years ago. Cody claimed I had moved in on a woman he was hitting on, and when he came back from the men's room, I'd already left with her. I had no recollection of the night in question.

"You look like you're staying busy," he said, nodding at the bandage above my eye. "Grab my duffel bag, would you?"

"How's everything, man?"

"Just living the dream," he said, as we walked inside. "I finished a case for Covie and Associates last week. They're defending a Russian mobster, and they hired me to dig up the dirt on the prosecution's chief witness, a twenty-two-year-old low-level Mafia douchebag. I tail him for five days, and he's got call girls running in and out of his place like he can't keep his dork in his pants for ten minutes without dialing up a blow job. Then he and his goombahs head to Vegas, and I bugged their hotel room. After two days there, you should have seen the report I wrote. It was the longest I've ever written—like a damn novel."

He paused, set the chow on the kitchen table, and walked over to my refrigerator. I heard a beer can open as I put plates and silverware on the table.

"What about you? Anything exciting?" He belched loudly and crushed the can in his fist.

"I told you I got my bounty hunting license renewed."

"And?" He cracked another beer while I began opening containers of potato salad, coleslaw, brisket, and cornbread.

"I captured a skip out of New Jersey last night. I had to pull him out of the mosh pit at Zeke's. Unfortunately, he was surrounded by a bunch of his pals."

"Things get a little rough?"

"I had to shoot him."

"Dead?"

"No, but he ain't gonna ever walk the same."

"What a shame."

"So, earlier today I was trying to relax over at Whiskey Dick's, and a couple of them showed up and tried to start something."

"Anything more than you could handle?"

"No."

He came around and sat at the table. "You want to go to the casino and play some poker tonight?"

"Sure, I'm up for a few hands."

I thought I heard the sound of a car idling out front, something I typically would have ignored. Though it was probably just a neighbor, I pushed myself out of my chair and went over to the front window. I peered out at a street empty and deep in shadow. In the distance I could see the sun clinging to a steep ridge over the lake, burning atop the granite face like a slice of molten steel. Stars were visible up high, but lower the sky was a florescent blue, glowing with the last of the day's heat. The small swath of lake visible from my window was still glittering in sunlight, the curl of the swells like silver confetti.

The rumble of a motor grew louder, and the same faded, black Buick I'd seen earlier in the day crept into view on the opposite side of the street. The muffler was either shot or the car had a high-performance exhaust system. It was too dark to see the driver, or if there was more than one person in the vehicle.

Cody thrust his mug next to mine, his hand on my shoulder.

"What's this?"

"We got visitors."

The Buick pulled forward and stopped, hidden from sight by Cody's truck. The driver killed the engine, and I heard the clunk of a door closing. A man's upper body appeared.

"You recognize him?" Cody said.

"Yeah, from last night, and earlier today. Let's go see what he wants."

We went out the front door. The man named Tom, the one from Whiskey Dick's a few hours before, stood near the back of Cody's truck.

"What's your interest with my rig?" Cody said. Tom appeared to be taking down the license plate on a small notepad.

"Nice ride you got," he said, glancing up and then back down to finish his scribbling.

Cody snatched the notepad from Tom's hand. When Tom reached out to try and take it back, Cody shoved him hard in the chest. Tom stumbled and fell to the pavement, then the doors of the Buick flew open and three men in white T-shirts, one of them Rabbit, jumped out. They tried to circle Cody and me, but Rabbit's eyes were wide in confusion, and he hovered near Tom as if he was a child unwilling to let go of his parent's sleeve. The other two men, average-size fellows, were trying to act tough, grimacing, spitting, flexing their muscles, but I didn't buy it. Cody feinted toward them and they scurried back, and then, embarrassed, resumed their positions.

I stepped up to Tom as he scrambled to his feet. "You sure you want to push this, buddy?" I said. "I don't like your odds."

"HCU takes care of its own, dickhead." He curled his lips in a snarl and his nostrils flared. But the belligerence of his tone was one more interested in saving face than fighting.

"You're starting to piss me off, Tom. Haul your sorry ass out of here," I said.

"I—I gonna kick your ass!" Rabbit said suddenly, one eye full of rage and the other fixed in its socket. "Right, Tom?"

Tom led Rabbit back to the Buick and waved his partners to the car. Once they were safely inside, Tom started the motor, but a moment later he opened the door. He stood, grabbed his crotch, and shot us the bone. "Have a nice night, pole smokers!" he yelled. Then he slammed the door shut and mashed the gas pedal, the gangbangers hooting and gesturing at us as they lurched forward in a shriek of burning rubber and tire smoke that left a single black strip down the street for as far as I could see.

"Come on, our dinner's getting cold," I said.

•　•　•

We finished eating and I cleared the mess of cartons and paper plates from the table while Cody sat at my desk, typing with two fingers and scanning the Internet for information on Hard Core United.

"Interesting little gang," he said. "They're based on the East Coast, and claim to be against drugs, alcohol, and racism."

"Against alcohol? They've been drinking like fish when I've seen them." I was on my couch, clicking back and forth between a boxing match and an old action movie starring Charles Bronson. "What do they do for money?"

"Here's a new one," Cody said, his eyes locked on the screen. "Their main gig appears to be shaking down heavy metal concerts. Not Led Zeppelin or Metallica, but the real death-rock stuff. Hardcore metal, they call it. Apparently hundreds of these bands are touring, and the local chapters of HCU offer protection to the clubs, or auditoriums, or whatever venues they play at."

"So they tell the people running the show, give us a cut, or else?"

"Yeah, something like that. They've even gone as far as enforcing where bands can play. One of the promoters, a band manager, didn't cooperate and got the shit kicked out of him. They put him in a wheelchair for life."

"Anybody do time for that?"

"Six HCU members were arrested, and evidence showed they all were involved in attacking him. But it was unclear who actually delivered the blows, so no one was convicted. They all skated."

"You know what doesn't jive—"

"Wait, there's more. They killed two guys in Philly last year. Gang beating is their specialty. It's how they typically go after their enemies. They know it's almost impossible to prosecute if it can't be specifically determined who committed the murder."

"Why would they bother with South Lake Tahoe, Cody? The only place here that would host a death-rock concert is Zeke's, and it could hold maybe a hundred people. I don't think that's enough to make for a decent payday for HCU, no matter how deep their cut."

"Huh," Cody said, rubbing the scruff of his beard. "They must have some other income source. I'd be surprised if any of those punks are working a legit job, especially that one guy. Was he mentally retarded?"

"They were the B-team. Some of the other dudes I saw at Zekes wouldn't have been as easy to handle."

"You got any names?"

"Why?"

"These guys come stir up shit at your home and you ask why?"

"Maybe they'll forget about it," I said, but the lack of conviction in my voice was plain. Cody stood and walked in front of the television. "Dirt, you shot one of them and now he's on his way to a federal penitentiary. They've already tried to mess with you twice, once at your bar and again at your house. Come on."

"What are you suggesting?"

"We need to know where they live. Then, if they decide to up the ante, we hit back—fast and hard."

I sat slumped on the sofa and rubbed a bruise on my thigh. Though I couldn't argue with Cody's logic, I wanted to discount the white trash gangbangers who had intruded on the idyllic mountain community where I'd bought my home and settled down. Hopefully, they'd find other targets for their energies, or better yet, go broke and move away. It was a nice thought, but probably one born from laziness. It was also the type of rationalization a man makes when he's acted out of anger or impatience, and has yet to accept that he has predicated his stake in the events to follow.

I hauled myself off the couch to get a beer, but instead tossed back a shot of Canadian Club. As usual, my problems were of my own design. A small part of me still clung to the idea I'd eventually become more like my father, a respected district attorney and devoted family man. That dream probably began to die shortly after the old man was murdered, back when I was thirteen years old. The trajectory of my life since then had been pocked with episodes of violence and retribution. My ex-wife once said she was sure I was subconsciously seeking vengeance for my father's death. That may have been true when I was younger, but I doubted it was behind my actions after all these years. Regardless, it looked like I'd not yet outgrown my inclinations.

I walked to the television and turned it off. Cody looked at me expectantly.

"Joe Norton," I said. "And run the Buick's license, too." I handed him a scrap of paper with the number. Cody went back to the computer and began typing.

• • •

We drove out of my dark neighborhood in Cody's truck, the diesel motor rattling softly. It was a quiet night, April being an off-season month for tourists. A mile up the road the glow from the casino lights in Nevada was faint, as if they'd conceded to slow business and dimmed the power.

Less than five minutes from my house, we turned into a subdivision of newer homes, mostly modern cabins on large lots. The peak-roofed structures looked new, the lawns mowed and free of leaves, the flowerbeds manicured and colorful. A few homes still had Christmas lights on, the bulbs twinkling and flashing against the old-growth pines in their yards.

"Turn left here," I said, looking at the map Cody had printed. When we came around the corner, we slowed in front of a large single-story home on a corner lot. It was painted white, in contrast to the natural wood finishes of the other houses on the street. Bright lights mounted on steel poles lit the place up garishly, as if it was an industrial compound of some sort.

We idled past the house. The backyard was enclosed by plank fencing, but the upper portion of a cinder block building in the back of the lot was visible. Cody drove away from the property, then made a U-turn and parked down the street, where we had a good view of the front.

"This is the address for John Switton, the registered owner of the Buick," he said.

"What else did you find on him?"

"Fifty-eight years old. No criminal record." I looked over the sheet Cody had pulled up on Switton. There wasn't a single blemish, not even a speeding ticket. But the data available was far less than a complete police file.

We sat looking at the house for a minute.

"Why would somebody light up their place like that?" Cody said, hunched over his steering wheel.

"Maybe they're paranoid about being robbed."

"You think Joe Norton's blue Chevy is in the garage?" Cody stared at the house while he spoke. We had been unable to come up with a local address for Norton.

I shrugged. "Who knows? Hell, maybe Jason Loohan is living there."

"Who?"

"He's another bail skip I'm looking for. A friend of Billy Morrison's."

"You want to knock on the door and ask for him?"

"It's tempting, but I don't even know if he's in town. Besides, I'd rather take him down when he's alone."

Cody started his truck. "There ought to be a law against all those lights," he said. I nodded as we slowly drove away.

4

BEHIND THE LOCKED DOOR of his office at Pistol Pete's Casino, John Switton was enjoying a prostitute while watching a Yankees game on the television he'd mounted in the corner. The whore was a small-breasted blonde with a nice ass, and he'd positioned her bent over his desk so he could take her from behind and still watch the game. Holding her hip with one hand, he used his free hand to alternatively sip from a glass of Chivas and puff on a stogie.

After he sent her away, he relaxed in his leather executive's chair and finished his drink. He'd left his slacks and shirt draped over the chair and sat in his shorts, his black socks clinging to his calves. Curls of coarse gray hair rose from around his wife-beater shirt. His upper body had thickened over the years, but he was not egg-shaped or fat like many men his age. He had wide shoulders and an eighteen-inch neck and his back was ramrod straight. When he walked into a room, his carriage still demanded respect from men half his age.

In the old days in Jersey, he had been one of the few non-Italians to make it to the inner circle of the Mafia. Although his Irish blood precluded him from ever being a made man, he was still a highly respected member of the Tuma family. He made his bones as a teenager and later earned a place in mob folklore when he beat a rival hit man to death with a claw hammer. Thus known as John the Hammer, he spent the next fifteen years reinforcing his reputation and amassing a sizable personal fortune, after investing his earnings in commercial real estate.

John was content working for the mob. The money was good, and his calculated, precise approach to the work minimized the risk. Then two events occurred that changed everything.

John's son Robert was ten years old when he came home from school one day complaining of a severe headache. John took him to the clinic and within a few hours a surgeon was drilling into his skull to relieve an aneurysm. The operation was successful, for the most part; the mental deficiencies Robert was born with had not worsened. But it was a bleak reminder to John that his only child would always rely on him. When Robert was released from the hospital, his head was wrapped in a huge ball of gauze. Tears welling in his eyes, John hugged his son and carried him to his Lincoln Continental. He carefully belted the small boy into the front seat and held his hand as he drove home.

The second event, in retrospect, may have been in some intangible way related to the first. It involved a contract on a bookie who was under investigation by the New Jersey anti-racketeering task force. John planned the hit meticulously. He spent seven days casing the target, following him around town, documenting his schedule and habits. When the man pulled up to the curb in front of his house at three in the morning on the eighth night, the timing couldn't have been better. John was parked across the street, waiting. As soon as his victim's car rolled to a stop, John slid from his Lincoln and crept up in the shadows. The man climbed from the driver's seat, and John stepped forward and parked two silenced .38 rounds behind the man's ear. Very smooth. Except when the body crumpled back into the car, the head came to rest on the center of the steering wheel. The horn bleated for only a second before John pushed him aside, but a light went on in the house. A small boy in pajamas stood staring out a bedroom window, his eyes unnaturally bright and fixed on John.

John moved back to his car and eased away from the curb, lights off. Just as he began to accelerate, he felt a bump and heard a screech of metal. He turned on the headlights and saw a mangled tricycle in the street. He stared at it, certain it had not been there earlier.

Driving across town through the deserted streets, John could not shake the image of the young child framed in the window. The horn had sounded only briefly, but the child appeared at almost that instant. The boy's face looked calm, his blond hair combed, his eyes still, as if the events taking place before him were preordained and unstoppable. It was goddamned eerie. And so was the tricycle that appeared out of nowhere, as if it had been pushed in front of his car by an unseen hand.

He told himself it was explainable, probably coincidental, and meant nothing. The important thing was he'd pulled off another job, and the payday would be nice this time. Robert had been asking for a drum set, and John had been putting it off. He decided as he drove that he would buy him one the next day.

When John pulled into his garage and turned off his motor, he sat in silence for a moment. Suddenly he was struck by an overwhelming sense that he was not alone. He whipped his head around toward his back seat, but it was empty.

"Jesus Christ," he muttered, wondering if he was losing it. His hair felt like it was standing on end. He got out of the Lincoln and his hand was on the doorknob to the house when he noticed something in his peripheral vision. Bending down to the front of his car, he saw a tuft of fine blond hair jammed in the crease of the steel bumper. Beside it, a wet smear of blood was streaked across the chrome.

John had never been a religious or spiritual man, but the sense of foreboding that plagued him after that night would not relent, and only grew worse as the weeks passed. He tried to ignore the dread in his heart, but it finally became so strong he concluded it must be a warning. He became convinced that not heeding it would precipitate his death. And that would leave Robert without a provider, something John would not allow to happen.

John thus made the decision to extricate himself from organized crime. It was a delicate matter, and there were some in the Tuma family who would view it as a traitorous act. In the end, it was John's Irish blood that saved him—the Italians never fully embraced him as a family member, despite his loyalty and unquestionable effectiveness. If he'd been Italian, they probably never would have let him go. Since he was not, his exodus had been begrudgingly granted.

For the next twenty years, John lived a quiet, peaceful existence. He forged a career in real estate, buying and selling small commercial buildings, and rarely thought of the life he'd left behind. With early retirement within his grasp, he decided to sell all his properties. He was waiting for the right moment when disaster struck. A severe recession took hold of the economy, causing the valuation of his holdings to plummet. John listed his properties for sale, but there were no takers. Companies began defaulting on their monthly lease payments, and John couldn't make his mortgages. Within six months he was wiped out; the banks sold off his buildings at cut-rate prices, and he was left with nothing.

John had adapted well to life as a legitimate businessman, but he needed cash flow, not only for his own needs, but also to take care of his son. Robert Switton was born mentally disabled and with physical deformities that made him a curiosity. His mother, an alcoholic, coke-addicted floozy who abandoned them once Robert was born, was the biggest mistake of John's life. She continued her drinking and cocaine habits after she knew she was pregnant, and by the time she was showing, it was too late. She gave birth to a baby that would never have a chance at a normal life. John alone had cared for Robert ever since.

Once worth millions, John lowered himself and called his contacts in real estate to ask for work. When that bore no fruit, he looked into careers outside of real estate, but people were losing their jobs at a rate unprecedented since the Great Depression, and no one was hiring. His checking account dangerously low, John considered selling his house, but recent foreclosures in his neighborhood caused his equity to vanish, and now he owed more on the home than it was worth.

John the Hammer Switton, ex-Mafia enforcer, felt himself coming apart at the seams. He found it impossible to concentrate on mundane tasks, and when he touched his face, it was either painfully dry or so oily his fingers shined with grease. No matter what he ate, his gut churned as if he'd swallowed a burrowing rodent, and he began to drop weight. He dreamt of blood and corpses and gunshots and often woke soaked in sweat. He finally reached his breaking point one afternoon when something inside him snapped while he tried to relax in the shade of his backyard. He leapt up and destroyed the bird bath on his lawn, smashing the heavy cement unit to pieces against the porch.

That evening John put in a call to Salvatore Tuma, once his closest friend from back in the day. John had lost all contact with his past life, and he wasn't surprised when the number he dialed was disconnected. He spent all evening trying to reach someone who could put him in touch with Sal. He finally spoke to some kid, probably a driver or a gopher for the Tumas, who said he would take a message.

Three days later John was playing cards with his son when the phone rang with a number he didn't recognize.

"Irish John the Hammer," the voice said. "It's been a long time, *Paisan*."

"That you, Sal?"

"It's me. How are you?"

"I've been better. How about yourself?"

"Ah, you know. Ups and downs."

"Yeah. Thanks for getting back to me, Sal. I appreciate it."

"What's on your mind, John?"

"I was thinking, maybe we could get together, have a drink, maybe something to eat, talk about old times."

The line went quiet for a moment. "My schedule's pretty busy, you know," Sal said. "Anything in particular you want to talk about?'

"I'm thinking, you know, maybe get back in the business."

"Huh? I thought you were doing good in real estate."

"Things change."

"Yeah, they do. I don't know what I can do for you, John. It's not like we're recession-proof here."

John suppressed a chuckle. "I know. But think about it, would you? I'm asking for a favor with this."

"You still living upstate?"

"Yeah, sure."

"I got some business midtown tomorrow. Drive into the city, meet me around four."

• • •

They met at a restaurant John knew well, a place that had been a favorite of the Tuma's for almost fifty years. The dark lounge had no windows and a musty odor particular to rooms that hadn't been redecorated for decades. The booths against the walls were upholstered in red vinyl sectioned by brass buttons. A small antique lamp lit each table.

John was grateful Sal Tuma agreed to meet with him. While they had been through a lot together, John knew any request on his part to reenter mob life would be tenuous. Sal's embrace of John in a traditional Italian hug surprised and pleased John. It was a good start. They took a booth, reminiscing and exchanging small talk for a while, feeling each other out. It was Sal who finally got to business.

"If you're interested in moving to Nevada, I might have something for you," Sal said.

"Nevada? You mean Vegas?"

"No. Lake Tahoe."

"Tell me more," John said.

The Tuma family had deep roots in gambling. They'd run a sports betting network along the eastern seaboard since the first world war, and when Vegas became the hot spot in the 1960s, Sal's father Leo bought two small casinos on The Strip, and later one in Stateline, Nevada. For two decades these casinos provided the ideal means to launder cash from the Tuma's other favorite enterprise, drug dealing.

When the Feds cracked down on Mafia casino interests in the late seventies, Leo Tuma was forced out of Vegas. But his casino in the smaller market on the shores of Lake Tahoe avoided the fallout, after certain payouts were made. Envelopes of cash went out monthly to gaming commission officials, who bought new cars, went on expensive vacations, and had their children's college tuition loans paid off. In return, Pistol Pete's Casino was allowed to remain under the ownership of the Tuma family. Until recently, it was managed by Sal, Leo's oldest son.

A series of unfortunate events in the last twelve months brought increased federal scrutiny on Pistol Pete's. A corrupt Tahoe County sheriff had run amuck, resulting in the imprisonment of Sal's son for running a local drug ring. The money trail led to the casino, and a team of government accountants was sent in to scour the books. The newspapers played it up, and public outcry forced Salvatore Tuma to flee to Italy to avoid a federal indictment. He returned to New Jersey when the uproar subsided and quietly paid off the necessary parties. But the damage had been done; the casino would not be allowed to continue under Tuma ownership.

"I've done a little checking since we spoke," Sal said. "You're a pretty unique guy, John. Not a single mark on your record. Not even a freaking traffic ticket."

"I've always been careful."

"From the outside, you look like a successful real estate investor."

"That's what I was, until the economy took a dump."

Sal uncrossed his legs and leaned forward. "I need to arrange a transfer of the ownership of Pistol Pete's Casino. Harrah's has offered to buy me out, but I'm not interested."

"Yeah, so?"

"How'd you like to own a casino?"

John cocked his head. "You want *me* to front points for you?"

"Your background is clean. Any links you had to us are too old to come up."

"Wouldn't the Feds need to approve of me first? I mean—"

"You let me worry about that."

"All right. Tell me more."

"We'll handle all the paperwork. The legal ownership of Pistol Pete's will be formally transferred to your name. You'll be given a monthly salary and health benefits. It will be enough for you to live comfortably."

John felt one of his eyebrows raise "What do I have to do?"

Sal Tuma pulled a cigar from his suit coat and offered one to John. "Just stay out of trouble, stay low key. That's it."

"Nothing else?" John asked.

A hint of a smile showed on Sal's mouth. "If anything comes up, I'll let you know."

Ice cubes rattled against his teeth as John drained his scotch. He knew what Sal meant. The day would come when Sal would call on John the Hammer, and when that day came, saying no would not be an option.

• • •

For the first three weeks after moving across the country to Stateline, Nevada, everything went smoothly. John leased a home a few minutes' drive from Pistol Pete's, a ranch-style house on a large lot, painted white, just the way he liked it. He'd developed a preference for well-lit, light-colored homes with minimal shrubbery after an incident when Robert was a toddler. A pair of thugs broke into the house where John and Robert lived, a brown Victorian surrounded by shade trees in Hoboken. They came on a moonless night and hid behind a hedge while jimmying the window. If not for one stepping on Robert's squeeze-activated stuffed animal, John might not have heard them.

When they opened his bedroom door, John blew them out of their socks with a silenced .45 automatic. By dawn their bodies were stuffed in metal barrels and resting on the bottom of the Hudson, and John was back home repainting the wall smeared with their blood. Robert never even woke up.

Having spent his entire life in Jersey or New York, John found the Lake Tahoe area a strange place to live. Clearly, the population was highly transient. Wealthy retirees spent weeks in vacation homes and then disappeared. Young men, often teenagers, showed up for the ski season and moved away when the resorts closed. The population seemed to expand or contract on a weekly basis as tourists flowed in and out of the casinos. The permanent residents were an odd blend of mountain men, outdoor adventurers, Birkenstock chicks, and miscellaneous escapees from California's suburbs.

John missed being able to walk into a good, old-fashioned, working-class bar where men born and raised in the community gathered. He tried a few local joints, but they were mostly hangouts for ski bums and assorted white trash. By default, he found himself spending his idle hours with the crew that ran Sal Tuma's casino. They were all East Coast transplants like him.

John knew two of them from his days working for the Tumas. Denny Totaglia and Carlo Bianchi were old-school boys about his age. Denny had been an odds maker in Queens. He'd always been overweight, but John almost didn't recognize him when he saw him sitting at the sports bar at Pistol Pete's. Fat Denny had to be pushing four hundred pounds.

Age had been easier on Carlo Bianchi. His head was hairless, but that's how John remembered him—he'd gone bald by the time he was twenty-five. He'd kept his body builder's physique after all these years, probably pumping iron daily by the looks of him. Carlo spent much of his career as a loan shark, and had also been active in enforcing labor contracts.

John also knew Pistol Pete's chief executive, Victor Severino. He was a tall, lean man, about fifty. His expertise was numbers—he managed the incoming cash from various Tuma enterprises, setting up systems to launder the money and make it invisible to the IRS. He was a master at cooking the books; the IRS had come after him on numerous occasions earlier in his career, but they had been unable to make anything stick.

But Vic Severino was more than a backroom bean counter. He'd done his share of wet work for the Tuma family, and was considered among the most valued and ruthless of Sal Tuma's men. Always wearing a business suit, his black hair slicked back, Severino was never seen having more than one drink at a sitting, smoked neither cigarettes nor cigars, and did not dally with prostitutes. He rarely changed expression and kept his own council, leaving John to wonder if maybe a traumatic childhood event had rendered him incapable of showing emotion. His taciturn nature made his associates wary and sometimes uncomfortable.

When John had learned he'd be working with Severino, he almost reconsidered his decision to accept Sal Tuma's offer. He'd crossed paths with Severino only a few times back in Jersey, but on one of those occasions

John had been ordered to whack a close friend of Severino's. The hit was legitimate, and John was just following orders—it was strictly business. But even though the killing was ordered by Don Tuma himself, Severino had still confronted John, let him know he was unhappy, made it personal. John had not given Severino's thinly veiled threats much credence at the time—after all, they worked for the same family—but John felt Severino was the type who could harbor a grudge for years. Given the opportunity, might Severino still be out for payback? It was possible.

The fourth member of Sal Tuma's team was his twenty-four-year-old nephew, Vinnie. He had a receding hairline, a hooked nose, close-set eyes, and a mouth that ran like a motor. John mostly ignored him. He suspected Sal sent Vinnie to Nevada because no one in Jersey could tolerate the weasel.

• • •

A few months after John got settled in his new home, he and Robert were relaxing on a Sunday afternoon, cooking a Bolognese sauce and a pot of pasta, when Sal Tuma called.

"I'm sending ten more men to Tahoe, John."

"To work at the casino?"

"No, it's for something else. Listen, I want you to help get them situated. They'll need to rent a couple houses. Until they do, let them stay at your place."

"Ten guys? What, I'm running a freakin' hotel?"

"It will be short term. Severino will take care of the finances, he knows all about it. I need you to help them find places to rent. In Nevada, right? Not California."

"When will they be here?"

"Some are flying in tomorrow. I'll send you their flights and you can pick them up at the Reno airport. A couple others are driving, so it'll take them a week or so."

John knew better than to ask questions. Since his brother Leo was in semiretirement, Sal was the next logical choice to be the big boss. If John played his cards right, he'd never have to worry about money again. Maybe he could eventually return to New York.

John hung up and drove to Pistol Pete's, where Vic Severino awaited him.

"Call a local furniture store and have them deliver mattresses," Severino said, his black eyes like lead balls, his complexion dark and grainy, like an Arab's. He handed John a wad of cash. "Better buy some groceries, too."

"What about finding these guys somewhere to live permanent?"

"The main man is named Joe Norton. You'll meet him tomorrow. Work with him on that."

The following afternoon John drove an hour to the airport in Reno. Robert followed him in the Buick John bought for him when they moved out west. Though Robert had a driver's license, John tried not to let him drive unless necessary. Sometimes it became awkward—at thirty-two, Robert was a grown man and wanted to be treated as such.

Leaning against his car at the curbside, John lit a stogie while Robert tried to describe a drum part he was learning. When Robert was a child, he put together a makeshift drum kit out of pots, pans, wood blocks, and cardboard boxes. The rhythms he created prompted John to ask the local high school's music teacher to assess his son's talent. Within a year, at the age of eight, Robert was declared a musical savant. His inability to turn his hands palm up did not detract from his skill at playing complex and difficult drum parts. His deformity actually allowed him to pound the skins with a power rarely seen. The speed and coordination of his feet was even more impressive. He took a liking to speed metal and could handle the genre's most demanding double bass pedal arrangements.

When Joe Norton and the half dozen men with him came out of the airport terminal, John had a brief moment of denial. The tattooed, T-shirted men were clearly drunk, trading profane insults and making a spectacle of themselves. One of them, a wire dangling from his ear, held his hand to his mouth and made noises that sounded like a gorilla grunting in anger. John squinted at the man.

"What the hell—"

"Hey, he's good," Robert said.

"At what?"

"It's called screaming. You've heard it in the music I listen to."

"You call that music, huh?"

"Ahh, Dad."

"Which one of you is Norton?" John said.

"I'm Joe Norton," the largest man said.

"John Switton. Load your gear in the trunks and let's go."

"We were thinking of going downtown, raising a little hell first." Norton smiled, his teeth reminding John of a horse's mouth.

"Suit yourself. You can take a cab to Tahoe then."

"What would that cost?"

"At least a hundred."

Norton knew nothing about John Switton, and he didn't like the man's dismissive tone, especially in front of his boys. But something about the gray light in the older man's eyes made Norton pause.

"You heard him," Norton said, his smile gone. "Load up."

5

As was my habit, I woke at dawn. Cody's chainsaw snoring was audible from the guest room while I brewed a pot of coffee. I poked around my refrigerator, hoping to find enough provisions to make an acceptable breakfast. Given Cody's appetite, it was an unlikely notion. I strapped on my full-size backpack and jogged a mile out to the supermarket and bought three dozen eggs, a couple pounds of bacon, some cartons of frozen hash browns, and two loaves of bread. As an afterthought I grabbed a dozen donuts from the bakery. I almost made it to the checkout counter before I turned around and picked up a fifth of vodka and a bottle of Bloody Mary mix.

Pine needles crackling beneath my shoes, I jogged home through streets still shrouded in the gray of dawn but randomly streaked with light where the early sun pierced the trees. My breath was steaming, and I had to ball my fists against the cold.

"Where the hell have you been?" Cody groused when I came inside. He was sitting at my kitchen table in his boxer shorts, a blanket over his shoulders, holding a coffee cup in front of him with both hands.

"Turn on the heat if you're cold," I said, and shrugged out of the pack and put a frying pan on the stove. Within a minute the kitchen was alive with the sizzle of eggs, potatoes, and bacon.

By the time we finished eating, the morning chill had dissipated and my yard was in full sunlight. We sat at the picnic table on my deck, reading the newspaper. A twenty-year-old compact Toyota pickup sputtered by, then turned around at the end of the street and came back, rolling to a stop in front of my house. The truck looked to have once been red, but it was now a hodgepodge of rust and primer. The passenger door opened, and we watched Juan Perez walk up my driveway carrying a black binder.

"Hey, Juan, what's happening?" I said.

"*Hola,* Mr. Reno."

"Just call me Dan, okay?"

"Okay."

"Cody, this is Juan Perez. I'm going to be speaking in front of his class for career day."

"Really?"

"That's right."

Cody stood and shook hands with Juan, who eyed Cody uncertainly.

"Who's that in your truck, young man?" Cody said, looking at the dark-haired woman sitting behind the wheel.

"It is my sister, Teresa."

"Well, invite her over. Maybe she'd like a cup of coffee."

Juan went back to his truck and after a minute I looked up from the sports page and saw them walking toward us. I blinked and folded the newspaper shut and stood when she stepped onto the deck.

"*Hola, senorita,*" Cody said. "*Mi nombre es* Cody Gibbons."

"*Buenos dias. Soy Teresa.*"

"Hi Teresa," I said. "I'm Dan Reno. I'm helping Juan on his school project." I held my eyes on hers, resisting the urge to stare down at her voluptuous body, which was clad in blue jeans and an orange cotton shirt that clung to her curves.

"Would you like coffee, or anything, Teresa?" Cody asked.

"No, thank you."

"I just brewed a fresh pot."

"Maybe a half-cup, then. With sugar, please." Cody went inside, and we sat and began reviewing the pages in Juan's binder.

"Juan tells me you're a private eye," Teresa said. She was sitting next to Juan and across from me, her hands folded under her chin.

"That's right. I also have a bounty hunting license."

"Bounty hunting? Do you work for the police?"

"No, but I frequently cross paths with them." I looked up from the sheet I was trying to read. Her hair was thick and jet-black and fell over her forehead and around her cheeks. The ends were lighter in color and rested where her shirt was pulled tight over her breasts. "I'm usually hired by private individuals, attorneys, or bail bondsmen."

"What do they hire you for?" She looked at me with frank interest, her eyes large and curious, her brown skin smooth and without the slightest blemish.

I smiled. "This will help me rehearse for talking to Juan's class, I guess. Sometimes I look for missing people. Other times, I try to collect information about people, usually information they'd rather keep secret."

"Like a man cheating on his wife?"

I nodded. "Divorce cases sometimes call for a private investigator."

"How about drug dealing?"

Cody walked out just then and placed a cup in front of Teresa, on one of the little saucers I never used. "Here you are," he said.

"*Gracias.*"

"Drug dealing is something I come across a lot in my work," I said. "It's a very common crime."

"What would you do if drugs were being dealt in your neighborhood?"

I rubbed my jaw. "Depends if it was bothersome."

"What if it was?"

"In that case I'd decide whether to call the police or discourage them myself."

"Why?" Cody said. "Do you have a problem where you live?"

"No, we don't," Juan said before Teresa could respond. "Can we work on my assignment?"

· · ·

When Juan and Teresa drove away a half hour later, Cody told me she worked as a cocktail waitress at Pistol Pete's.

"We talked when we went to look at the meadow. She's working tonight. Why don't we drop by and say hello?"

"She's got to be fifteen years younger than you," I said.

"So? Your last broad, uh..." He snapped his fingers a few times.

"Beverly."

"Right. How old was she? Twenty-one?"

"Look, Cody. These people came from one of the poorest areas of southern Mexico. If not for their parents sacrificing everything they had to send them here, they'd probably be dying of malnutrition somewhere, or worse."

"Where'd you hear this?"

"The owner of the restaurant where Juan works told me. He hired Juan out of charity, and says the kid is the hardest worker he's ever seen."

"Their English is almost perfect."

"Juan said his parents made them study it every day."

"I see."

"I don't think he was very happy with you talking to her," I said.

"Yeah, I saw the looks he was giving me. But he's gonna have a tough time keeping the horn dogs away from her."

"Are you speaking for yourself?"

"Now, come on, Dan. I've got no dishonorable intentions here. What's wrong with being friendly? Besides, she told me about a gang of Mexicans selling dope and basically bringing down the standard of living at her apartment complex. I was thinking you and me might take a spin over there and piss in their punch bowl."

"What? I can't think of anything I'd rather do less. What do you expect to accomplish?"

"From what Teresa says, these guys sit out in the apartment's common area, getting shitfaced, throwing knives at trees, intimidating the tenants, and claiming the area as their own."

"Sounds like someone should call the cops."

"Apparently someone did. One of the gangbangers got busted a couple days ago, but the others are still there as if nothing happened."

I stacked the papers Juan had left me. "I've already got one fine group of citizens on my ass, Cody. Isn't that enough?

"Hey, I just want to persuade them to tone it down a bit. What harm can come of that?"

I walked inside, hoping he could answer that on his own.

• • •

Later that afternoon, we parked on the street outside the apartment complex where Juan and Teresa Perez lived. Graffiti covered the walls and derelict vehicles lined the street, but flowers hung from the balconies and the sidewalks were chalked with hopscotch games. Two women pushing baby carriages stood chatting on the corner.

We knocked on the door to the Perez's unit. Teresa opened it in her cocktail waitress outfit, a short, frilly skirt beneath a low-cut top showing ample cleavage. I didn't see Juan anywhere. I said hello and averted my gaze.

"*Hola*, Teresa, you look lovely, absolutely gorgeous," Cody said, staring at her breasts as if his eyes could spring them free of her blouse.

The apartment was clean and looked well organized. The old kitchen table was scratched and marred but polished to a shine, and I could see where a tear in the sofa had been mended with needle and thread.

"They are here," Teresa said without preamble. She pulled back the curtain over the sliding glass door, and we looked out at the common area. A group of Latino men in red bandanas sat at a picnic table on the edge of the grass, heckling an elderly couple who were hobbling by. The old folks hunched over their walkers, doing their best to ignore the taunts. A minute later two longhaired white dudes approached the table and exchanged cash for small packages hidden in their palms. After they walked away, two of the gangbangers stood and hit off their beer bottles, then began sparring, throwing slaps at each other until one backed off.

"Let's go suggest a change of scenery to these *pendajos*," Cody said, sliding open the glass door. We walked across the grassy area to where they stood.

"What's going on, boys?" Cody said. The men stared at us with blank eyes. A couple of them were probably teenagers, the rest in their twenties. Tattoos covered their brown skin, their teeth flashed with silver caps, and the pants they wore sagged low on their hips.

"You want something?" said the largest of the bunch, his torso fat and barrel shaped. He stepped to within an arm's length of Cody and gave him the dead eye.

"You want to sell drugs, go find somewhere else to do it," I said, addressing a man with angular eyes and a square jaw. "The people living here have a right to this area."

"You a funny man, homes," he replied. "Maybe not too smart, though."

"I think you're the one with an intelligence issue," Cody said. The fat man started to say something, but Cody shoved him and sent him sprawling over the table.

The *cholos* jumped at us, circling, getting in position to rush from all sides. I heard the flick of a knife, and saw a blade in the hand of one of the younger gangbangers. He came at me and I kicked his wrist, my foot extending over his head. The knife flew from his hand, then I grabbed him by the hair and pounded his face into the large pine tree shadowing the table. He flailed, but after the third blow he dropped to the ground, bleeding from the mouth and unconscious. Before I could turn, another one jumped on my back. I hit him hard in the ribs with an elbow, peeled his hand from my throat, and slapped him into a wrist lock. When he bent to keep his arm from breaking, I kicked him in the gut, and he collapsed and lay in the fetal position.

Two of the gang ran at Cody. One got behind him and swung a forty-ounce Budweiser bottle, shattering it over his skull. Cody turned and grabbed the man's neck, then picked him up by the crotch and launched him into the other Latino. They went down in a heap.

The Mexicans regrouped, waving bottles and knives, circling. Cody and I were waiting for their attack when two men in street clothes walked into the square.

"Looks like cops," Cody said, a thin trickle of blood running beside his ear.

Four of the gangbangers bolted, leaving the unconscious member lying near the tree. The two Cody and I had spoken to remained, apparently unconcerned about the arrival of whoever was coming our way. Probably because they weren't holding drugs, I guessed.

"You recognize them?" Cody said, nodding at the white men walking toward us.

"I've seen the bigger guy before. Pretty sure he works for Douglas County."

"What's he doing in California, then?"

The two men approached and flashed badges.

"What happened to him?" said the smaller one, a pock-faced man with black hair. He pointed at the prone Latino, who lay near the picnic bench, blood trickling from his mouth.

"He was playing Frisbee and ran into the tree," I said.

The man glared at me, but his big partner's freckled face split into a grin.

"Don't you hate it when that happens?" he said.

"If you two are here buying dope, you're out of luck," Pock Face said. "So get lost." He began searching the two gangbangers, ignoring us as Cody and I backed away to the small patio of the Perez apartment. Theresa opened the sliding door while we watched the cops handcuff their suspects.

"It's Rodrigo," Theresa said. "Their leader." She pointed to the slim man being led away. He was walking in starts and stops and leaning unexpectedly, making it difficult for the cop to guide him smoothly. It was an old prison trick.

"I guess our work is done here, huh?" I said to Cody.

"For now, I suppose," he replied.

"Looks like the police are taking care of those guys, Teresa," I said.

"I appreciate you coming." She bowed her head and smiled shyly, standing with her small feet together. She wore black flats, her calves full and well shaped, her thighs curving invitingly into the ruffles of her short dress.

"Of course," Cody said grandly. "We are at your service, *senorita*."

"Oh, Mr. Gibbons, you are bleeding."

"It's nothing, just a scratch."

"You have glass in your hair. Sit, and let me clean it for you."

Cody sat at the kitchen table and Teresa began combing out the shards from the broken bottle. Soon a small pile of bloody slivers lay on the newspaper she'd laid on the table.

"You have some cuts," she said. "I will clean them with alcohol."

When she finished, Cody said, "Thank you, Teresa. If you have any trouble, ever, you can call me."

"Okay, Mr. Gibbons," she laughed. "I will remember that."

We left after Cody said a prolonged good-bye, and drove out to Highway 50, heading toward the state line.

"I should call Marcus Grier," I said.

"Grier? Does he still hate my guts?"

"Probably."

"I could never figure out what his problem was."

"He's a lawman, Cody. Every time he's met you, it's been in the middle of a shit storm you created."

"What? That's the biggest bunch of bullshit I've ever heard."

"I'm sure you've heard worse," I said, pulling into Whiskey Dick's. He gave me a curious look as I left him at the bar and went to a table in the corner to call the sheriff. After a minute I was connected to Grier.

"*Say that again?*" he said.

"A couple plainclothesmen just arrested two Mexican gangbangers at the Pine Mountain Apartments," I said. "I recognized one of them—about six-four, with a face like a fish. I ran into him once in Douglas County."

I could hear Grier breathing in the phone. "Describe the other one."

"Five-nine, dark hair, acne scars."

"Thanks for the information," he said, and hung up.

At the bar, Cody was shaking a dice cup and eating a bag of potato chips. "What'd your buddy have to say?" he said.

"He didn't sound too happy."

"You mean he didn't like the concept of out-of-state cops coming into his backyard and making arrests?"

"Apparently not."

"No wonder he's pissed."

"Those cops didn't read those guys their rights," I said.

"Yeah, and did you like how they left that one who's face you pounded lying there?"

"Something ain't kosher with those guys."

"No shit, Sherlock. Any idea what's behind it?"

"Nope." I sipped my beer and took a few chips from Cody's bag. The blatant misconduct we witnessed was hard to ignore, but whatever trouble might be brewing between Marcus Grier's office and the cops from Nevada was none of my business. Cody would surely understand that, I hoped.

6

THE WHITE POLICE VAN rolled across the state line and came to a stop at the police complex in Nevada. Pete Saxton and Dave Boyce opened the rear doors and brought their suspects into the booking room.

"Put 'em in the drunk tank," Saxton said to the jailer, a grizzled ex-prison guard nearing retirement. "I wouldn't feed them anything unless you want to clean up their barf."

"We aren't drunk, *officer*," Rodrigo sneered, his brown face reddened.

"You sure were having a hard time walking ten minutes ago. What was in those forty-ouncers you were drinking, fruit juice?"

Boyce finished writing on a sheet of paper and handed it to the jailer. "Don't let them out until we show up in the morning, okay, Sam?"

"You got it, hoss."

•   •   •

When Pete Saxton woke the next morning, he made sure to put his shoes on before leaving his bedroom. The workers remodeling his kitchen had turned his home into a shambles. Sawdust coated the hardwood floors, and the other day he had stepped on a nail, the tip jabbing into his heel and drawing blood. He would talk with the contractor the next chance he got, tell him to keep the place cleaned up or he'd take it out of his pay.

He took his coffee out to his new deck, the freshly stained redwood shiny and smooth. The hot tub he had installed a week ago gurgled quietly. He'd not yet had a woman in there, but planned to bring one home soon, preferably some young thing for a little soak and poke action.

Saxton finished his coffee and picked the dried mucus from the corner of his eyes. So far, his arrangement with the greaseballs from Pistol Pete's was going better than expected. They wanted some low-rung pushers cleared out of town, a pretty easy task, especially given what they were willing to pay. It might get a little sticky since the Mexicans were operating out of California, but he was sure he could handle whatever issues came up. Who would complain too loudly about a group of crystal meth-dealing beaners getting shit-canned?

The best part, though, was the deal was ongoing. After the Diablos Sierra was done with, the mob would move their boys in, on the Nevada side of the state line. Saxton would receive an envelope weekly for making sure they were not harassed. He looked at his watch. In an hour he'd meet with Joe Norton and his crew. The heavy-metal gangbangers from Jersey were strictly white trash, but what do you expect from a group of drug dealers recruited by the mob? At least Norton seemed reasonably intelligent and sane.

But intelligence and sanity are relative terms, Saxton thought, a smirk on his face. When Norton had told him about a local bounty hunter named Reno shooting Billy Morrison, Norton's right hand man, Saxton was incredulous. An accused rapist jumps bail, gets shot and captured, and takes the big bounce. What's the issue here? Sounds like Billy Morrison's life was circling the drain anyway. But now Norton had a hard-on for Reno, and Saxton said he'd do him a favor and look into it. So he'd talked to the black sheriff, who apparently had some history with Reno. What had that accomplished? Probably nothing.

Saxton drove his SUV to Dave Boyce's house, a mobile home in a trailer park that was once a haven for prostitutes. Boyce's ex-wife had cleaned him out when they divorced and was still taking half his paycheck. The good news was she wouldn't be able to touch the crisp twenties stuffed in those weekly envelopes. Still, Saxton was a bit worried about his partner. Since his wife left him, Dave Boyce spent two hours each evening working out at a martial arts club, beating the shit out of heavy bags, speed bags, sparring partners, whatever and whoever was available. On weekends he hung out at the casino nightclubs, trying to seduce every woman he could find. To Saxton's knowledge, Boyce hadn't had a piece of ass in months. A week ago Boyce admitted as much, adding that the fact he couldn't get laid despite being the most handsome and personable bachelor in South Lake Tahoe was a testament to how screwed his life had become.

Boyce was waiting on the street when Saxton drove up. "Thanks for the ride," he said. "The mechanic said my motor is seized, so my truck's headed for the scrap heap."

"What you gonna do for wheels?"

"Ever hear of a ten-speed?"

They drove a few miles around the lake and parked in the Douglas County PD lot.

"Go check out the van," Saxton said. "I'll get the wetbacks."

Five minutes later Boyce pulled up to the curb, and Saxton emerged from the building with the gangbangers. Both were cuffed behind the back.

"Where are you taking us?" Rodrigo said.

"To the bus stop. You're going back to Mexico."

"You can't tell us where to go," said the other *cholo,* the stocky one with a crew cut.

"Just keep on telling me what I can and can't do," Boyce said, steering out of the police complex and onto the highway.

Five miles into Nevada, they turned onto a dirt road leading away from the lake. They drove down a rutted trail into the forest and stopped when the path ended in a dirt circle serving as a turnaround.

From the trees, Joe Norton and six HCU members appeared, carrying bats and lengths of two-by-four.

Saxton opened the rear doors and pulled the gangbangers out into the crisp morning air.

Rodrigo looked around, taking stock of the situation. He stuck his chin out, gesturing at the men standing in front of him.

"It takes that many of you to take me, even with my hands cuffed?" Rodrigo spat, his saliva spraying the ground.

Norton walked up to Rodrigo and slapped him across the face, not hard, just enough to taunt him. "Shut up, you little bitch," Norton said.

"Take my cuffs off and we'll see who the bitch is."

Dave Boyce stepped between Rodrigo and Norton. "How about you and me? I'm about your size, *cholo. Mano e mano.*"

"You want to fight me? What happens if I beat your ass?"

"Then no one will mess with you. You have my word. My partner will even give you a ride home."

Rodrigo stared at Boyce. "I don't believe you, but you wanna fight, let's do it, homes."

Boyce removed the cuffs from Rodrigo's wrists. The moment he was free Rodrigo tried to stomp Boyce's foot, but Boyce danced away, then came back and feinted with a left jab. Rodrigo sidestepped and rushed forward with a series of furious punches, one clipping Boyce's head and drawing blood above the eye.

Boyce moved laterally and smiled. "That all you got?"

Rodrigo came at him again, wild with adrenalin, punching and kicking in a blur. Boyce blocked a left hook and stunned Rodrigo with a hard jab to the face, then threw a snap kick, the ball of his foot driving into his opponent's midsection.

Rodrigo staggered back, blood streaming from his nose, his features contorted in pain. Boyce flew at him with a spinning back kick, the point of his heel spiking into the gangbanger's thigh. Rodrigo dropped to a knee.

"Get up, *puta,* or I'll beat you to death," Boyce said.

Rodrigo pushed himself up, his eyes feral and black with rage, but as soon as he stood, Boyce whipped a kick into his ribs, then threw a right hand that broke Rodrigo's jaw with a sickening crunch. Boyce followed with an uppercut before Saxton grabbed him from behind, pinning his arms and walking him backward.

"Easy, Dave, no need to kill him."

Saxton waited until he could feel the tension in Boyce's body ease before letting him free. They stood looking at Rodrigo, who lay in a bloody mess on the dirt.

"What about this piece of shit?" Norton said, pointing at the remaining Mexican, a man almost Norton's size.

"Don't hurt him too bad," Saxton said. "No broken bones or blows to the head or face, got it?"

The big *cholo* was expressionless, his fear hidden. Saxton turned to him. "You'll be dropped off at the apartments with your *Mero Mero* there, or what's left of him. Then you collect your friends, get on a bus, and vamoose. *Comprende?* I'm telling you to get out of town. We don't tolerate drug-dealing scum like you in Lake Tahoe—and I'm talking South Lake, North Lake, Truckee, and I work in Reno, too. That means you and your gang need to disappear from the whole region. I've told these boys to take it easy on you so you'll be able to clearly communicate to your fellow gangbangers that you are done here. Do you get what I'm saying?"

The man swallowed and nodded. Saxton removed the cuffs from his wrists, then climbed into the white van along with Boyce. He made a U-turn and slowly drove away, looking in his rearview mirror, watching Rodrigo crawl to a sitting position while the HCU team knocked the other Latino to the ground and took their boots to him.

7

THE MONTH THE DOZEN HCU members spent at John Switton's house had pushed John the Hammer to his breaking point. None of them lifted a finger to clean up after themselves; most lacked even the common decency to flush the toilet. The trail of food wrappers, soiled laundry, and dirty dishes they left in their wake reminded John of pictures he'd seen of a capsized garbage barge. Within two days, the tidy residential home became a filthy, chaotic flophouse. John talked to Vic Servino and Joe Norton, and when he got nowhere, he hired a full-time maid and spent his waking hours in his office at Pistol Pete's.

When he finally found suitable rental properties and Norton and his boys split, John learned three of the gang members had left their guitars and amps behind, in the detached cinder block building where Robert played the drums. Switton wasn't thrilled when his son told him they had formed a band and would be rehearsing three times a week. But John decided not to meddle, as Robert's social life was limited, and he seemed excited about the prospect of his first metal band. At least the freaking room was mostly soundproof.

The previous night, when John came home from the casino and saw Robert wasn't on the couch watching television, he went out to the back building. The blast of sound that greeted him when he opened the door was startling. The guitars howled over Robert's driving beat, the bass drum propelling the rhythm at a speed John had never heard in any form of music. The singer, if that's what he was to be called, was growling in a thick, horrible tone, as if Satan himself was speaking through his vocal chords.

The room's walls and ceiling were carpeted, and sections were covered with yellow foam mattress pads. A coffee table was shoved in a corner and looked ready to collapse under the weight of empty beer cans and bottles and an ashtray overflowing with cigarette butts. John stood with his fingers in his ears until the onslaught finally ended.

"What do you think, Dad?" Robert said, wiping the sweat from his face.

"It ain't exactly the Bee Gees."

"Who?"

John turned to the singer. "Do people actually listen to this?"

The lead guitar player put his beer down after a long swig. "No one your age, pops," he said.

"No one my age would wear a ring in their nose, either."

"It's called fashion. You don't know what it means? Try a dictionary."

"Hey, Tom," Robert said.

"Look, you can wear a ring through your scrotum if you want," John said. "And I don't really care what kind of noise you make, as long as I don't have to listen to it. All I ask is you treat my property with respect. That means clean up after yourselves when you're done playing." John pointed at the coffee table.

The second guitarist, wearing a billy goat beard to hide his weak chin, began tuning his instrument. John reached over and yanked the power chord from the man's guitar. "You need to clean the place before you leave tonight. Or you can find someplace else to play." John flung the chord at the man and walked out.

An hour later Robert's bandmates were talking loudly in front of the house. John waited for them to drive off, then went out to his back patio and stood in the shadows. After a minute Robert appeared from the structure, his deformed physique and unnatural gait silhouetted as he walked across the dark yard, carrying a small box clinking with beer bottles. He dumped the bottles into a garbage can on the far side of the house, then returned to the room, and a minute later began the trek again. After the third time, John wheeled the garbage can over to the cinder block building and helped Robert clear the trash from the interior. Then he led his son inside the main house, made him a snack, and they watched television together before going to bed.

•   •   •

By the time John left for the casino the next morning, the frost had given way to a spring sun that bathed the meadows along Highway 50 in light. Clumps of purple wildflowers spotted the glistening, dew-covered fields. Between stands of pine, John could see two white plumes reflected on the blue surface of the lake, as if painted on a sheet of glass.

Driving with his window open, John tried to enjoy the scenery. But it felt artificial, as if he was watching a movie, and once it ended, an ugly reality would resume. He shook his head at the thought. The gig in Tahoe had saved his ass from financial ruin. Sal Tuma had personally extended himself, offering John a deal he should be grateful for. So why couldn't John accept the situation and be content?

The answer was obvious, he thought, walking to the Employees Only entrance at Pistol Pete's. It was bad enough he was forced to board the HCU jackasses for a month. Now three of them had befriended Robert, and it seemed they would become frequent visitors to his home. If they showed John a modicum of deference, that would be one thing. But instead they displayed an utter lack of respect, in effect dismissing him as an old man whose comments and opinions carried no more weight than a child's. In his prior life, it was an offense no sane man would make.

John had not asked Sal Tuma or Vic Severino why the HCU goons had been brought from Jersey to South Lake Tahoe. In truth, John didn't give a shit, as long as they weren't stupid enough to draw Robert into any trouble. But they were stupid, and that was the heart of the problem. No doubt HCU would be involved in criminal activity. If Robert was hanging around with these bozos, trouble would be inevitable. Go to bed with dogs, wake up with fleas.

Clearly it was time to have a serious chat with the so-called musicians who'd enlisted Robert as their drummer. John would start with the guitarist with the nose ring - Tom, if he remembered right. Nothing physical, just a one-on-one conversation to let him know the issues. And if he copped an attitude, then what? John felt a delicious rush course through his veins. How long had it been since he'd been involved in a violent situation? Twenty years, at least. He'd left his life as a mob hitman after what he'd thought was a supernatural warning. In retrospect, maybe it was just nerves. Regardless, his life as a legitimate businessman had suited him fine. But the situation in Tahoe might call for different tactics.

John sat at his desk until his emotions subsided and the impulse to crush Tom's skull with a crowbar faded. He was surprised he would so readily contemplate reverting to his old ways. His career as a real estate investor had sometimes involved dealing with difficult adversaries, but from the beginning, he'd squelched any temptation to use muscle. All things considered, it had simply not been necessary.

But now he was playing in a different league, one where the rules of lawful citizenry might not apply. If Robert's new friends weren't the types to respond to reason, so be it. There were other ways to make a point.

John thumbed the cap off his scotch bottle and poured himself a short drink. Strong-arming any member of HCU presented a few problems. They were under the domain of Vic Severino and Sal Tuma, and pissing off either mobster would be a bad strategy. Severino signed his checks, and

Tuma was John's gravy train. So he would have to show restraint when the time came—he might rough up Tom a bit, but nothing heavy, no broken bones, just slap him around and send a message.

Whatever happened, John reminded himself he must avoid the police radar. As the paper owner of Pistol Pete's, he could not afford problems with the law. Sal Tuma would have his ass if he didn't keep his nose clean.

John spent the next hours handling miscellaneous paperwork. His signature was required on various documents on a daily basis. Besides the actual casino operation, in itself a complex undertaking, Pistol Pete's also ran its own restaurants, gift shops, video arcade, and theatre, each managed as a separate profit center. The theatre alone was a large business, a two thousand-seat venue for pop concerts, comedy acts, cabarets, and the like. The hundreds of people employed by Pistol Pete's reported up to a dozen senior managers responsible for their own respective departments (slots, card tables, security, dining, entertainment, etc.). These managers worked directly for Vic Severino.

It was late afternoon when John took a break. Though his role didn't require any real decision making, he found himself spending an increasing portion of most days involved in the routines of the business. This was by choice, he realized. Still in his fifties, John had no desire to be retired. His habits were those of a professional businessman, and he enjoyed learning the nuances of Pistol Pete's operations, and applying himself, if only to a minor degree, to the successful running of the company. And there was no mistaking his role was to be minor—Vic Severino had made it clear John was to remain outside of the enterprise's true inner workings.

John turned on the Yankees game and dialed the number for the young, talkative prostitute he'd taken a liking to. She was also a Yankees fan, and he'd bought her dinner once, after she hung around in his office and watched a game with him. He felt his genitals react to the thought of her arrival—she was a wonderful piece of ass—but he also looked forward to her bubbly company. He got her voice mail and left a message.

When he called an hour later and she didn't pick up, he headed out to the sports book, disappointed and fighting a surge of irritation. As usual, Denny Totaglia and Carlo Bianchi were parked at the mostly empty bar. Denny's massive flab hid the bar stool, making it appear as if four steel posts were shoved up his ass.

"Gentlemen," John said, sitting next to Carlo, who was wearing a powder blue polo shirt that looked a size too small, the sleeves tight around his pumped biceps.

"Johnny, have a drink, baby," Denny slurred, his eyes red and hollow. "We were just talking about that time in the Bronx when we ran the Caluso brothers out of town. Those rat bastards. Goddamn, remember that?"

John glanced at his watch, then at Carlo. Denny loved reminiscing about the old days, but usually didn't do so until late in the evening, after a number of drinks. It was only four, but Denny's heavy jowls were flushed and his eyes were slits in his fleshy face.

"Severino around?" John said.

"He's in Reno for the night." Carlo pointed at Denny with his thumb. "He's celebrating his absence by getting ripped."

"Goddamn right," Denny said.

"Let's go across the street to Caesars." John stood and patted Denny's shoulder.

"Why?"

"You want Severino to know you're soused this early?"

"What do I give a shit?" Denny said, but he glanced nervously over his shoulder.

"The walls have eyes. Be smart, Denny."

Before Denny could respond, Vinnie Tuma walked into the sports book flanked by two bimbos. Vinnie was wearing a gray suit with wide lapels, and his feet were wedged into shiny two-toned loafers, as if he was a gangster out of the fifties. A smarmy smile was plastered on his face, interrupted by frequent drags off a cigarette. Despite his youth, he already had a noticeable potbelly beneath his shallow chest. The women with him, in high heels and short dresses, were obvious hookers. One was a curly-haired brunette with cannonball-sized breasts, and the other a slender blonde. Both wore a shiny gleam in their eyes, like they'd just been worked over real good in bed, or, more likely, were blasted to the gills on cocaine.

Vinnie acknowledged the men, pointing and winking, and sat with the women at a center table. John tried to ignore them, but the brunette had a shrill voice, and Vinnie began babbling loudly about his system to beat the roulette wheel.

"Jesus Christ, look at that fucking clown," Denny said.

A burst of laughter erupted from the table, and John turned and saw Vinnie bury his head in the brunette's cleavage. Then Vinnie reached in his pocket and took a quick snort from a small object cupped in his palm. He passed it around the table, the girls hitting off the vial before returning it to him.

"We got to get him out of here," Carlo said, as a group of gamblers walked in and began scrutinizing the latest odds above the betting counter.

John watched Vinnie's hand reach under the table, between the legs of the blonde. He hadn't recognized her before—she'd done something different with her hair—but now John saw she was the call girl he'd been trying to reach. He felt his face redden as his eyes clicked with hers. She gave him a little smile and busied herself lighting a cigarette.

Carlo walked to the table and stood over Vinnie. "Come with me for a second. I need to talk to you."

"Hey, Carlo, make it another time, huh?"

"No, right now, Vinnie."

"Gimme a break, man—"

"Now, Vinnie." Carlo dropped his hand to Vinnie's shoulder, his thumb digging into the nerve above the collarbone. Vinnie tried unsuccessfully to smile through it. "Hang loose, ladies, need to take care of some business real quick." He stood and went with Carlo to the far end of the bar.

Staring at the televised ballgame behind the bar, John heard Denny chattering at him, and he nodded and grunted, but none of the words registered. Of all the call girls in the area, what were the chances Vinnie just happened upon John's regular squeeze? Slim and none, John thought, remembering how Vinnie had been eyeing the blonde when she and John were having dinner in the casino coffee shop. The weasel had probably come by to get her number when John used the men's room.

And then he shows up in the sports book in this ridiculous suit, with the two girls, whacked on booze and blow, knowing John would likely be there. Vinnie flaunting it, as if he were a real high roller, a kingpin mob boss celebrating a big score. If he'd pulled a stunt like this back in Jersey, he would have gotten the shit slapped out of him, on the spot.

John walked to where Carlo and Vinnie were having a hushed conversation. A sheen of sweat glowed on Vinnie's big forehead, and a crusty ring of white encircled one of his nostrils. Carlo let go of Vinnie's arm as John approached.

"You need to show a little respect," John said.

Vinnie blinked as the words bounced off his face. "What? Who the fuck are you to talk down to me?"

"Shut up, Vinnie," Carlo said.

"No, seriously. From what I understand, you're a failed real estate agent working here as a charity case."

"I was working for your uncle's father before you were born." John's voice was quiet and even.

"Oh, I get it, more of this old-school bullshit. I got news for you. Who do you think is in line to take over this operation? That's right, you're looking at him. So get out of my face or I'll have you scrubbing toilets."

"You want to stuff drugs up your nose, I don't care," John said. "Just have the common sense not to do it on the casino floor."

"Take your whores and bring them to a room," Carlo said. "Or go someplace else."

Vinnie stared them down, then strode back to his table. He took his time finishing his drink, before gathering up the prostitutes and walking out.

"I hate to rain on the little prick's parade, but Jesus Christ," Carlo said.

John ordered a scotch. "He's got a mouth on him, doesn't he?"

"A mouth like that is asking to lose its teeth," Denny said.

John shrugged. "He's a kid. He'll come around when he sobers up."

Carlo looked at John and felt an eerie sense of déjà vu, but he couldn't place it. The three left Pistol Pete's and had drinks and dinner at a local restaurant before heading to Caesars to watch the topless show. Then they shot some craps and had a nightcap at the VIP lounge. By the time they left, the incident with Vinnie seemed an old memory.

It wasn't until Carlo was driving home near midnight that he remembered what it was about John's demeanor that was gnawing at him. The casual dismissal of the insult, the unnatural calm, the impression of being unflappable. Carlo now made the connection from two decades past. It was how Irish John the Hammer acted while planning an execution.

8

STUART GOLD, PRODUCER OF the dance troupe performing at Pistol Pete's, nipped at his gin fizz and contemplated the fickle and unfair world that led him to South Lake Tahoe. A year ago he'd been walking on air, managing one of Las Vegas's most successful A-list shows and dating the male lead, a lad in his twenties built like a Greek god. Stuart took off his glasses and cleaned the lenses, which fogged up every time he thought of the handsome young stud. He'd thought he was in love, and when their affair ended after three months, he was devastated. To be so brutally abandoned was not only a horrible affront to his ego, but it also left a yawning emptiness in his soul. He'd wandered around Vegas in a daze, unable to think of anything but how hurt and miserable he was.

But that wasn't the worst of it. When Stuart found out his boyfriend had left him for Bobby Porter, ex-Broadway bigwig and the most powerful producer in Vegas, Stuart simply lost it. Porter, known as Cornhole Porter, or CHP for short, was a raging queen with a notorious reputation for wielding his influence in return for sex. After learning Porter was shuttle-cocking his ex-love, Stuart flew into a hysterical rage and stormed past security into Porter's office. Eventually he was hauled away by the police, and spent the night in a cell in the Las Vegas county jail.

It wasn't long afterward that Stuart found he'd become *persona non grata* in Las Vegas. Cornhole Porter had put out the word that Stuart was dangerously unstable and only a fool would hire him. In Vegas, this amounted to a virtual blacklisting. He was fired from his job, his contract declared void, and everyone in the city shunned him. He couldn't even have a drink at a casino bar without feeling like a social pariah.

The opportunity to direct *I SPY*, a silly little second-rate show targeted at smaller markets, was something Stuart would have snickered at before his downfall. But he didn't have any better options, and realized a break from Vegas was probably necessary to rebuild his career. So he took the job and drove his Mercedes to Hollywood, where the troupe was assembled. Stuart rewrote the script, fired half the performers, and trashed and replaced all the choreographed dance numbers before he was satisfied it was ready for the stage. Sure, it was a less talented group than he was used to working with, but at least he'd molded the production into something original, something that would be recognizable as his work. It was a starting point.

Just when he was beginning to feel better about things, fate dealt him another blow. The headline gig at Caesars in South Lake Tahoe was cancelled, and the best the producer could do was secure a Sunday through Thursday slot at Pistol Pete's, a casino Stuart had never heard of. Fearing the worst, he drove to Tahoe to check it out. To his relief, Pistol Pete's was a decent-sized establishment, of course nothing compared to the Vegas casinos, but not bad for Lake Tahoe. And the showroom itself was respectably large. Stuart cringed at the thought of the small audiences that would populate the cavernous hall. Maybe they could curtain off much of the seating to create a more intimate feel.

The show had opened six weeks ago to generally favorable reviews, but those were by small-time critics writing for local papers and magazines that no one in Vegas would ever read. Stuart tried reaching a half dozen Vegas reporters, people he used to take to dinner and gossip with at parties. Some friends they turned out to be—not one took his call. He considered mailing them the positive write-ups, but knew it would only make him look desperate. Those so-called writers were nothing more than a pack of parasites, and they probably enjoyed witnessing his downfall.

The only thing positive to report was at least the damn weather in Tahoe was turning warmer. Stuart hated the cold, and he always associated the most positive developments in his life with sunny days. So it was only fitting it was a warm spring twilight when Teresa Perez shyly approached him at the casino bar.

She was wearing the same outfit as the other cocktail waitresses, a tacky, forest-green-over-lime ensemble most of the girls despised. Although Stuart had not the slightest sexual interest in women, he was stunned at how dignified yet sensual Teresa looked in the outfit. The green tones contrasted wonderfully with her skin, a flawless deep bronze glowing with youth and life. Stuart appraised her figure with a glance—large breasts, slender waist, full hips, and the type of ass he knew drove men wild.

"Mr. Gold?" she said. "My name is Teresa Perez. I was wondering if you would listen to me sing."

Stuart smiled at the brazen request. In Vegas, he was hounded by aspiring performers, most whom he sent away, and sometimes not politely. But when Teresa spoke, her gold eyes meeting his, a tiny jolt ran through him. It was a feeling he recognized—he had a radar-like instinct for talent, and when he was in its presence, it struck him like a tiny electric shock. It had been a long time since he felt the ping, but he recognized it as clearly as a crash of cymbals. A twinge of euphoria coursed through his body—his sensor was rarely wrong.

He took her to the empty concert hall and led her to the stage.

"What do you want to sing, my dear?"

"How about 'Amazing Grace?'"

Stuart raised his eyebrows. "Interesting choice. I'm all ears."

Before she was halfway done, Stuart's face was on fire and tears were welling in his eyes. Her voice filled the hall, echoing in the expanse, lovely and majestic. His heart thudded, and he thought this was what it must feel like to have a religious experience. He wanted to tell her to stop, but when he tried to motion at her, his arms were like jelly. Surrendering, he closed his eyes and let her voice take him away.

When she finished, Stuart noticed two janitors standing transfixed. He shooed them off and joined Teresa on the stage. She looked at him expectantly, hope and concern in her eyes.

"Have you performed in public before, my dear?" Stuart said.

"Only at my church."

"Have you ever been under contract?"

"What?"

"I mean, have you had an agent?"

"No."

"Ahh," Stuart said. "In this business you'll go nowhere without a good agent. Come sit with me, Teresa. We have much to talk about."

• • •

Juan Perez went to his bedroom where he kept his weight set and pumped out six sets of curls with a forty-pound bar. He checked his biceps in the mirror and moved to the bench press. Born a frail child, he had to work hard to build his muscles. But hard work was not something he was afraid of. The desire to work, the will to overcome and become something—that's what separated real men from the Diablos Sierra gangbangers. Sure, they acted tough when they were in a pack, but individually they were just sad Chicanos who would end up dead or in jail.

When he was done with his workout, he hurriedly showered and pedaled his bike through the back roads to the restaurant where he worked as a busboy. The Redwood Tavern was an upscale steakhouse, catering to wealthy tourists and locals who liked to hang out in the adjoining bar.

The waitresses at the restaurant loved to tease Juan. They found his doe-like eyes irresistible, and they knew he was a virgin. One of them, a slinky, dirty blonde who recently turned twenty-one and now drank at the bar after her shift every night, told Juan she would catch him one day and screw his brains out. Another one, a buxom woman almost old enough to be his mother, told him to stay away from the blonde, she was unclean. Though he knew they were mostly kidding him, sometimes when Juan looked at the women, he would feel a lump in his throat, and his genitals would get hot and swollen and he would become so hard he'd have to go to the men's room to adjust himself.

Juan knew the fire that burned in his loins was a sign of weakness. He did his best to ignore it, and secretly wished all women were more like his sister, Teresa. When she came home from her job at night, she would share stories of middle-aged white men who tipped her with twenty-dollar bills, seemingly in return for only her smile. It was no surprise to Juan that men were smitten by her. She had lustrous black hair surrounding her heart-shaped face and dark eyes that sparkled with delight when she laughed. As for her body, Juan simply considered her athletic. He never thought of her as a sensual being. Teresa did not flaunt her figure, and Juan knew if men lusted after her, they would be disappointed. His sister was pure, as was he.

When Juan returned home after finishing his shift, he waited up for Teresa, like always. They had come to the United States together three years ago, their parents saving and putting up all they owned to buy their children's way across the border. On the day they left their village for good, Juan's father, a stout, stoic man, gave his son a brief hug. Juan and Teresa promised their parents they'd always look out for each other, before they climbed aboard the bus idling on the dirt road in front of their home. As they drove away, Juan looked back one last time and saw his father's face had changed, as if the muscles that held his features in place had quit and surrendered to gravity.

. . .

Sometime after eleven the door lock clicked and Teresa walked into the apartment. Juan could immediately feel her excitement. Her eyes were lit up and instead of sitting after many hours on her feet, she stood in front of the couch where he watched TV.

"I had an audition today for the variety show," she exclaimed. "The director wants to be my agent!"

Juan jumped up and hugged his sister. It had long been Teresa's dream to be on stage. She had a truly unique singing voice, deep and lovely and full of life. In church they sometimes asked her to sing a hymn, and when she did, even the youngest of children became still and listened as if hypnotized. At these moments Juan would close his eyes and believe her singing was that of an angel descending from the heavens.

But she had been blessed with more than a wonderful voice. She was also a natural dancer, and could move to the rhythms of any musical style with ease, her hips gyrating as if the pulse of the songs were born from within her. Juan would sometimes see her in her room, practicing various dance steps on the threadbare carpet, her hair flailing about her face, her body a portrait of fluid exuberance.

That Teresa was destined for fame, Juan felt confident. But he was also concerned, now that the opportunity had arrived for her to take the next step. Juan may have been immature in dealing with the opposite sex, but in other ways, he possessed a wisdom that belied his youth. His childhood had been fraught with the threat of bandits, kidnappers, and corrupt police and officials that preyed upon the people of his remote village. He knew once Teresa's talent was discovered, there would be many seeking to manipulate her for their own benefit.

But tonight was not a time to worry about such matters. It was occasion for celebration. Juan prepared a plate of nachos, the tortilla chips hot and crispy when he removed them from the oven. He sat with Teresa until well past midnight, speaking of their hopes and dreams—Teresa's aspirations to be a star, and Juan's plans to go to college after graduating from high school. And then, once they became successful and wealthy, they would bring their parents from their poor village to America, so they could once again live together as a family.

•   •   •

Three days later Teresa again stood on the stage, this time with some of the *I SPY* cast members. The three women and one man were clearly pissed at being called in for the unscheduled afternoon rehearsal. When they met Teresa, they stared at her, their faces incredulous, as Stuart told them the agenda.

"The final scene in the second act, she'll appear, dressed in black, and sing a slow, haunting number, to punctuate the demise of the Russian spy."

"But this is a light comedy!" blurted the man, his face hot and pouty beneath his curly blond hair.

"And that's why it will work." Stuart patted the man's rear. "Now let's get to the blocking."

"As long as my songs aren't changed, I really don't care," said a red-haired woman.

"You've got nothing to worry about, Desi. Everyone, take your places. Chop-chop."

Teresa memorized the stage movements after three tries. On the fourth run-through, Stuart told her to be ready, the sound man would play the musical score she'd sing to. She thought she'd be nervous, but when the music started, Teresa felt calm and confident. As she sang she noticed the looks of surprise, then envy, and from one of the gals, a nod of begrudging respect.

"Fabulous, you, simply fabulous," Stuart said, standing and clapping when the song ended. The cast members couldn't help smiling. Stuart Gold had not been a big time Vegas producer by accident. The man had his faults, but by god, he had a nose for talent.

"One week from today, people, Teresa will go live."

Before Teresa left, she handed Stuart the signed contract, granting him the right to represent her, and awarding him a percentage of her income for the next five years. He knew most agents would have taken a much larger cut, but Stuart didn't need the money—he'd already socked away enough to retire comfortably. His motivations were of a different ilk. Once Teresa Perez became a star, he planned to launch himself back to the forefront of the Las Vegas entertainment business. And then, if he played his cards right, the time would come when he would pay back Cornhole Porter, the pompous, beguiling prick. Teresa Perez would be Stuart's vehicle for both success and revenge. The young Latina would be the next Jennifer Lopez, or maybe even bigger. Stuart had never felt so sure of anything in his life.

9

COMING UP WITH NO solid leads in my search for Jason Loohan, I called the bondsman in New Jersey to ask if Loohan had surfaced there.

"He's vanished. If he was in town, I'd know it. That's why I offered you his paper."

"Well, he's not turning up out here," I said. "I need something more to go on. How about his affiliation with Hard Core United? Is he part of the gang?"

"I don't think so."

"You said he was best friends with Billy Morrison, right?"

"That's right—they go back a ways. But that doesn't mean they shared the same taste in music. Or were in the same gang, for that matter."

"What about hobbies, or habits?"

"Hold on, I'll pull my notes."

I waited a few minutes, listening to papers shuffle and his mumbling and grumbling.

"All right, one source said he likes to hustle pool in bars. Another guy told me he's a real whoremonger. Said if he was starving and had to choose between a meal and getting his crank turned, it'd be a toss-up."

"How reliable would you consider these sources?"

"About as reliable as all the other pus bags I deal with."

"What about his police record? You have a copy, right?"

"I should, but I don't."

"Why the hell not?"

"My relationship's a bit strained with some of detectives at the precinct, if it's any of your business."

"It is my business. Jason Loohan could be in Canada for all you know." I started to say something else, but he interrupted me.

"Look, the bounty on Loohan is three grand, Reno. It's coming out of my pocket, too. Finding him may require a little detective work. If that's too much to ask, just let me know."

"You tell me you have a hunch he *might* have come with Morrison to Tahoe, just because they're buddies? And based on that, you want me to canvass every bar with a pool table in the region? Oh, and in my spare time, also search for prostitutes he may have boned? That's pretty damn slim. Tell you what—I'll pass."

"Whoa, whoa, slow down there. Look, Loohan's a career criminal. He's also got a face that's easy to recognize. Spend a day or two on this, would you? Start with the seediest joints and the streetwalkers, and maybe he'll pop up."

"It's a long shot."

"It's also a nice payday. What's the matter, are you too busy?"

He had me there. Except for dodging whatever grief Cody tried to pull me into, I didn't have a goddamned thing on my plate. Maybe I'd gotten lazy, after running into a chunk of money that allowed me a break from the pressure of making my bills every month. I felt a creeping shame at having spent the entire winter skiing at my leisure, not working, and then complaining when offered a job that probably would require some real effort. Shit, when I was broke, as I had been most of my career, I would have jumped at the chance for a three grand bounty.

"All right, I'll pound the pavement for you," I said, resolved to resume my old work habits. "Okay? Just call me if you hear anything that might help."

I hung up and printed fifty copies of the picture the bondsman had provided of Loohan. He had a ruddy complexion, like you'd expect of an Irishman, but beneath his coal-black hair his eyes were 100 percent Asian. The incongruity of his features reminded me of an unfinished computer-generated police sketch.

It was still not nine A.M., and since touring the bars and looking for hookers would be pointless until later in the day, I went out to my garage to lift weights and kill some time. I was lying on my bench press when Cody opened the door.

"My boiler is giving me grief," he said, holding his gut.

I sat up. "Maybe you ought to cut down on the consumption." The dozen donuts I'd bought two days ago were gone, as was the case of beer and fifth of vodka.

"Thanks, doc," he said, and went back inside.

By noon I was ready to hit the road, but as I was leaving, Cody came out of the bathroom.

"I just puked. I feel a lot better already. Wait up and I'll go with you."

"Bad idea," I said. "Why don't you rest up, maybe dry out for the afternoon?"

"I told you I feel fine."

"I got a long day in front of me, Cody. If things don't pan out in town, I'll probably head over to Carson, and maybe even to Reno."

"Don't worry about me, I'm good," he said. "I don't even feel like drinking."

"I've heard that one before."

Cody smiled like a man all too familiar with his own weaknesses. I waited while he put on a fresh shirt and gargled with the mouthwash I kept in the bathroom. Then we drove off to the nearest bar.

Whiskey Dick's had just opened and was empty. The bartender came around from the back with a tub of ice.

"Hi, Pam," I said. She dumped the ice into the bin next to the well bottles and wiped her brow.

"Little early for you, ain't it?"

I put a picture of Jason Loohan on the bar. "Ever seen this dude?"

She picked it up with wet fingers and studied the printed photo.

"Nope, can't say I have. He's not related to those freaks that came in the other day, is he?"

"He might be. Do me a favor and call me if he comes in, okay?"

She sighed, folded the picture, and propped it between two spigots on the back bar. Then she gave me a look, her resigned face accusing me of transgressions past and future. I left quickly, hurrying to escape her scornful eyes, and memories of my divorce.

Next we hit Houlihan's, a large hotel bar on Highway 50 that used to be called O'Shay's, and before that it was Mulligan's. It looked like it was originally a banquet hall, but the owners decided pool tables, video games, and air hockey would be a better use of the real estate. I'd never seen any cars in the parking lot, and the last time I'd stopped in, on a Friday night, the place was like a morgue.

There was no bartender on duty, and when we went to the adjoining hotel lobby, the kid at the reservations counter said the bar was only open on weekends.

We walked outside, squinting into the bright heat of the day. I put on my sunglasses and said, "Let's go check out the local knife and gun club." We drove to the west end of town and stopped at South Lake Tahoe's only true biker bar, a ramshackle, red-painted A-frame called The Ho-down Club. A rust-bucket Chrysler and a collection of Harleys were parked out front, where a bearded, overweight man in a black leather vest tended to a smoking barbeque. He eyed us as we walked to the entrance.

"What's going on, kemosabe?" Cody said.

Inside, cigarette smoke swirled in the shaft of light from the doorway. Apparently The Ho-down was not buying into California's anti-smoking laws. We sat at a corner of the bar waiting for the bartender, an older fellow who looked like country singer Willie Nelson, to finish his conversation with a long-haired biker and his bitch, a bleached blonde with huge breasts that had to be implants. She caught my eyes on her and shot me an evil smile. I nodded and looked away, thinking this one belonged to the clan, for their use whenever the mood struck.

After a minute the bartender made his way to us. "What's drinkin', men?"

"Diet Coke."

"Two," Cody said.

I paid with a ten, and pushed the change onto the tip rail. The bartender scooped up the cash and dropped it into a glass pitcher behind the bar.

"You guys want lunch? We got five-dollar burgers fresh off the grill."

I shook my head. "I'm looking for a guy, name's Jason. An Irishman with black hair and Asian eyes. Shoots a good game of pool. Seen him around by chance?"

"Don't sound familiar. He a local?"

"No, he's new in town."

He shrugged and started walking away.

"Hey," I said, pulling a folded sheet from the pocket of my Levis. "Take a look at his picture, would you?"

He gave the page a cursory glance, then raised his eyes to mine. His face was screwed up in a grimace, the skin age-spotted and folded, his stained teeth clenched inside his gray beard like rotted eggs in an abandoned nest. He put his paw over the paper and learned forward on his elbows, his voice not much above a whisper. "We get all sorts in here, but I haven't seen anyone resembling your friend. You're free to ask around, but

I wish you wouldn't, you know what I mean?" He cut his eyes toward a handful of bikers sitting on the other side of the place. They were in full road gear—boots, black leather chaps, arms wrapped in ink, their faces grainy and wind burnt.

"How about one of them burgers, boss?" Cody said.

"Make you a deal—I'll give you one on the house, just take it to go."

"We mean no trouble," I said.

"Mister, you don't look like you'd back away from it either. And sometimes it don't take much to bring it on here."

"Call me if you see him. I'll make it worth your while."

He looked at me with bleak eyes. The biker and his female friend were now staring at us.

"You can get your lunch from Frank," the bartender said, motioning toward the front door. "On your way out."

"Let's boogie," I said to Cody.

"It's a little too early for heavy metal anyway, Dirt." Cody eased himself off the barstool, looked around the room, and said, "Y'all have a nice afternoon now, ya hear?" He grinned and waved, then followed me outside.

We watched the man at the grill wrap a couple cheeseburgers in tinfoil, then drove across the street to a public campground and ate at a picnic table in a grove of pine trees.

"Not bad," Cody said, balling the foil and tossing it in a trash can. "What was the barkeep's problem?"

"He's the owner, and the ABC put his liquor license on probation."

"Serving minors?"

"That, and crank was being dealt out of the bathroom. And a month ago a man was stabbed near where we were sitting."

"A quaint, charming place, known for its discerning clientele and gourmet menu." Cody stood and blew his nose in a napkin. "Let's roll."

We spent the rest of the afternoon bouncing around local hangouts on the California side of the border, before crossing into Nevada.

"Are we gonna hit the casinos?" Cody asked.

"Just the security offices. I know a couple of the managers. Do me a favor and play it low key, would you? I want to stay on good terms with these people."

"Isn't it getting close to happy hour?"

"I thought you didn't feel like drinking."

"Did I say that?"

"You want to wait in a bar while I take care of this?"

"Naw, I'm good."

I parked in the back of Harrah's, Tahoe's largest casino. The casino conglomerate that owned Harrah's also owned Harvey's, and a smaller adjoining casino that targeted a younger crowd. The security chief at Harrah's, a sexless black woman in her fifties, oversaw security for all three casinos, and we'd gotten along well the one time we'd met. But that was a while ago, and I didn't know if she'd remember me.

I went to a half-door next to the cashier's cage, where a sign said SECURITY in large, gold letters. A balding man with a mustache stood behind the door, writing on a clipboard.

"Joan Wallace, please." I handed him my card and he glanced at it, his lips downturned, his eyes shaded with disinterest. Then he handed it back. Maybe he felt the big boss had more important things to do than talk to the likes of me.

"What's it pertaining to?" he said.

"An armed robbery suspect jumped bail and we think he's in the area." I held up a picture of Jason Loohan's face. "Ever seen him?"

"Nope." He continued writing on his clipboard.

"How about Ms. Wallace?"

"She's a busy woman, buddy. Do you have an appointment?"

I felt Cody move closer.

"I'll just call her then," I said, punching numbers into my cell. "What did you say your name was?"

He raised an eyebrow. "Hold up there. Let me go see if she's in her office."

"What's his deal?" Cody said, watching him walk away.

"His wife's blowing the milkman, his hemorrhoids are killing him, and the cat shit in his shoes."

"Really?"

I shrugged. "Just my overactive imagination."

We waited for a few minutes until the man came back and opened the door for us. We followed him into the bowels of the casino, past a team of workers counting and recounting stacks of cash, until we came to an office. He knocked lightly and let us in.

The African American woman behind the desk looked at me from over her glasses, her grayish eyes steady and penetrating.

"Mr. *Reno*, as in, no problemo. What can I do for you?"

"You have a good memory, ma'am."

"I never forget a face."

"I imagine that's an occupational hazard at times."

"Who's this?" she said, ignoring my remark and shifting her eyes to Cody.

"Cody Gibbons, ex-San Jose PD," he said. "Pleased to meet you."

She dismissed him with a nod. "I hear you were involved in a shooting a few nights ago," she said.

I scratched my ear. "Word gets around, huh?"

"I'm connected to law enforcement agencies on both sides of the border, Mr. Reno. It's part of my job to stay informed of local criminality."

"Maybe you can help me, then. I'm looking for Jason Loohan, a known felon from New Jersey. He's a friend of the man I shot, a rapist from New

Jersey." I handed her Loohan's picture. "He jumped bail on rape and armed robbery charges."

She studied his face, then ran the sheet of paper through a device next to her computer monitor.

"I'll send it out and have his picture posted on our bulletin boards. If he's spotted, I'll contact the authorities."

"I'd appreciate it if you'd contact me directly, Ms. Wallace. I don't believe there's a warrant for him in Nevada yet, so the local police can't do much."

"Sure they can. A phone call to New Jersey is all it takes."

"Maybe so, maybe not. Anyway, if I catch him, there will be no doubt to the conclusion—he'll be on a plane back to the East Coast within twenty-four hours."

"Whether you have to shoot him or not."

"I'm sure that won't be necessary."

"Really? In your case, Mr. Reno, shooting seems like an occupational hazard."

• • •

We left after I convinced her to at least call me along with the Nevada PD, should Jason Loohan show up in one of Harrah's establishments.

"Sounds like you're not exactly a local hero," Cody said, as we crossed the street toward Pistol Pete's.

"What else is new?"

"Not my patience, that's for sure. Let's say we give it a rest after this joint, huh? Go get some chow and have a drink or two."

"All right. But after that I'm heading to Carson City."

"My friend the workaholic," he sighed.

We went through the street-side glass doors into Pistol Pete's, a place I avoided after Cody and I were involved in a case last year that resulted in the death of a corrupt sheriff and the disappearance of Salvatore Tuma, a Mafioso and previous owner of the casino. I'd later learned the business was under new ownership, but I suspected there were still those at Pistol Pete's who'd be less than happy to see me on the premises. To say that applied to Cody would be an understatement.

"Cody, why don't you chill out at the bar while I take care of this? I shouldn't be long."

"What, you think I might start something if we run into one of Sal Tuma's old buddies?"

"Tuma's long gone. So is his crew. The Nevada Gaming Commission forced him to sell out."

"Who's the new owner?"

"Beats me. What does it matter?"

"I'm gonna play a few hands of blackjack," Cody said. "Call my cell if you can't find me." He walked away, and I began searching for the security desk, without luck, until a janitor guided me to the opposite side of the casino, to an unattended counter near the sports book. I waited there for another few minutes before spotting a uniformed guard with a walkie-talkie.

"Can I talk to your head of security?" I said.

He looked at his watch. "He's probably gone home for the day."

"Anyone on duty I can talk to?"

"Try him." He pointed at a fellow in a short-sleeved shirt coming out of the adjacent bar.

"Excuse me," I said, walking over to intercept the man as he strode into the maw of the casino floor.

"Yes?"

His bald head shone under the lights, and the wrinkles on his face were those of a man in his fifties, but his flat stomach and the thick veins that ran up his forearms and oversized biceps belonged to someone younger.

Steroids and human growth hormone were now being marketed as the fountain of youth. It looked like he'd bought into the dream.

I handed him a picture of Jason Loohan. "We think he's in the area. He's jumped bail and is considered armed and dangerous."

He looked up from the picture, the lines across his forehead like rows of dry riverbeds. "Are you Nevada PD?"

"No. Private investigations." I hesitated for a second, trying to place his accent, before handing him a business card. "If you see him, would you call me?"

I waited while he studied my card. "Yeah, sure," he said. "No problem." His eyes met mine, and there was a hint of levity there, as if we were sharing a joke.

"Thanks," I said, and was about to walk away when I paused. "Your accent reminds me of someone I used to know. New York, right?"

He smiled thinly, his teeth barely visible. "No, I'm from Detroit. Born and raised."

"Go Red Wings."

He blinked, and I could almost hear the file cards shuffling in his head. He looked away for a second before his eyes came back to me, no longer amused.

"I was always more of a Tigers fan," he said. Then he slid my card into his pocket and walked away, the picture of Loohan rolled up in his hand like a length of pipe.

•   •   •

As I moved toward the card tables, I considered the possible meaning of a continuing mob presence at Pistol Pete's. An indirect consequence of the case I handled a year ago was the arrest of Sal Tuma's son, Jake, for his role in a drug ring. The enterprise had fattened a lot of wallets, including those of some former South Lake Tahoe cops. When Jake Tuma went down, I imagine it created a void, a situation where demand was greater than supply, a business opportunity. It looked like the Mexicans operating out of the Pinewood Apartments had moved in to take advantage.

When I spotted Cody, he wasn't playing cards, but instead was sitting at an inactive roulette table, highball glass in hand, chatting with a dark-haired cocktail waitress. For a second I hoped it wasn't Teresa Perez, but then she turned, and though I still couldn't see her face, her bust line gave her away.

"Hi, Teresa."

"Oh, Mr. Reno. Hi."

"Dan, Teresa tells me she'll be singing at the show here next week," Cody said. "Can you believe this girl?"

"I didn't know you were a singer," I said.

"I've always sang. But this is the first time I'll be doing so professionally."

"Well, congratulations, Teresa. That sounds wonderful."

"I told her we'd be there," Cody said, beaming. "We can buy tickets tonight."

"Sure," I said.

"Cody just asked me to dinner," Teresa said. "I'd like to invite you both to my place tomorrow night. Juan and I will cook you a real Mexican meal."

Cody's mouth fell open, but he recovered quickly. "Why, that sounds splendid," he said.

"I don't know," I said. "I'm working a case and I might be over in Reno…"

"Juan and I would be really disappointed if you can't make it," Teresa said, looking up at me with her brown eyes.

"He'll be there," Cody said, slapping me on the back. "We have to go now, dear, we have work to do. But we'll see you tomorrow."

We headed toward the exit, and once we were out of earshot, Cody said, "I know what you're thinking, but it's not like that."

"Like what?"

"Like I got designs on her for a piece of ass."

"What is it, then?"

He didn't speak until we were outside. The sun had fallen, and the thirty-foot cowboy above Pistol Pete's main entrance was alive with neon light against the darkening sky, the six-shooter flashing orange and red at the end of the barrel.

"You remember when I told you I got Stacy Hicks pregnant, right before we graduated from Oakbrook?"

"Vaguely."

"So, she didn't want to get an abortion."

"And?"

"About a year ago she wrote me a letter, out of the blue. Said I have a sixteen-year-old daughter. She included a picture."

"Wow. Is she looking for child support?"

"No, I don't think so. She just asked if I was interested in meeting her."

"What did you say?"

"Nothing, yet. I mean, I haven't responded."

"I'm not sure what this has to do with Teresa Perez, Cody."

"What I'm saying is, I have a daughter that's not much younger than her, all right? So maybe I feel a little guilty about it."

"So now you've sworn off younger women?"

"No—listen, my point is, Teresa seems vulnerable. Maybe she could use someone around to help out, if needed."

"And it's just a coincidence she's beautiful with a body that walked off the pages of *Playboy*?"

"Christ, get your mind out of the gutter, would you, Dirt?"

We stopped at the corner to wait for the light to change, and when I looked at Cody, the confident, cavalier expression he usually wore had collapsed, replaced by an uncertain grimace.

In law enforcement circles, Cody Gibbons was seen as a larger-than-life, quick-to-violence cartoon character, a grim sight indeed for criminals unfortunate enough to cross his path. He treated legal convention as a mere suggestion, much in the way traffic lights are viewed in some third world countries. His reputation as an out-of-control confrontation junkie hiding behind a bounty hunter's license was no doubt warranted to a large degree, but Cody could always justify his actions by pointing to the end result. He'd been officially fired from the San Jose police force for shooting a PCP-crazed suspect, but he had done so to stop the man from beating a fellow officer to death. In another episode, he shot dead a Latino gang-banger holding a rifle to the head of a naked and battered woman. And two winters ago, he'd saved my life by blowing away a hired assassin who was trying to kill me.

As for his personal life, he never spoke much about his divorce from a woman I considered a normal, mainstream type. Since then, his relationships consisted of strippers who moved into his apartment for a couple weeks then vanished, drunken one-nighters, and a brief affair with the wife of the SJPD lieutenant who was behind his firing.

Not a man drawn to introspection, at least that he let on, Cody seemed mostly oblivious to his public persona. If it was suggested to him that he was an emotionally shallow womanizer who no respectable lady would have, or, perhaps, a drunken bear happily frolicking among and waging war against society's worst criminal elements, Cody would probably shrug and say, "What's your point?"

But there was another side of Cody Gibbons few knew of. I'd met Cody when he was a fifteen-year-old kid, abandoned by an alcoholic father and left to forge his way on the streets. I remember him at our high school in middle class suburbia, wearing the same pair of pants and shirt for the entire semester. We'd become friends on the football team and worked together on weekends at odd jobs, mostly physical labor. There were times he'd come to work with no lunch and pull an eight hour shift hauling rubbish at a construction site, a job so back breaking everyone they hired quit except us. Cody often worked without a break, and though I always offered to split my lunch with him, he never accepted.

In our senior year, Cody's play on the defensive line won him a scholarship to Utah State, which he almost lost after tossing our head coach into a garbage bin. On the last day of high school, he proposed marriage to a cheerleader he'd been dating, and when she declined, he left town on the spot and hitchhiked to Salt Lake City.

Five years later he landed back in San Jose as a rookie patrolman. It was during that time my marriage was dissolving, due in part to my inability to deal with my emotions after killing a man. I'd woke up one morning in the parking lot of a seedy wino bar, my life unhinged, my job lost, my wife gone. Cody was there for me then, lending me enough to make my rent, and helping me land employment at a local bail bonds company. Since then, I learned I could always rely on Cody in the darkest of times. He'd put his life on the line for my cause more than once, and I had no doubt he'd do it again if need be. Loyalty was as much part of his nature as his more debatable traits.

The light turned green and Cody stepped into the crosswalk, but I stopped him.

"We forgot to pick up the tickets for Teresa's debut," I said, and started walking back to Pistol Pete's. "Come on, man."

He looked at me like a vindicated soul.

• • •

Afterward we drove to Sam's place, a small tavern off 50, for tacos, beers, and french fries, then proceeded around the lake until turning where the road forked east toward Spooner Pass. Within a minute or two, the forest was replaced by treeless hills dotted with sagebrush. Above us a sky splattered with stars illuminated the colorless terrain, which looked as forlorn and cold as a moonscape.

"I figure I'll give this two more days," I said. "I'll cover Carson City tonight and Reno tomorrow. If I don't come up with anything solid on Loohan, I'll cut my losses."

"You ever consider maybe Loohan might like to catch up with *you* and get some payback for what you did to his best buddy?"

I watched Cody light a cigarette, then turned my eyes back to the road. "Sounds farfetched," I said. "He's running from the law, not looking for it."

"Never know. Let me ask you a question: What would you do if you skipped bail?"

"Get a fake ID and keep a low profile, maybe leave the country."

"And how many bail jumps actually do that?"

I steered deftly to avoid a jackrabbit bounding across the road. "Not many."

"Right. Because most of these douchebags couldn't logic their way out of a wet paper bag if their lives depended on it. You try to apply logic to their behavior, next thing you know they do something completely opposite."

"Contrarian theory, huh?"

"Call it a fancy name if you want, but it happens."

"I'll keep that in mind."

We came around a bend and over the pass and watched a brightly lit roadway appear in the dark valley below. We glided off the grade and hung a left when we reached the lights, onto Highway 395, Carson's main drag.

Carson City is an armpit of a town, exactly the kind of place you don't want to wake with a hangover. If not for being the Nevada state capital, I suspect it would be no more than an anonymous blip on the map. But the city employed large numbers of government workers, and the storefronts serving them were lined up for miles on Highway 395, like a testament to cheap consumerism. Fast food restaurants, car dealerships, furniture outlets, gas stations, minimarts, RV centers, and cut-rate hotels for as far as the eye could see. Like a long, oversized strip mall. The effect was broken briefly by a couple blocks that passed for a downtown, consisting of ancient bars, a trio of run-down casinos, and the capitol building, a brown, domed structure that looked like it needed a good washing.

The single notable attraction of Carson City, and in truth the main reason most visitors ever came here, was a smattering of legal brothels outside the city limits. That was the extent of Carson City's Old West charm—a few whorehouses relegated to the outskirts of town.

We stopped at every pool hall and bar on 395, and not a single bartender or patron claimed to have ever seen Jason Loohan. We left the last bar, a depressing dump that reeked of rotten teeth and vomit, and stood outside my truck in the cold shadows. My eyes burned with weariness, and the muscles between my shoulder blades were in a knot. I rolled my head and flexed my arms behind me.

"It's past ten, Dirt. You ready to head back?"

"No. Not yet."

Five minutes later I turned off 395 at the intersection where Highway 50 reconvened, heading east across hundreds of miles of barren Nevada desert.

"Here we are again, the loneliest road in America," Cody said.

"Don't sweat it, we're just heading to the cathouses."

"That's what I figured, but with you I never know."

I drove for eight miles into the emptiness until the low, faded billboard for Darla's Ranch, The Velvet Parlor, and Tumbleweeds flashed in my headlights. The half-paved road we turned onto was dark and narrow. We rumbled over a short bridge and around a tight corner before pulling into a large, well-lit gravel parking lot.

Four chain link-fenced trailer homes arranged in a horseshoe surrounded us. One was a strip club that replaced a brothel that burnt to the ground some years back. The others were places where men went to tear off a piece of ass that would cost them nothing more than money.

We started at Darla's, a no-frills ranch for the budget conscious. Inside was a small lobby crowded by a cigarette machine and a jukebox, and further in a weathered madam stood behind a four-stool bar.

"Company," she rasped, and a half-dozen whores filed out from of an adjoining room where they'd been smoking and watching TV. They stood in a lineup for us.

Carla, a frizzy blonde with cottage cheese thighs and deflated breasts, smiled big, hoping to win us over with her personality. Her friend Zelda was a pretty brunette with an inviting cleavage, but her lower body looked borrowed from a circus fat lady. Beside her, a dour American Indian woman built like a skinny man stared us down as if plotting revenge for the massacre of her people. Next, a frail, bikinied thing mumbled her name, her blurred tattoos from a different era. Standing a head above her was a short-haired girl who reminded me of Alfalfa from the Lil' Rascals. She may have been the cutest of the bunch, especially compared to the last in line, a female version of ex-Packers linebacker Ray Nitzke.

I produced one of my last remaining pictures of Jason Loohan, but before I could say anything, Cody stepped forward.

"Okay, ladies, who wants to pay me fifty bucks to get laid?"

Fortunately no one took great offense, especially after I bought a round for the house. But none of them recognized Loohan.

After that it was off to The Velvet, a more upscale brothel with at least a few ladies I wouldn't kick out of bed for eating crackers. We had a couple drinks at their bar, and I let my head fall forward, the alcohol melting away the fatigue of the day's work, my purpose slipping behind me. But the day wasn't over yet, I reminded myself. I chugged a caffeinated drink and pulled Cody out of there, not an easy task after he'd become enamored with a stunning redhead who saw him as a hot prospect.

The remaining bordello was Tumbleweeds, a sprawling building with a fifty-foot mahogany bar overlooking a garish red parlor sectioned by circular couches.

"Whoever did this interior decorating should be shot," Cody said.

At the corner of the bar stood a gangly man in a security guard uniform. He had a bit of a gut and a mustache that looked silly, but I'd seen him in action once, and he was quite competent with a billy club. I decided to steer clear of him. The jolt from the energy drink had already faded, and it was past midnight. I wanted to rid myself of my remaining pictures of Loohan and head home.

Cody seemed to have other ideas, though. We'd only been at the bar for a minute before he was on his second drink and had a slinky blonde perched on his lap. I handed her a sheet of paper and asked if she recognized Loohan. She whispered something in Cody's ear, and they broke into giggles.

"Get a room," I sighed.

"Don't look now, but here comes Blackula," she said, looking over Cody's shoulder. I turned and watched a tall Negress with a beehive hairdo and cowabunga breasts approach us. Her lipstick was Christmas red and she wore black lingerie that brushed her ankles.

"You two look rough and ready," she said. "Y'all ready to party?"

I handed her my last, crumpled picture of Loohan. "Ever see this guy?"

She looked at the picture and back at me. "You messin' wit' me?"

"No, why?"

"This chump offered me twenty dollars for a blow job."

"When?"

"My rates start at three hundred, honey buns."

"And I'm sure you're worth every penny. When was he here?"

"Maybe half hour ago. I told him, he on a budget, head across the way to Darla's."

At that moment my cell rang. Cody looked at my phone, his eyes narrowed.

"That man whose picture you're passing around," a female voice said. "He's out front, getting on a motorcycle."

Cody lifted the girl from his lap and set her on the bar, and we raced out the front door. About fifty feet from us a man in blue jeans and a black leather jacket kick-started a blue Yamaha, a street legal dirt bike. His face was clearly visible under the lights attached to the chain link gate in front of Darla's.

I handed Cody my keys. "Start my truck," I said. Then I walked across the gravel to where Jason Loohan sat on the idling bike, his black hair hanging low over his forehead. He pulled his helmet on as I grew near.

"Man, that's a sweet bike, dude," I said. "I was thinking of getting one—"

I reached for his arm, but he juiced the throttle and the cycle leapt forward, the back tire digging into the gravel and spraying me with a shower of rocks and grit.

"Son of a bitch," I said, spitting dust.

A second later Cody skidded to a stop next to me, and I jumped into the passenger seat. He mashed the gas pedal, and we roared after Loohan.

The dirt bike launched over a berm and caught big air, the rear tire pitched sideways in classic motocross form. Cody steered into the jump, and we careened over it, my head bouncing off the ceiling. I jammed on my seatbelt and watched Loohan wheelie down the straightaway leading from the cathouses.

"He's playing with us," I said. "We'll never catch him."

Cody ignored me and buried the throttle. We gained on the bike but had to slam the brakes to navigate a tight corner, which Loohan power slid around and exited as if shot from a sling. The motorcycle's taillight began to grow dim. The road was now a straight shot to the highway, maybe half a mile, but much of it was uneven, paved smooth one second, then pot holed and rutted, then we'd slam up onto the concrete again, hitting so hard the entire chassis shuddered.

"You're gonna blow a tire," I said. Cody lost control of the truck for a second and took out a couple fence posts, the old wood snapping and flying behind us.

"Sorry about that," he said.

Before I could reply, Loohan hit a dicey section at speed and almost went down. We made up some ground and were perhaps fifty yards behind him when he reached Highway 50. He turned right, heading away from town. We bounced up onto the pavement in pursuit, the motor revving against the red line, the tires howling until we caught traction and launched ahead.

"Not gonna catch him, my ass," Cody said. The motorcycle was built for off-road and probably topped out around eighty. Within twenty seconds we were right on his rear fender, Loohan tucked over the handlebars, his right elbow cranked low, holding the throttle wide open.

"Your call. You want to take him now?" Cody said.

We were on a straight, two-lane ribbon of black asphalt. To each side of the road the terrain dipped low, the soft shoulders bordered by barbed-wire fencing. Beyond the fence line lay open desert plains.

"Pull up alongside of him. Put the bumper right on his leg and push him into the dirt."

Cody swerved close to Loohan, near enough for me to reach out and touch him. Loohan stole a quick glance at us, and I saw his fingers reach for the brake lever.

"He's gonna brake," I said, and Cody edged closer, forcing Loohan to the last inch of pavement. In a second he would either brake and risk getting run over, or drop off into the dirt at eighty. *Now we'll see how good a rider you are.*

A long moment went by, then Loohan rose from his seat and steered off the road, his tires dropping into the void. He hit the loose dirt with his weight back, spraying us with a blast of dirt clods, then flew up the opposite side of the embankment and jumped the fence cleanly. Cody skidded to a stop and we got out and watched Loohan dart away through the scrub. His headlight flashed in the dark expanse for a minute, until it grew dim and disappeared. We stood on the side of the road underneath the stars as the last rumble of his motor faded.

"Got to hand it to him, he's quite the acrobat," Cody said.

"He's got balls, I'll give him that." I got a flashlight and a map from my glove box and opened the map on the warm hood.

"There's nothing for thirty miles in the direction he's headed, and that's pretty rough terrain, especially at night," I said. "I think he's got two choices—head back west, past the whorehouses to 50, or cut across further east, maybe surface in Silver Springs. Either way he's got to get back on the highway tonight."

"Or spend the night out there."

"I doubt it. It's too cold, and now that he knows he's being hunted, I don't think he's gonna sit still."

"Back west then?"

"I think that's the best bet. We find somewhere to park off 50 and wait him out."

"Let's get coffee. There was a gas station back about five miles."

We drove off, and while Cody was inside the filling station minimart, I unlocked the steel box in my truck bed and pulled out the suitcase containing my gear. My Beretta .40 cal. automatic lay on my bulletproof vest, along with a Panther stun baton, a spray can of mace, plastic ties that served as handcuffs, binoculars, and a 35mm camera. When Cody came back and handed me a steaming sixteen-ounce cup, the suitcase was between us on the seats, and I had just inserted an eleven-round clip into the Beretta.

"You still keep your backup piece under the seat?"

"Yeah," I said. Cody reached between his legs and removed my Glock 9mm from its hiding place. He checked the chamber and put the weapon in the glove compartment.

I found the perfect spot without much searching, a brief rise in the highway where a small street intersected, maybe leading to a private residence, or a quarry, or some infrequent destination. I backed my truck down the street, giving us a wide view of the highway and the desert beyond.

"The goal here is to disable his bike," I said. "If we see him, aim for his tires."

"And if he runs?"

"I don't lose foot races."

Cody laughed. "Still got your speed, huh?"

"Enough of it, anyway."

An hour went by. Clouds moved in, and the air felt damp. I kept my window down and listened for the low tones of Loohan's four-stroke motor while scanning the desert for a solitary headlight. Cody flicked a cigarette butt out the window. "I gotta take a leak," he said. He wandered a few steps from the truck, and I heard him urinating. Then I jumped as a shot broke the stillness of the night.

"I'm hit!" Cody barreled back into the front seat, his hand holding his shoulder, blood coming from between his fingers. Another shot, and the plastic cab window behind us split and my windshield spider webbed.

Crouched low, I started the motor and jammed the accelerator. A third shot sounded, winging off my window frame. I screeched onto 50 and floored it. Cody popped the glove box and wrapped his bloody paw around the Glock. A half mile down the road I slowed and turned to him.

"How bad is it?" I said.

"Just winged me. Stings like a bitch, though."

I looked at the amount of blood soaking through his shirt. "You need stitches."

"It's a scratch. Turn around and let's go find that mother."

"Wrong. I'm taking you to Carson City General."

I slouched in my seat and peered out of the portion of the windshield still clear. I didn't like the look of all that blood flowing from my partner's shoulder.

"How the hell did he get behind us?" Cody said.

I paused. "He must have stopped in the desert and waited for us to drive away, then came back and followed us. Probably rode with his headlight off, or we would have spotted him."

"I can't believe we're running from him," Cody said, his face pale.

"You need a doctor." I turned my eyes to the road and hit the gas.

. . .

I sat in the waiting area at the Carson City emergency room, dozing and waking every few minutes. The bullet Cody claimed scratched him had torn a trench along the meat of his left shoulder, and the doctor wanted to keep him overnight. I was dubious. As soon as Cody was stitched up, I expected him to come barging through the doors, ready to hit the road.

I dozed off again, and this time I was out for a couple hours, because the nurse who rousted me said it was five in the morning.

"Your friend's asleep," she said. "He'll be fine, but he's lost some blood, and we have him on an IV. He'll be here at least another few hours."

I rubbed my eyes and walked out into the predawn. It had drizzled, and the lights over the parking lot glowed through a foggy mist. I found my truck and stared at the ruined windshield. Down the street was a cheap hotel. I checked in and fell into bed in my clothes, but sleep would not come. After a while I got up and sat in the room's single wooden chair, staring into the darkness.

Cody's perspective on criminal behavior was rooted in his upbringing on the streets and the seven years he'd spent as a cop. His insight could be uncanny, probably because he so often operated on the fringes of legality himself. But I thought his idea that most crooks behaved illogically was misguided, much like assigning racial stereotypes to any individual. The reality was some criminals were predictable, and others were not. In the case of Jason Loohan, it was the latter.

I had considered it a given Loohan would hightail once he'd lost us. Instead, he'd doubled back and attacked while our guard was down. As a result, Cody was hospitalized and my truck disabled. It was only by virtue of luck the outcome hadn't been worse. Fortunately his aim was less than dead-on, but Loohan had outrun and outsmarted us. What did that teach me about him? He was armed, for one. And resourceful and stealthy, and capable of rapidly shifting from a defensive position to the offensive. And he was willing to kill to maintain his freedom.

The morning was gray and wet when I went outside, the low hills to the west dusted with snow. The quiet was broken by a solitary big rig rumbling slowly through town, like a funeral procession. I grabbed the gear case from my truck, stepped back into my room, and pulled on my bulletproof vest. If Loohan was now hunting me, I wouldn't be a hard man to find. Especially when I considered that, based on his friendship with Billy Morrison, Loohan probably knew Joe Norton, and Norton's boys had already paid me a social call.

Eventually I slept and dreamt I was back in San Jose, employed as a pencil pusher by some nameless company. My father was involved somehow, in a suit and tie, as I always remember him. There was a vague notion of evil men up to no good, but I was distanced from it by many layers and felt no concern. Then Cody showed up, talking to my old man about how to resolve the situation, and the threat began to seem more real. I was just starting to feel a sense of danger when my cell phone jolted me awake.

"Hey," I croaked. "What's up?"

"My blood pressure, my insurance rates, the usual. Where are you?"

"A few minutes away."

"Come get me, man."

Cody was waiting five minutes later outside the emergency room entrance, his shoulder wrapped in gauze and his arm in a sling.

"Let's go get some grind," he said. "They tried to feed me a tray of dog food in there."

"How's the arm feel?"

"Just a flesh wound. Bled a lot because the bullet broke a bunch of little veins. Are you gonna drive back home with your windshield like that?"

"Not if I can get it fixed here without waiting too long."

"Don't forget we have dinner tonight at Teresa's."

"You still want to?"

"Why wouldn't I?"

I didn't answer and drove us to a Denny's. We sat in a booth drinking coffee, while I looked through the phone book for an auto glass shop.

"What are you thinking?" Cody said.

"Those HCU boys seemed to think it was real clever getting our license plate numbers. But there's no way for an ordinary citizen to trace a license plate."

"Who cares about those jackoffs?"

"I do, because Loohan's linked to them, through Billy Morrison. HCU found where I lived the same night I brought down Morrison. And I ain't in the phone book."

"They'd have to have a connection to trace your plates."

"To the police, right? Doesn't sound logical, does it?"

Cody smiled, his eyes crinkling with irony. Then his smile faded. "You still got that sawed-off in your closet?"

"Yeah, why?"

"Because if I see Loohan in your neighborhood, I'm gonna paste him to the sidewalk." He winked. "That's a promise."

"It's a nice thought," I said, as our breakfast arrived. "But I think a better plan is to find him before he finds us."

10

THE DODGE SUV PULLED into the alley behind the Pine Mountain Apartments. Two HCU members yanked Rodrigo and Pedro from the back of the vehicle, dumped them near the garbage bins, then drove off in a spray of gravel. Pedro crawled to his knees, his face contorted in pain. He thought maybe his ribs were broken, but he was more concerned about Rodrigo. The leader of the Diablos Sierra faded in and out of consciousness, blood bubbling from his mouth with each labored breath.

Struggling to his feet, Pedro left Rodrigo curled on the cracked pavement, and limped to the apartment he shared with two other gang members. They were watching television, oblivious to what had happened.

"Get up and bring the car around back. We need to get Rodrigo to a doctor." The men jumped up and a minute later eight of them hovered over Rodrigo, lifting him as gently as they could into the back seat of a Chevy Impala.

"I will kill whoever did this," said one of the teenage *cholos*.

"Shut up, Luis," Pedro said. "Go make me some icepacks."

Just then Juan Perez came around the corner on his bike, returning from the supermarket with a backpack loaded with groceries. The narrow easement was blocked by the Impala. Juan hit his brakes and caught a glimpse of Rodrigo's bloody face as he disappeared into the Chevy. He stared wide-eyed, straddling his bike until the young gangbanger named Luis looked up and said, "What are you looking at, *maricon*?"

The Impala drove past Juan, nearly hitting him. Juan tried to turn his bike around and follow the car out of the alley, but the backpack was heavy and his efforts were awkward. Luis picked up a pinecone the size of a softball and winged it from twenty feet. It was a perfect shot, the cone smacking off Juan's cheek, the spines leaving flecks of blood on his skin.

"Get lost, you *puta*!" Luis yelled, then ran up, stripped the pack from Juan's back, and flung the contents to the ground. "Your sister has nice tits!" he added, kicking a head of lettuce over the fence behind the Dumpsters. "Tell her I want to shoot my load on them!" The remaining *cholos* laughed nervously until Pedro hissed at them to quit messing around and led them through the common to his apartment.

Juan set his bike against a stucco wall and salvaged the groceries. A quart of milk had burst, but otherwise the food was intact. He walked his bike to his apartment, his face burning with shame. Once inside he gagged, choking back the bile rising in his throat. He was sickened by his fear and cowardice. He had allowed his sister's name to be defiled without the slightest objection. A real man would never allow himself and his family to be so humiliated. Why did he not have the *cojones* to stand up to those losers? They thought they were so tough, never alone, never without each other's protection.

Squeezing his eyes shut against tears of frustration, Juan sat huddled on his couch. Who was he trying to fool? Any of the gang could kick his ass one on one. Aside from a few harmless wrestling matches as a small boy, Juan had never even been in a fight. Confronting the Diablos Sierra would be like asking to have chili juice poured in his eyes.

Born malnourished and weak, Juan was used to being the slightest among his peers, and a target of bullies. He hoped the time would come when he'd outgrow his physical limitations, and he'd already begun to see results from his weight lifting regimen. Maybe it wouldn't be long before he was ready to make a stand and unleash years of repressed anger on those who provoked him. He'd start with the gangbanger Luis, if he was still around. Especially if he ever said anything about Teresa again.

Heading to his room, Juan wondered what happened to Rodrigo. Possibly he was in a car accident. The only other thing Juan could think was he'd been in a fight, but he couldn't imagine the gang letting him take a beating. Rodrigo looked near death.

He added plates to his curl bar and pounded out ten reps, trying not to arch his back. It seemed things might be getting shaky for the gangbangers, he thought, the idea providing a bit of solace. The cops had arrested one of them, and Teresa had told him, after she got home last night and woke him from the couch, something about Dan Reno and his big friend paying the gang a visit. Juan had been too drowsy to pay much attention, but now it seemed important. He'd get the details from Teresa as soon as she returned from her errands.

Juan was finishing his workout, pleased he reached a new max on the bench, when Teresa came through the door in high heels. He stared at her in surprise.

"You look so tall—why are you wearing those shoes?"

"They were on sale. Do you like them? I feel like a real lady."

A lady? You're my sister, not a lady. But when he looked at her again he could no longer deny the obvious; Teresa was grown up. The realization brought a twinge of fear and sadness. They'd always cared for each other, but since she'd told him about her upcoming performance at Pistol Pete's, he'd noticed a change in her personality. In the past they'd shared stories, finding something to laugh about, but now she'd become less responsive, seemingly absorbed in her thoughts. When she did talk, it was always about her, her hopes, ambitions, and concerns. As if his own were secondary. He'd begun to feel invisible, and sensed she'd already taken the first steps on a journey to a world where he would have no place. How long would it be before her career bloomed and she became immersed in her new life? How long before she found a man? And what of their family—what about the plan to bring them to the United States?

He swallowed his apprehension and steeled himself. He was sixteen, older than many boys in his native land who had full adult responsibilities. The time had come for him to stand up and put his boyhood behind him. Teresa's life was her own, and he needed to start acting like a man.

"What were you telling me last night about Dan Reno?" he said, deciding to not mention his humiliation at the hands of the gang.

"Two things. First, while you were at work, Dan and his friend Cody came here. They went to talk with the gang and a fight started. Then two policemen arrived and arrested Rodrigo and the fat one, Pedro."

"Arrested? I just saw Rodrigo and Pedro this morning. Rodrigo was bloody and I think going to the hospital."

They were silent for a moment. "Good," Teresa said. "Maybe they will all go away."

Juan sat on the couch, his elbows on the knees. Maybe the gangbangers *would* disappear. Trouble from both the police and Dan Reno and his giant *amigo* might be more than they could handle.

"What was the second thing?" Juan said.

"I invited Cody and Dan to dinner tonight"

"*You what?*"

"You can work on your project with Dan."

"While you…" Juan said, the implication in his sister's remark not escaping him. Juan had noted Teresa's interest in the bear with the straw-colored hair the morning on Dan Reno's deck. Now it appeared she wanted to take it to the next level. What could she be thinking?

He went to the kitchen, hiding his face in the refrigerator. "What will we cook?"

She came up from behind and hugged him, his head squeezed between her breasts.

"You shouldn't worry so much, my little brother."

"I'm not worrying. About what?"

"The future. There will be great things in store for you, I'm sure."

Juan squirmed, not wanting his sister's body so close. He knew she just wanted to show her affection for him, but the physical contact made him uncomfortable.

"You don't need to worry about me," he said, peeling her hands from his arms. "I'm more grown up than you think."

With those words a quiet surge of confidence resonated inside Juan. In his mind he saw himself leaping a river, to a place where square-jawed men shouldered burdens of family and work and fought for what they believed in and never shied from adversity, their constitutions as formidable as the granite faces surrounding the valley in which the events of Juan's young life would unfold.

• • •

Three doors away, Pedro lay on his bed, a bag of frozen corn on his elbow, another on his ankle. He washed down a handful of pain pills with a pull of tequila, and began punching numbers on Rodrigo's cell phone, dreading the call he knew he must make.

"Senor Santos?"

"Yes, Rodrigo."

"*Pardon*, it's not Rodrigo. This is Pedro. Forgive me for calling, I know I shouldn't be."

"Where is Rodrigo?"

"He's been taken to the hospital."

"What happened?"

"Two policemen arrested us yesterday. They released us this morning, but first took us to the forest, where a detective beat Rodrigo very badly. Then another group of men beat me."

"Did the police ask for money?"

"No. But they told us we must leave the area."

"Did they file charges against you?"

"No."

"Who were the other men who beat you? Were they *la policia*?"

"No, sir, they were not."

"When can I speak to Rodrigo?"

"I don't know. He's at the hospital. I think his jaw is broken."

"Keep Rodrigo's phone with you. You will be called back."

Pedro hung up and breathed a sigh of relief. The call had been easier than he expected. Santos was a lieutenant in Juarez's largest drug cartel, two levels removed from Ivan Ramos, the cartel's leader, a man whose very name caused Pedro's heart rate to quicken. Pedro had glimpsed Ramos just once, behind the huge desk in his hacienda office. Machine guns hung from the shoulders of his bodyguards, and dozens of soldiers patrolled the grounds outside. The daily decisions made in Ramos's office often determined who would live and prosper, and who would die. If he felt it expedient to his grand scheme, Ramos would not hesitate to order the deaths of every member of Diablos Sierra.

Pedro could only hope the recent setbacks wouldn't bode too grimly for him and the gang. He knew of Ramos's plan to penetrate the retail drug trade in the United States, and South Lake Tahoe was considered a key launch point in the west. Ramos was not content limiting his business to wholesale markets. There was as much money to be made at the street level, and there was no shortage of soldiers eager to cross the border from Juarez to work in US cities. Pedro had been happy to leave the poverty of Juarez for a chance at a better life when the opportunity came.

Making sure Rodrigo's phone was fully charged, Pedro placed it on his chest and closed his eyes, hoping that when he woke the circumstances of his life would still hold promise.

11

THE MANAGER AT THE auto glass shop said he'd have my windshield replaced by early afternoon. Cody and I went from the shop into the cold, overcast day and took a cab back to the hotel. I fell asleep watching TV, and when I woke, Cody was in bed snoring, his bandaged shoulder protruding from the blankets. I walked outside and started down the road, looking for coffee. The streets were still soaked and the cars that passed left oily mists in the damp air. I huddled in my coat and kept walking, my boots kicking at the wet gravel on the side of the pavement.

My initial career path was the result of a happenstance event. If not for being offered a job as an apprentice investigator by an old friend of my father's, I likely would have ended up in some other field. But employment prospects for sociology majors weren't exactly abounding, so when the opportunity for a steady job came, I took it.

I worked for three investigation firms before setting out on my own. My last boss was a penny-pinching clock-watcher named Rick Wenger, a man I tolerated for three long years before I left San Jose for Lake Tahoe. Wenger was incompetent, and I finally concluded that if he could run a successful investigations agency, how hard could it be?

Pretty goddamned hard, I learned. There were a handful of well-established private eyes in the Tahoe area, and for the most part, I picked up their scraps. A divorce case here, a missing person there, just enough to call it a job. But my recent return to bounty hunting was turning out to be a little more interesting.

Combat tactics are usually inevitable when tracking down miscreants like Billy Morrison or Jason Loohan. Though I wasn't quick to admit it, my capabilities seemed best suited for these types of cases. Of course, with Cody Gibbons around, violence became almost a foregone conclusion.

Somewhere in my psyche, though, I clung to the idea that a truly intelligent thought process could produce an amicable and just solution to any matter. A reasonable negotiation was certainly preferable to the use of force. I always hoped reason would carry the day. After all, we live in a modern society, one that grants unprecedented rights and freedom to its people, right? Striving for peaceful conclusions seemed not only sensible, but also in accordance with higher civilization.

I rolled my eyes and smirked as I walked. I don't know why I had these types of conversations with myself. With most of the scumbags I dealt with, diplomacy was about as effective as trying to change a set of spark plugs with a garden rake. It was also a good way to give a subject an opportunity to escape, or worse.

When I first got into the profession, I never envisioned what it would entail. I didn't expect to be dealing with individuals who committed the most heinous of crimes, then enjoyed a slice of pie and a glass of milk before a good night's sleep. I also didn't anticipate being put in the position where the only alternative to being shot was to shoot someone to death.

But, I rationalized, I was just filling a necessary social function. Our prison systems are bursting with recidivists, criminal gangs run rampant in cities of every size, and reports of murder on the streets are so commonplace they're barely newsworthy. Ask any law-abiding citizen who's had the misfortune of car trouble in the wrong part of town, or had a daughter pulled into a van while walking to school, or perhaps come home to find drug-crazed men ransacking their house. The perspective of a first-time victim can be illuminating.

To protect our country's more or less decent civilians, a large, clattery machinery of judges, lawyers, policemen, private investigators, and licensed bounty hunters exist. We all get paid, to varying degrees, to keep the discordant elements at bay. If fate had dictated otherwise, I might have been immune from this world, instead selling insurance or maybe counseling couples in failing marriages. Christ, given those options, maybe I was luckier than I thought.

•　•　•

Later that day, as we came over the pass and the landscape turned green with fir and pine, my phone rang. Sheriff Marcus Grier.

"Good afternoon, Marcus."

"Reno, I just got a call from Lieutenant DeHart in Carson City."

"My old friend."

"He said the hospital there reported treating Cody Gibbons for a gunshot wound."

"Yes, that's true."

"I know it's true, damn it. What the hell is Gibbons doing in town?"

"Vacationing."

"Forgive me, I'm not in the mood for your attempts at humor today. Why didn't he report the incident to the police?"

"I don't know. Let me ask him." I put my phone on mute. "Marcus Grier wants to know why you didn't alert Carson City PD you'd been shot."

Cody pulled on his ear. "Tell him I got distracted by a riveting episode of *Keeping Up With the Kardashians*."

"Marcus? He's been on pain killers and sleeping."

"Where are you two?"

"Coming around the lake into town."

"How long will it take you to be at my office?"

"What for?"

"I'll ask the questions. What time?"

I checked my watch. "Four o'clock."

"What's his problem?" Cody said after I hung up.

"I don't know. Maybe something to do with those Nevada cops."

"That all?"

"I'm sure he wants to know why you were shot."

"What are you going to tell him?"

"The truth. I got nothing to hide."

The skies turned blue as we crossed into California. The lower half of an orange sun peeked from below a stubborn bank of purple and gray clouds, like a half-lidded pupil under a thick eyebrow. I opened my window and the forest air was heavy and warm.

I left Cody at my place and walked into the stuffy lobby of the sheriff's office at four sharp. Marcus Grier opened a door and motioned for me to follow him into the complex. The salt-and-pepper hair on his scalp was cut short, to the point his head looked shaved from beyond a few feet. We went into his office, and he sat and pointed toward my chest with his pencil.

"Care to explain the body armor?"

"Sure. I'm hunting for an ex-convict named Jason Loohan, a friend of Billy Morrison's. I found him in Carson last night, and he took a couple shots at Cody and me."

"He got away, I take it?"

"For now."

"A friend of Billy Morrison's—is he a member of HCU?"

"I'm not sure."

Grier stood and stared out his window. A deputy pulled up, stomped a cigarette out in the dirt, and scratched his crotch.

"So, why the vest? You think Loohan's still hanging around?"

"It's possible."

"I don't like the idea of an armed criminal on my streets."

"I don't either."

Grier sat back down and started to write on a piece of paper but snapped the lead. He broke the pencil between his fingers and tossed it in his garbage can.

"HCU is bad news," he said. "They all live in Nevada, but seem to spend as much time on this side of the border. If I get half a chance, I'll have them behind bars."

"For what?"

"Jaywalking, drunk in public, whatever."

"It'd be nice to find something a little more substantial," I said.

"Let me know if you have any ideas."

I crossed my legs and rubbed at the stubble on my chin. "Depends how far you want to take it."

"I play by the book," he said, his voice a thick baritone. "But if you're aware they're involved in anything illegal, I need to know."

I paused, letting Grier's comment sink in. "Here's something," I said. "When I popped Billy Morrison, one of Joe Norton's boys took down my license number. They had my address later that evening, almost as if they had access to a police database."

Grier's bloodshot eyes narrowed, and his skin took on an almost purplish hue.

"Look, Jason Loohan probably has ties to HCU," I said. "I want to cut him off at the knees. It would help if I could get ahold of his police file."

He glanced at the clock on the wall. "Is Loohan from New Jersey?"

"Yeah."

"I'll see what I can do. Call me in the morning." I got up to leave, but he stopped me. "How's Gibbons?"

"He'll live."

"Good. Try not to let him get too crazy, would you?" Grier smiled and patted me on the back, as if we were chatting about a harmless old friend.

I shrugged. "I'll try."

. . .

When I got home, Cody had removed the bulky hospital bandages and was wearing a pressed, button-down shirt.

"You gonna shower?" he asked. "We need to leave in about twenty minutes."

"Marcus Grier asked how you were."

"For real?"

I shrugged. "He seemed genuine about it."

"So what, I'm his good buddy now?"

"I think he wants our help with HCU. Sounds like they've pissed him off."

"What are they up to now?"

"Nothing Grier can bust them for, apparently."

"What does he want us to do about it?"

"I told him they were able to trace my license number somehow. He didn't seem all that surprised."

"That's not good."

"I'm getting the impression that if we killed them all and loaded their corpses on a wagon heading out of town, he'd be a happy camper."

"Sounds a little extreme. Come on, hurry up. I don't want to be late."

The sun was setting as we drove to the Pine Mountain Apartments in Cody's rig. It was a bright, still night, the mountains blue, early stars appearing above a wave of low clouds backlit with red light. The type of night made for backyard barbeques, bonfires on the beach, and dancing under moonlit skies. Except I didn't feel any of that mojo. My chest was heavy with my Beretta, my thoughts preoccupied with an armed, convicted felon lurking on the edges of the twilight.

Teresa opened the door for us, dressed in stonewashed jeans and a red shirt tied at the waist. She smiled and curtsied shyly. "Welcome to the *casa de Perez*," she said. The apartment was fragrant with corn tortillas, *chiles*, and roasted chicken.

"Smells great," Cody said, hefting a brown bag clinking with expensive tequila and margarita mix. "You look lovely, *senorita*. How about a drink?"

I heard the clang of steel weights. "Juan, our guests are here," Teresa said, as Cody followed her into the kitchen.

Juan appeared at a doorway down the hall, wearing gym shorts and a tank top.

"Pumping some iron?" I said.

He nodded. "Hi, Dan."

"You look like you're bulking up. How much are you benching?"

"One sixty."

"Not bad."

"Next semester I have wrestling in PE."

"You keep on lifting, you'll be a handful."

Juan smiled and walked out to the living room. "I heard you and Mr. Gibbons fought the Diablos Sierra."

"Who?"

"It's what they call themselves. The gang."

"You seen them around lately?"

"This morning. Their leader, Rodrigo, was injured, I think badly."

"Injured?"

"Yes, and so was Pedro, but not like Rodrigo."

"Describe these guys, Juan," I said over Cody's boisterous voice and Teresa's giggles from the kitchen.

"Rodrigo is about five-nine with no fat. Pedro is a little taller and over two hundred pounds." *The same two that the Nevada plainclothesmen arrested.*

"I think they were either in a car accident or lost a fight," Juan said.

I went over to the curtain and pulled it aside. At the picnic bench sat two Caucasians in white T-shirts and knee-length black shorts.

"You ever see these guys before?"

Juan peered out beneath my arm. "No."

"Supper time!" Teresa walked out of the kitchen holding a casserole pan. Cody followed her, a black pot in one hand, a drink in the other.

The dinner conversation was a blur of light chatter, which remained genteel despite Cody's occasional flirtatious remarks. Teresa was obviously excited about her upcoming debut at Pistol Pete's, and talked of her hopes to launch a career as a singer or actress. It was easy to see why Cody was taken with her, despite his claims otherwise. She seemed to realize her aspirations were what most only dreamed of, but she spoke of them unflinchingly. I sensed a quiet confidence at her center, as if she'd faced long odds all her life but knew eventually she could overcome any obstacle. There wasn't a hint of arrogance or conceit in her voice—just a calm, steadfast determination. It was almost mesmerizing, especially from someone so young. How old was she? Twenty-one? Twenty-two?

As we ate Juan stayed quiet for the most part, sipping what was supposed to be a virgin margarita, but I'd spotted him spiking it with a bolt from Cody's bottle. When he went to the kitchen again, I joined him.

"Slow down there, kid," I said, taking the bottle from his hands. "You want to get me busted for contributing to the delinquency of a minor?"

"I'll drink you under the table," he said.

"No, you won't."

After we finished eating, Cody helped Teresa with the dishes and Juan showed me some paperwork he'd prepared for my presentation to his class.

"Please use this as your guide, okay?"

"Looks straightforward."

"What will you bring for visual aids?"

"Well, handcuffs, I suppose. Maybe my bulletproof vest…"

"How about that?" Juan said, pointing to where I'd hung my jacket. I'd taken off my shoulder holster and thought I'd hidden my piece, but my coat had fallen open.

"I don't think your school would be too happy if I brought it on campus."

"Do you always carry it?"

"No. Sometimes."

"Show me some of your moves."

"Huh?"

"Like when you kick someone's ass."

"I don't kick anyone's ass. I think you're talking about self-defense."

"Yeah. Show me what to do."

"Why? You got people messing with you?" He didn't answer, but then I noticed some little cuts on his face. "Come here," I said.

"Let's say some tough guy grabs you by the collar. Grab me." Juan reached up to my neck and held my shirt. I crossed my left hand over his arms and grasped his left wrist. "If anyone ever grabs you by the collar, just do this, and punch him in the nose with your right. They'll never know what hit them."

"Wow," he said, trying it on me in slow motion. "Show me another one."

"If you can get behind your opponent, try getting your arm around their neck, like this. Then grab your wrist with your other hand and hold it tight. It's called a sleeper hold."

"Why?"

"Because if you hold as tight as you can for about ten seconds, the person will lose consciousness."

"I will remember that one."

"Don't use it unless you're really in trouble, understand?"

"How about boxing? Do you know how to?"

"It takes some training," I said as Cody walked up. "We ready to go?" he asked, his hand on his stomach.

I finished my drink. "Sure."

We thanked Juan and Teresa and promised to return the favor. Before we left their doorway, I surveyed the dark street, looking where someone might hide, scanning for movement. We walked through the night to Cody's truck, my hand itching to reach into my coat.

"Food was good," I said as we drove away.

"Teresa signed a contract with an agent. Hopefully the guy's legit."

"You feeling okay?"

"Nothing a few vics and another drink won't cure."

"Take it easy on the pills."

"No worries."

Famous last words, I thought.

"Juan told me he saw the two Mexicans the cops arrested this morning at the apartments," I said. "They were in bad shape."

"Meaning?"

"Like maybe they had the shit kicked out of them."

"By the cops?"

"Could be. And that's not all. Guess who was sitting out at the picnic bench?"

Cody turned onto my street and cut his eyes at me.

"A couple of the HCU metal heads," I said.

"What the hell?"

"I think we just found out what HCU does for money."

"Sounds like trouble in paradise."

We pulled into my driveway, Cody's headlights illuminating the house.

"Yes, it does," I said.

We sat idling, staring at the garage door. Someone had spray painted the word, COCKSUCKER, across the panels in bright red. The letters were poorly spaced, the last two shrunk to fit. The paint had dripped off every letter, reminding me of something out of a slasher horror movie.

My initial shock gave way to a churning sensation in my gut, as if I'd eaten something that might not stay down. The nausea lasted only a few seconds, before it ballooned into a black lump of fury in my throat. I swallowed and took a deep breath. Outrage and anger were emotions I couldn't afford at the moment. I needed to think clearly.

"Kill the lights," I said. I clicked off the Beretta's safety, and Cody reached over and pulled his .44 revolver from the glove box. I slid out of the truck, creeping in the shadows leading to my front door. Cody flared to the perimeter of the yard and covered me from the trees.

The front door was locked, no signs of tampering. We made our way to the back of the house, checking the windows and back door. After a few minutes, we came back around to Cody's truck.

"If anyone's inside, they would have to have a key," Cody whispered.

"Or know how to pick locks."

"Let's go in."

We flattened our bodies against the walls on either side while I unlocked the front door and swung it open. The interior was dark and silent. I reached in and flicked the light switch. A quiet moment passed, then we burst inside, covering the room with our weapons. Nothing moved. A minute later we'd searched the house and found it empty. We stood, not speaking, in my living room.

"They shouldn't have done that," Cody said finally.

It was 9:30. I dialed Marcus Grier's cell number.

"It's late, Dan. What's up?"

"You said you wanted to bust HCU? I believe they've vandalized my house with spray paint. If you want to investigate the crime scene, be here by eight in the morning. That's what time I'll start repainting."

"How do you know it's them?"

"If you don't want to check it out, suit yourself."

"I'll be there in ten minutes," he said.

I washed the dishes in my sink and sponged up a few dirt smudges on the kitchen floor. Then I went out to the garage to check on painting supplies. The roller I'd used last summer was caked hard with paint. I tried removing it from the metal handle, but it wouldn't budge. I threw the whole thing in the trashcan. When I went back inside and sat on the couch, Cody asked if I wanted a drink, but I shook my head and walked out to the front yard. Except for the chirping of crickets, it was quiet, almost serene. A mile past the meadow behind my property, I could see a line of lights from the gondola that ran up the mountainside to the ridge-top restaurant at the ski resort.

A moment later Cody came up behind me, his huge paw on my shoulder.

"Easy, Dirt, easy. Here, drink this." He handed me a shot glass.

"I'm all right."

"Drink it, man."

I took the glass from his fingers and gunned it, the whiskey bitter on my throat.

"The only question I have is whether HCU did this, or if it was Loohan on his own," I said.

"We'll find out tomorrow."

"How so?"

Cody smiled, his face bisected by light and shadow, his teeth glistening and feral against the course stubble on his cheeks. "It's time to go have a serious chat with the HCU homos. They shouldn't be hard to find."

We waited on the porch, listening to the night. Headlights appeared down the street, and a moment later Marcus Grier's squad car rolled to a stop in front of my driveway. Grier aimed his spotlight at the garage, lighting the crime scene with an artificial intensity that struck me as unnecessary and obscene. He got out of his car and Cody and I walked over to where he stood surveying the spray-painted letters.

"Any other damage, or is this it?" Grier said. He wore khaki pants, jogging shoes, and a crème-colored sweatshirt.

"Just this," I said. He snapped a couple photos and turned his attention to Cody.

"It's been a long time, Mr. Gibbons. Enjoying your visit?"

"Sure, why not?"

"You don't look bad for someone who's been shot."

"I heal quick."

Grier started to say something but apparently thought better of it. He shifted his spotlight to the side of the house. "You didn't by chance find a spray can?"

"Nope," I said.

"Let's check your yard," he said, handing me a flashlight. Cody leaned against Grier's cruiser and watched us begin to comb through the shrubs.

"I think there's something going on between HCU and some Mexican gangbangers that operate out of the Pine Mountain Apartments," I said.

"Like what?"

"Like HCU is moving in on their drug territory."

"How'd you find this out?"

"The common area where I saw the Nevada plainclothesmen arrest those two Mexicans, guess who's hanging out there now?"

Grier looked up and stared at me.

"That's right. A couple of the HCU tough guys."

"Thanks for the tip," he said, as we moved toward the back fence.

"What's up with the Nevada cops?" When Grier didn't respond, I added, "They seemed to have made a special trip into California just to harass the Mexicans."

"You know how difficult it is to bust a cop?"

"Yeah?"

"Yeah," he said. "Maybe I'm an idealist, or maybe I'm just naïve, but the corruption up here never fails to amaze me."

"We're not gonna find a spray can," I said. Grier shrugged, and we walked back to his car.

"I'll ask your neighbors if they saw anything tomorrow morning," he said.

"Appreciate it," I said. "Then you'll call New Jersey and see about getting Loohan's record sent over?"

He nodded, his face tired, exasperated, a little sad maybe, or perhaps just plain unhappy at the recent developments on his plate. I watched him drive away, heading home to his wife and two daughters. I was sure there were times Marcus Grier questioned his career choice, and this was probably one of them. From my perspective, Grier was a cop equally suited to serve as a reverend or a social worker. I believed his most natural inclinations were to make people happy rather than to arrest them. This did not in itself make him a bad sheriff, but when things got rough, and I had no doubt they would continue to, Grier wasn't always willing to shift into overdrive.

I watched Grier's taillights disappear, then looked again at my defaced garage door. The obscene epithet and dripping paint made me think of cocktail party conversations I've overheard on the nature of criminal behavior. People outside law enforcement seem perpetually perplexed at human deviance and seek to answer the basic question, what makes a person go bad? It usually ends up as a nature versus nurture debate, and no matter how well schooled the discussions, no real clarity is ever drawn on the subject. To me and others in the trade, it's a stupid conversation, really, moot and pointless. Criminality has countless manifestations, and every act has its own unique gestation, sometimes dating back to the womb.

I once knew a devout Mormon man who did not smoke, drink, gamble, or use profanity, and had never slept with a woman besides his wife. He worked like a fiend, supporting six children and tithing 10 percent of his earnings to his church. His vice? Speeding. An impatient man, he couldn't help it. He tailgated on the freeways, drove down residential streets at forty-five, and one day ran a red light and T-boned a car packed with teenagers. Three died, and he's still in prison. Figure that one out.

As for gangs like HCU, I imagine their members probably came from low-income, broken families, where violent crime is learned at a young age, as a survival tactic if nothing else. How do their backgrounds compare to those of the flocks of Wall Street executives accused of fleecing billions from ordinary citizens, including pseudo-intellectual liberals who voted for more lenient laws every chance they got?

Marcus Grier had fled the racism and depravity of a large Southern city to be sheriff in a relatively small resort town on the California-Nevada border. In the three years I'd known him, I hadn't seen much evidence he'd been granted a reprieve from his past. South Lake Tahoe seemed an unlikely magnet for mobsters, drug dealers, and corruption. At least I'm sure that's what Grier thought when he moved here. Unfortunately, he was wrong. Next time I run into a group of armchair sociologists, maybe I'll ask them to explain it.

12

ABOUT THIRTY MILES WEST of Yuma, Arizona, sat the remains of a deserted border town. At the sole intersection, a few abandoned buildings stood, windows busted out, paint colorless and peeling, a rusted weather vane silhouetted against the dusk and creaking in the wind. The only sign of life was an emancipated yellow dog trotting woefully along the street. Farther out, a handful of decrepit structures dotted the flatlands, dust-colored and collapsing into the earth. The narrow road through town dead-ended near the fence along the border, where coils of razor wire spiraled off into a fading light. Beyond the boundary a bank of hills met a blood-red sky. The clouds above were like smoke, as if the earth was afire.

A solitary tumbleweed drifted by the idling SUV like an apparition searching for its grave. Vinnie Tuma pointed his finger and said, "Bang, bang."

Joe Norton shook his head and turned onto a dirt side street. The inclusion of Tuma on the trip had been a last-minute development, and putting up with him for the long drive felt like something out of a bad reality show. It was like *Romper Room* with the freaking guy, Tuma whining he needed to take a leak, complaining about the fast food, talking about blow jobs, driving Norton and Loohan out of their gourds. And for what? What did Severino hope to accomplish by sending this dipshit gumball with them? The answer was obvious; Tuma was there as a watch guard, to assure the drug buy made its way back to Tahoe. He was perfect for the job—he was untouchable, and Severino knew it.

But the problem gnawing at Norton was of a different nature, and it made his head feel like it was in a vice. With Tuma there, any potential for scoring the drugs *and* keeping the hundred grand Severino provided was fried. Did Loohan understand that? Besides a brief flicker in his dark eyes, Loohan hadn't reacted when Norton told him, an hour before they took off, that Tuma was coming with them.

"No point in even considering a rip-off," Norton had said, "because Tuma would just bring the cash back to Severino. So there's nothing we can gain."

Loohan shrugged.

"Don't get any ideas," Norton said. "We cannot fuck with these people."

"You worry too much." Loohan brushed some lint from his black jeans.

"Too much, my ass. Are you hearing me, Loohan? We make the buy, deliver the goods, and you get your five grand and head for the hills. That's the deal."

The conversation ended there, leaving Norton to wonder what capacity for mayhem might be simmering within Loohan. Norton had never worked with him, in fact had only met him twice back in Jersey, but Billy Morrison had considered him an indispensable ally. Although Norton didn't want to bring in an outsider for the run south, without a competent gunman in HCU's ranks, he had little choice. His head-banging soldiers might be able to terrorize a mosh pit, but pitted against armed men with enough Colombian flake to generate a million in street sales—forget it. And Norton sure as hell wasn't going to walk into a deserted border town alone with a hundred grand of mob cash.

They had spent the previous morning together, Norton wanting to get to know Loohan better before offering him the job. Hoping to gain some level of confidence that Loohan was trustworthy, that he would provide what was needed and then vanish. They had driven around town in Norton's Chevelle, up and down Highway 50, stopping for coffee at a convenience store, and then paying a quick visit to the Pine Mountain Apartments. A couple of Norton's men were positioned in the common, telling the visitors who wandered in they would need to drive just a few minutes into Nevada to score reefer or blow.

Loohan hadn't said much during their time together, answering questions in monosyllables, rarely raising his eyes. In fact, the only time he'd shown the slightest animation was when a pretty Latina in a frilly green cocktail waitress getup walked through the common.

"Who is that?" he'd said, drawing his hair from his face.

"I don't know. Some beaner bimbo."

Loohan watched her until she disappeared into her apartment, an undisguised lust radiating from his black eyes. Norton looked at him, slightly disconcerted with the intensity of Loohan's stare. Almost like a cat stalking its prey.

"Like that stuff, huh?" Norton said.

An hour later Norton dropped off Loohan behind a gas station. Loohan was probably not someone he'd want to hang out with. Some dark, weird shit smoldering in the dude. But he was definitely a guy who knew how to keep his mouth shut. Maybe the perfect guy for the job. And Norton had no better alternatives.

• • •

Norton rubbed his temples, trying to ease the pressure that had been growing during the long hours on the road. Then he craned his neck to the rear seat where Loohan sat.

Loohan gestured with his head, his black hair covering his eyes. "Those lights down there? About half a mile. Probably border patrol."

"Which way they headed?"

"Away."

Next to Norton, Tuma fidgeted, his shoes scraping against the gray lunch box tucked behind his heels. The box was stuffed with cash, the bills bundled and neatly arranged.

Tuma punched a text message on his cell phone as Norton turned down a street that dead-ended at a wood-sided building that looked like it had once been a warehouse.

"You ever put that thing down?"

"What's it to you?" Tuma said. "Severino wants me to stay in touch. Hey, when we get back to civilization, I'm gonna buy you guys a real Italian dinner." Tuma snorted a quick laugh. "Pasta, veal, red wine, the works. That ought to cheer you up."

His fists griping the steering wheel, Norton rolled to a stop and shut off the motor.

"You know what a Mexican stand-off is?" Loohan asked.

"What, you eat a bunch of beans and see who can fart the loudest?" Tuma laughed again, loud as a bark in the close confines of the vehicle.

"Not quite."

"What then?"

A pickup truck was parked down the street, a hundred feet away. Its headlights flashed on and off, bright in the dwindling twilight.

"You're about to find out."

Norton glanced at Tuma. "You get to be the taster," he said, then shifted his eyes back to the pickup.

"Not a problem. Bring the blow back here and I'll be glad to take a rip."

"Doesn't work that way, my friend," Loohan said, leaning forward, his hand on Tuma's shoulder. "I need you with me."

"Hey, Severino said I should wait in the car. You guys would handle it."

"That .38 you keep in your coat pocket?" Loohan said.

"Yeah?"

"You know how to shoot it?"

Tuma looked at Norton, his eyebrows lifted, a frown forming on his mouth.

"What the fuck I do to deserve this disrespect?"

"You don't *get* respect," Loohan said, his voice flat. "You earn it,"

"You heard him," Norton said, reaching under the seat and sliding free a pistol grip shotgun.

"Hold on, now—"

"You ain't got the balls for this shit, is that it?" Loohan's face up close, his breath hot against Tuma's ear. "What would your fellow mobsters think?"

The doors to the pickup opened and three men stepped out onto the hardpan street. The darkening skies made it difficult to see them in much detail. Vinnie Tuma swallowed, his hand in his pocket holding his gun, his palm slick with sweat.

Norton and Loohan climbed out on the driver's side, leaving Tuma standing near the passenger side fender. They began walking toward the three figures, who waited like dark statues. Norton and Loohan stopped after a few paces.

"I have the money," Norton yelled. "We inspect the goods, and if we like it, we make the exchange." He pointed with his arm. "Here, in the middle of the street."

"Okay," came the reply. "We have the goods."

Norton retreated to the SUV, while Loohan walked toward the pickup. Tuma froze where he stood. "Come on," Loohan said.

"What about Norton?"

Loohan stopped. "We got nothing to worry about as long as he's back here holding the money, so quit sniveling."

When they neared the truck, two of the men spread to the sides, leaving a tall man with lank blonde hair leaning against the cab. He wore a black overcoat, his arms crossed, the cavalier expression on his face betrayed by deep creases at the sides of his mouth and a quarter-moon shaped scar on his nose.

"I'll need to test the purity," Loohan said. The blond shifted his eyes, first left to where a small Asian man stood, then right to his other cohort, a Hispanic with a Pancho Villa mustache. He looked back to Loohan and nodded.

"I'm going to reach in my pocket for a flashlight, a piece of tinfoil, a razor blade, and a lighter." Loohan raised his head and drew his hair from his eyes with a middle finger. "Okay?"

The men to the sides took a step closer.

"Go ahead," said the blond. "Do it slow, nice and easy."

Loohan slipped his hand to the inside pocket of his coat and pulled out a plastic baggie containing the instruments. The Asian man was now pointing a pistol at him, a semiautomatic of some make. Holding the bag up, Loohan looked to either side. "Cool?"

"Pull him out a key," the blond said to the mustachioed man. Walking around the far side of the pickup, the mustache stepped over the side-wall into the bed, his cowboy boots clunking against the steel floor. He unlocked a toolbox bolted behind the cab and withdrew a brown, paper-wrapped package.

"How about one from the bottom of the pile?" Loohan said.

The blond frowned, his eyes flickering with impatience. "Get another one," he said. When the mustache produced a second brick of cocaine, Loohan stepped to the rear of the truck.

"Open the tailgate and I can test it here." The blond released the gate, and Loohan carefully unwrapped the bale. He held it in his hands and broke it in half with a dull thud.

All the while, Tuma had been standing as if paralyzed, but the sound seemed to snap him out of his stupor. He walked to where Loohan scraped a few flakes from the middle of the white mass onto the piece of tinfoil. Loohan chopped it into powder with the razor blade. Tuma and the blond stood waiting, the mustache back on the ground next to the Asian, whose gun was still trained on Loohan.

"Snort it," Loohan said. Using a rolled dollar bill, Tuma inhaled the pile in a quick motion. He twitched his nose, swallowed, and sighed. "Tastes good."

Loohan scraped a bit more onto the foil and handed the flashlight to Tuma. Then he held his lighter underneath the small pile and watched as it began to smolder, the smoke nearly colorless. After a minute he set it down and looked at Tuma, whose eyes were wide. "That's got to be the best blow I've ever had, man. I'm freaking flying. Whew!"

Loohan put the flashlight and lighter back in the baggie. "Hey," he said, to the man pointing the pistol. "You're from Laos, right?"

The man's eyes clicked. "What's it to you?"

"I was born there, man." Loohan spread the fingers on his left hand, showing the burn scars on the webs. "Survived three years at Kompong Thom."

"You did?" he said, stepping forward, the gun lowering. "My brother is still—"

As the man spoke, Loohan replaced the baggie in his coat, and when his right hand reappeared, no one saw the small, black .25 he held. No one had a chance to. Three shots rang out in a quick cadence, Loohan's arm a blur as he pulled the trigger. The report echoed thinly in the desert air, like a tack hammer hitting a nail. The Asian crumpled, a red dot the size of a dime on his forehead, dead before he hit the ground. The blond took a round in the ear, spinning in a circle as he dropped, the expression on his face perplexed for an instant before the light faded from his eyes. The mustache was last, shot in the heart. He flopped flat on his back, his heels dug into the dirt, his torso soaking in blood. They went down so fast they seemed to fall like dominoes.

Vinnie Tuma stared slack jawed at the bodies. It was quiet and nothing moved. He couldn't quite process what had happened and stood there as if a spike had been driven into his mind's gears. Loohan climbed onto the truck bed and began removing the ten kilos from the lock box. His fingers shaking, Tuma fumbled a cigarette into his mouth.

A few seconds later they watched Norton race up in the SUV and jump out, holding his sawed-off at port arms. "Goddamn," he said.

"Put the drugs in the back of our ride," Loohan said to Tuma.

Norton moved about the scene coiled in a crouch, his head low, his eyes darting, never looking away from Loohan for long. After inspecting each victim and moving around the perimeter, he finally sighed and straightened. He stared hard at Loohan, who stood in the pickup, overlooking the scene like a vulture waiting for the right moment to swoop down on a carcass.

"This wasn't the plan, man," Norton said.

"Sure it was." Loohan hopped off the tailgate.

Tuma finished moving the bricks to the SUV and stood looking at them expectantly.

"We need to get the hell out of here," Norton said.

"Yeah, Jesus Christ, no shit," Tuma said. He opened the passenger side door, but before he could get in, Loohan said, "Hold on. Need your help with one more thing." He motioned with his arm and Tuma stepped away from the vehicle.

Norton watched Loohan's arm straighten, and Norton's lips had already started forming the word *no* when the pistol bucked and a sudden geyser of blood and brains blew out the back of Tuma's skull. Tuma fell as if his legs were kicked out from under him, and hit the ground flat on his back.

"Aagh!" Norton thrust up his hands, his face contorted and red. "What the motherfucking Christ are you doing?"

"Calm down."

"Fuck calm down! Do you know who you just blew away?"

"Do you think I'm stupid?"

"I think you're out of your goddamn mind!"

"You're wrong." Loohan opened the rear hatch of the SUV and pulled open the panel to the storage bay. He removed a large roll of clear plastic wrap, the type used by warehousemen to secure boxes on pallets, then handed Norton a pair of rubber gloves.

"The hell are these for?"

"We're going to wrap Tuma and move him somewhere we can bury him. You don't want any blood showing up in the car, do you?"

Norton's hand twitched on his shotgun as he glared at Loohan. Killing the nephew of a high-ranking mob boss was an almost suicidal act. And now Norton was complicit, thanks to Loohan's homicidal frenzy. Recruiting Loohan for the drug score seemed a good idea at first, but from the minute Vinnie Tuma got involved, Norton could feel it moving irrevocably toward disaster. Norton closed his eyes tightly and spat. Now his worst fears were confirmed—Loohan had turned out to be a complete lunatic.

For a second Norton considered raising his weapon and blasting Loohan into oblivion. Then he could tell Severino the deal went bad, and Norton was the only one to survive. Would Severino buy that? Maybe, maybe not. What was the alternative? There was a lunch pail packed with a hundred large, plus ten keys of high-grade blow in the SUV. That kind of weight could solve a lot of problems, but it would be tricky.

When he looked up again, if Loohan's back had been turned, Norton might have killed him. But Loohan was watching, his goddamned oriental eyes calm and calculating. Did Loohan plan on shooting him? If so, Norton thought he'd already be dead.

Peeling the plastic sheathing from the roll, Norton began wrapping Tuma's bloody face, first removing the still lit cigarette from his lips.

Loohan reached in Tuma's jacket pocket and found his cell phone, then raised Tuma's shoulders, and soon the corpse was mummified, tightly bound and unrecognizable. They lifted the body and jammed it into the back of the SUV, shoving to make it fit. Ten minutes later they were on a dark two-lane road, heading north. Save for a thirty-minute stop in the Imperial Sand Dunes National Park, they drove thirteen straight hours back to Lake Tahoe, arriving just as the sun rose and cast a blinding swath of white over the deep waters.

13

WHEN THE PHONE RANG, Pedro jerked awake, his breath caught in his throat. His ribs were on fire, as if he'd been stabbed with a heated blade and every motion caused it to twist.

"This is Pedro," he gasped.

"Have you heard from Rodrigo yet?"

"No."

"Until he returns, you'll be in charge."

"Okay."

"You'll be contacted by one of our men in a day or so. Until then, lie low."

"I'll keep Rodrigo's phone with me."

"You'll be contacted in person."

"By who?" Pedro asked, risking a question.

There was a long pause on the line. "The Angel is coming," the voice said.

Pedro took the cellphone from his ear and stared at it, his eyes trance-like and unbelieving. He shook his head, hoping he could somehow reverse what he'd just heard. A bitter taste flooded his throat and he took several shallow breaths, fighting a bolt of nausea. Then he rolled off the bed, staggered to the bathroom, and puked his guts out, his viscera roiling, his ribs cracking with every heave.

"Hey, Pedro, you okay?" one of the younger gangbangers said, standing in the doorway.

Pedro finished spitting and turned his bloodshot eyes to the kid. "Bring the car around. I need to go visit Rodrigo."

"It's too soon, Pedro. He's in bad shape, man. They got to wire his jaw. The nurse said not to come until tomorrow, maybe the day after."

The tattoos on his fingers blurring in his vision, Pedro pushed himself up and shuffled back to his room. He lay on the bed, staring at the textured pattern on the ceiling. Back in Juarez, he could have been relaxing in the small cantina his mother ran, eating enchiladas and drinking a margarita. The sun would go down and his friends would join him to play cards and talk about girls. A stray Chihuahua that came around would be curled up in the corner of the restaurant, enjoying the warm odors and the sounds of friendly conversation. Every now and then Pedro would reach down, holding a tortilla chip for the dog to take from his hand.

But that life hadn't been good enough. Not when men were making more in a day than his family made in a month. Everyone there was getting rich from the drug trade, including the local police. Teenagers fresh out of poverty were cruising the streets in shiny Cadillac SUVs, smirking at the poor working-class shop owners and the factory laborers. The best-looking *senoritas* in town hit the streets parading in new wardrobes and sparkling jewelry, and their parents knew it was wrong but said nothing. The lure of the drug money was simply too much for the impoverished people of Juarez to resist.

Pedro rolled to his side and tried to get comfortable. He had known of the shootouts and seen the dead bodies in the streets and heard the stories of men abducted in the night and found decapitated. The reports of torture and of entire families massacred became frequent and no one doubted their authenticity. Juarez had become the murder capital of the world. The cartels owned the city.

He talked with his family about moving away from the violence. To Baja perhaps, maybe all the way to Cabo San Lucas, where the tourist trade was booming. He'd heard the American-owned hotels and resorts paid well. His English was decent, and the coastline along the Sea of Cortez was said to be the most beautiful on earth.

But then Pedro learned Juarez's most powerful cartel was recruiting men, offering a chance to work not in Mexico, but in an American town 1,200 miles away. The money offered was incredible. If he was paid as promised, it would only take six months to put away enough to launch a new life, perhaps open his own cantina in Cabo. In the end, it was his dreams that seduced him. Pedro felt it was the best chance he'd ever have to escape the squalor of the violent border city where he'd been born and raised.

And now the most feared killer in Juarez was making a special trip to Lake Tahoe, coming to meet face to face with Pedro. It was rumored very few had actually seen The Angel in person and lived to speak of it. Would Pedro be considered a liability once he laid eyes on him? It was a too real possibility. Pedro knew working for the cartel would be risky. He had accepted this, but did not anticipate his dreams of escape would turn so quickly into a nightmare.

· · ·

The hardware store didn't open until nine, and by the time I finished repainting the garage door, it was almost noon. I sat at my picnic table and closed my eyes for a moment, letting the sun warm my face. Through the screen door I could hear a mixed martial arts match on TV. When I went in, Cody had my Remington pump shotgun disassembled on the kitchen table and was cleaning the shortened barrel.

"You got ammo for this bad boy?"

"There's a box of shells in the closet."

"How about lunch?" he said, eyeballing the breech.

We drove down 50 toward a sandwich place and were passing Zeke's when Cody said, "Whoa, pull in here." I hit the brakes and bounced over the curb into a parking lot split by a huge redwood, its bark chipped away where countless drunk patrons had scraped their bumpers against it. I had a hazy recollection I might have been one of them, back before Zeke Papas died and his son gutted the dining room.

"You hoping they'll fire up the kitchen for us?" I said.

"Let's just see if anyone's around."

The large two-story building, painted an odd peach color, looked like it may have been a fancy home in the past, just shy of a mansion. Neon beer signs lit up every window, and no one had bothered unplugging one that advertised *BBQ chicken*. On the siding next to the front entry, a hodge-podge of concert flyers were pasted over one another.

"Looks like the moral majority have an event planned for tonight," I said, pointing at an advertisement for a headlining band named Blood Screw, and a backup act that called itself Suicide Pact.

The sign on the door said CLOSED, but a couple cars were parked out front, and I could hear laughter from inside.

"Must be early cocktail hour," Cody said, pushing open the door.

"And they didn't even invite us." I followed him in, leaving behind a bright spring afternoon and wading into the gloom of what was once the best Old West-style restaurant and saloon in the region. At least the bar was still intact, but the floor planks had been pulled out to reveal a sunken concrete foundation. The area was cleared of tables and the chairs shoved to the walls, I assumed for death metal fans to stand on to better view the mosh pit and stage. The cacophony of odors inside was a potent brew of mildew, beer, sweat, unwashed clothes, and skanky sex. The latter emanated from the single female in the place, a shorthaired brunette with a face studded and ringed through the nose and eyebrows. She sat on the bar, her breasts perky, the nipples visible through a skimpy halter. Her legs were spread lazily and dark public hair curled from around the frayed crotch of her cut-off jeans.

"Hey," said one of the three men at the bar, a scraggly dude with long hair. "We're closed. Can't you read?" His buddy pulled a mirror smeared with white powder off the bar top and moved it out of sight.

"I must have left my reading glasses at home," Cody said. "How's tricks, toots?" he said to the woman. She blew a stream of smoke at him and shifted her heavily lidded eyes away, feigning boredom.

"I'm looking for Zak Papas," I said.

The men eyed us, maybe figuring we were cops, but it was hard to say with this bunch. They were unshaven, eyes dilated, chewing their cuds like cokeheads do, blown away on blow and not particularly concerned we'd wandered in.

"You got him," said the shortest of them, a rotund, prematurely balding fellow with a red goatee.

"You got somewhere we can talk in private?"

"Why don't you weirdos split, man?" the lady said. "You're bringing me down."

"Have another drink, then," I replied. Zak Papas looked at me uncertainly, then shrugged and motioned for me to follow him. We climbed a narrow flight of stairs to his office, a room lined with bookshelves and cluttered with model replicas of schooners and countless dust-coated knickknacks.

"I'd met your old man a few times," I said, as he sat behind a relic of a desk. "He was a good guy."

"Some people say that."

"Served damn good food, too."

"Yeah, yeah. What is it you want, mister?"

"Besides a good plate of BBQ? I want to know about your relationship with Hard Core United. They your buddies?"

His jaw fell a bit, but his eyes didn't leave mine. "My buddies? I wouldn't say that. We dig the same music, but that's about it."

"You got no problem with them coming to your club, skimming the door, and raising hell?"

"Huh? I get the raising hell part, but what about the door?"

"It's their MO. They take a cut of the ticket prices from you, right?"

"No, hell no. That's never happened."

I stared at him.

"Why would I lie, man?" he said. "You a cop, or what?"

"Private." I pulled a picture of Jason Loohan from my pocket. "Ever seen him?"

He studied the picture. "Freaky-looking dude, ain't he?" He handed it back to me. "I've never seen him. I'd remember if I did."

"You've never seen him here with any of the HCU boys, huh?"

"Like I said, I've never seen him, period. Why, what's he done?"

"All sorts of bad shit, Zak. He needs to be taken off the street."

He thought that over for a bit, then moved his hand from his mouth. "Look, I'm a good citizen," he said. "A businessman. You think he's part of HCU? Then come by tonight—three of them are in the warm-up band. They kind of suck, but their drummer is this psycho-retard who's smoking hot."

"Is that right? You know where they might be hanging out?"

"No clue. I never see them outside of here."

"All right. In the meantime, call me if you see him, would you?" I tapped Loohan's picture and handed him my card. He glanced at it, then looked back again, his eyes widening.

"Oh, shit! You're the whack job who shot up my bar! I can't believe I'm so damn stupid!"

"Blame it on the dummy dust."

"Oh, fuck me. Man, you ain't allowed back here, you stay clear of my business, you—"

"Hey, Zak." He stopped and looked at me with red-rimmed eyes, like he was ready to cry. "I can't say I blame you for not wanting me around," I said. "And to be honest, I think the music you guys listen to is the shits, so I really don't want to come back tonight. Give me a couple of the right answers and maybe I won't have to."

"What? What do you want?"

"An HCU member named Tom. Wears a ring in his nose. Sound familiar?"

"Sure. He plays guitar."

"Know where he lives?"

"No."

"I'm sure he'll be here tonight anyway, right?"

"No, bullshit. Listen to me. His band rehearses at the drummer's house. They're probably over there loading their gear."

"You got an address?"

"No—"

"How about a name?"

"Okay, yeah. The drummer, Rabbit. Rabbit Switton. He's a freak, man, plays as good as anyone, I mean Vinnie Paul, Joey Jordison…"

"Why's he called Rabbit?"

"His real name's Robert. His dad has some funky East Coast accent. When he says Robert, it sounds like Rabbit. So that's what everyone calls him."

"He's the 'psycho-retard,' huh?"

"Look, he's got some kind of mental disability, call it whatever you want." He stood. "We straight here?"

"Look, Zak," I said. "I don't mean to be a life coach or anything, but I got some advice for you. This death metal thing attracts trouble like flies on shit. You like the music, fine. But you want to base your business around it? Bad move."

"Opinions are like assholes—"

"Yeah, I know. Everyone's got one."

When we got back downstairs, Cody was talking with the lady on the bar, who had lost the attitude and seemed to be enjoying his attention. The other two dudes were distracted by a TV newscast covering an earthquake in Haiti that had left tens of thousands dead. They were giggling at a scene showing corpses strewn like trash in the street. "Those spooks are up shit creek," one said.

"Let's go," I said, interrupting Cody's conversation.

"What's your name, anyway?" the girl said, grasping Cody's hand and leaning her head near his.

"Lance Romance," I interjected.

Cody winked. "See you, babe."

"Anytime," she purred.

"What'd you find out?" he asked, once we'd walked into the fresh air.

"One of the bands playing tonight is made up of HCU members. I think they rehearse at the house we checked out the other day."

"Let's pick up lunch and drop by, then."

"Sounds like a plan, Stan."

"What happened to Lance?"

Twenty minutes later we sat eating sandwiches in my truck down the street from the white house listed as John Switton's residence. I assumed he was the father of Rabbit Switton, the man I'd watched smash a bar glass to smithereens at Whiskey Dick's. Despite his physical deformities and mental issues, Rabbit was supposedly a great drummer. It was hard to imagine, but I'd seen stranger things. Regardless, I didn't think he was the one who vandalized my home, unless others put him up to it.

We opened the windows and waited, listening to birds chirp and the occasional jet pass overhead. The afternoon had turned balmy, and Cody lit a cigarette. I considered bumming one out of boredom.

"What time you got?" he asked.

"Two."

The minutes passed slowly, until a little before three a Ford pickup with Nevada plates drove up the street and parked in the driveway of the Switton house. From our spot a football field away, I could see the three men who climbed out wore black shorts and white T-shirts. I started my truck, but they quickly disappeared into the house.

"Come on, let's go straighten their shit out," Cody said. I drove up and parked in front. He started to get out, but I stopped him.

"Let's wait for them to come out. I want to do this in the street."

"Who knows how long they'll be inside?"

"Be patient. I have a feeling it won't be long."

I was right. Within five minutes the garage door opened, and the man named Tom wheeled out a large speaker cabinet on a dolly. Following him, a lanky, bearded man lugged a smaller amplifier, and then came Rabbit Switton, straining under the weight of a black bass drum. Before Tom spotted us, Cody and I were across the lawn and on the driveway. Tom's expression went blank with surprise and fear, but he regained his composure quickly and smirked.

"Hey, it's the douchebag patrol."

I walked up to him, my legs energized, blood pounding in my temples. I caught his right wrist and twisted it until I could see the tip of his index finger was stained with red paint. He tried to jerk away, but I cranked his arm behind his back and tripped him to the ground, my knee on his spine.

"You think you can spray paint my house and get away with it, asshole?"

"Get the off me, man, or I swear to god, we will fuck you up."

I yanked him to his feet by the collar. "Go ahead, fuck me up."

He froze, and in my peripheral vision the bearded man and Rabbit were staring open-mouthed, as if witnessing a bad traffic accident. I saw in Tom's eyes a brief glimmer of regret, like maybe he was remembering a turning point in his life, perhaps a choice he made years ago that was now irreversible. Then he let out a yell, his eyes round with rage, and threw a roundhouse right. The punch was telegraphed from a different time zone, and I easily blocked it, then stepped forward and hit him with an uppercut to the midsection that made his feet come off the ground. He would have collapsed, but I snatched him by the hair and grabbed his right hand. I squeezed, feeling his finger bones shift under the pressure.

"I'm in a charitable mood today, Tom, so I'm going to give you a chance to right this situation. Then you can go play your gig and everyone will think you're a badass heavy metal man, and you can pretend this never happened. You hear me?"

He gagged and I thought he might puke. I waited until the color returned to his face as Cody discouraged the other two, who had snapped out of it and were talking and gesturing, trying to figure how to come to the aid of their buddy.

"I'm looking for Jason Loohan," I said. "Yeah, Billy Morrison's best friend, asshole, so don't tell me you don't know him."

"I, I got no idea…"

I squeezed harder. "Think on it, Tom. I'm sure you can come up with something. Where can I find him?"

"You're gonna break my hand," he cried.

"Wouldn't that be a shame, you'll never play guitar again. What a loss for the music industry."

He dropped to his knees. "I don't know, I don't know," he whimpered.

"Last chance, Tom." I tightened my grip, feeling the connective tissue ready to snap.

"Stop!" he screamed, sweat beaded on his forehead. "Jesus, Joe Norton, please let go. He's been with Norton, shit, let go—"

"Where's Norton live?"

"Green house, the only green house on Zane Ave, in Nevada behind the Safeway."

I eased my hold. "All right, Tom, I'll go check it out. If I find out you lied to me, I'll come see you at Zeke's tonight."

"I ain't lying."

"Good boy. One more thing. Don't even think of calling Norton. That would be a life-threatening mistake. You clear on that?"

He stood slowly. "Yes."

"You also owe me for paint and my time," I said, and spun him around and yanked his wallet out of his back pocket. When I saw it contained only three one-dollar bills, I rolled my eyes and flung it onto the roof of the house. "Let's go," I said to Cody, but as I started for my truck, a white Lincoln pulled up to the curb. The door swung open and a man dressed in gray slacks, dress shoes, and a lavender polo shirt stepped onto the asphalt. He was in his fifties, wide shoulders, neck like a bull, his eyes small in his meaty face.

"What's going on here?"

"Who are you?" I said.

"John Switton. I live here."

"Hey, Pop, we're loading our gear for the gig."

"I can see that, Rabbit. What's your problem?" he said to Tom.

"Nothing," Tom mumbled, and walked back to where he'd left the dolly. Switton shifted his eyes back to me.

"He vandalized my house," I said. "We've just been discussing the matter. I consider it resolved, for now."

"*Vandalized?* Was Rabbit part of this?" He addressed me, then turned and looked at the others. Cody was standing next to Rabbit, whose mouth moved silently, as if he was trying to formulate a sentence but the words escaped him.

John Switton moved in a blur, and in a second had his hands on Tom, who yelled in protest as the older man grabbed his collar and slammed him down on the hood of the Ford truck.

"What kind of shit are you dragging my son into?" he snarled, holding Tom by the neck. The bearded man took a step forward, but Cody stopped him with a forearm to the chest.

Tom got out a few strangled words before Switton lifted him and again slammed him on the hood. "Rabbit doesn't think too well," Switton said through clenched teeth. "He's easily influenced. I hold you personally responsible for any trouble he gets into. Understand?" Before Tom could answer, Switton pivoted at the hip and flung him through the air. Tom landed on the lawn with a snort.

"Well done," Cody said, walking between them to my rig.

Switton and I met eyes but neither of us spoke. I felt an odd bond, as if we shared an agenda beyond our dislike of Tom, but it was probably nothing more than a random thought. I nodded at Switton, and for a second, a smile began on his face. Then it was gone, and I climbed into my cab and drove away.

•   •   •

As we crossed the state line, I found myself thinking back to earlier in my career, to the eccentric personalities, the neurotics, the cavalier, the violent. My last boss, Rick Wenger, had motivations straightforward and without complexity—he was in it for the money. Wenger was obsessed by wealth, and judged all individuals solely on their financial status. If someone was relatively poor, he considered them a dirtbag. Conversely, if a person was wealthier than he was, Wenger was wracked with envy. There was no middle ground, no moral or ethical considerations in Wenger's equation. A hospice nurse making fifty thousand a year helping terminally ill patients die in comfort was simply inferior to a used car salesman pulling down sixty grand. In applying his perspective to his job, Wenger sought out cases posing minimal risk and high potential for billable hours. As long as he got paid, he had no philosophical concern as to the resolution of any case.

Before my career with Wenger, I worked for a bail bondsman named Ray Loretta. A man of extraordinary physical and mental energy, Loretta loved the challenges of the job. For him, pitting his skills against the criminals he worked with was great fun. He provided bond to the highest risk crooks, and eagerly chased them down when they fled. He pepper-sprayed con artists, beat murder suspects bloody with his fists, kicked gangbangers in the balls and laughed at them, and once shot a rapist in the head during a hundred-mile-per-hour chase through downtown San Jose. In his spare time, he was a prolific ladies' man and had multiple affairs ongoing at any given moment. How he managed all this while maintaining his wife and three kids was beyond me.

A mile into Nevada, I stopped in an empty parking lot, and as I assembled my gear, I considered my own motivations. It would have been easy to assume Jason Loohan was long gone by now, so why not forget about him? I wasn't in dire straits for money, and the three-grand bounty seemed a paltry fee for chasing a man I knew would kill me given the chance. Instead, Cody and I could turn around and head over to Pistol Pete's, play some cards, maybe say hello to Teresa Perez. Maybe get drunk, then tomorrow I could work on revitalizing my investigations business, solicit the local attorneys, try to land a divorce case or two. I felt the weight of my automatic in my hand, and thought, "Why not?"

Years ago, a district attorney had taken exception to my involvement in a shooting. The charges were eventually dropped, but in the process, I was sent to a court-appointed psychologist. After a couple sessions on the couch, the shrink submitted his report, professing that I suffered from "social vengeance syndrome, a desire to rid society of its ills by violent means." He went on to elaborate: "This behavior is classic overcompensation for anger and feelings of loss due to his father's murder. His tendency to proactively defend what is near and dear to him is extreme and borderline antisocial. He displays a lack of faith in the legal justice system, and if threatened will likely respond with extreme prejudice."

This kind of psychobabble always made me chuckle, because it ignored a fundamental reality; when dealing with criminals who'd gladly see me dead, the best defense, and actually the safest tact, was a full-blown offense. A passive approach was almost always foolhardy. It was as simple as that.

Bottom line: Jason Loohan had shot my best friend and the bullet meant for me had blown out my truck's windshield. He may have left for parts unknown, or he could be lying in wait for the right moment to finish the job. As much as I might have liked to find a rationale to discount the threat he represented, I knew I wouldn't. Loohan needed to be found and dealt with.

Body armor on, stun gun, handcuffs, mace, and my Beretta .40 cal. in place, I watched Cody strap on his vest and secure his shoulder holster. He swung my sawed-off to an upright position, the barrel resting on his shoulder.

"If he runs, shoot for his legs," I said.

Five minutes later we drove down the street where I'd been told Joe Norton lived. It was a neighborhood of working-class tract homes, probably thirty or forty years old, most shabby and unkempt, some with faded

FOR RENT placards in the windows, all anonymous and unremarkable. Abrupt late afternoon clouds had moved in, blotting out the sun and casting a dreary grayness over the residences and the scattering of aged vehicles parked along the curb. Toward the end of the street was an olive-green house, its front lawn dead and a familiar blue Chevy Chevelle in the driveway. A *BEWARE OF DOG* sign hung on a chain link gate barricading the side yard.

"Got any doggy treats?" Cody asked.

"Yeah." I handed him a plastic container from my gear case. We parked a few doors down and watched the neighborhood for a while. The quiet and stillness left me with the impression this was a place where people kept to themselves, greeting their neighbors with blank stares and nods but nothing more. No block parties, gleeful children's voices, or Fourth of July fireworks here. No Christmas lights either, just the occasional kaleidoscope of spinning red-and-blue lights atop a police cruiser. Peel away the weathered siding and brittle roofs on these houses, and you'd find plenty of dirty secrets and unhappy lives.

Nothing stirred at the green house. We left my truck and once we were close enough, Cody winged some nuggets of dog food into the side yard. When no dog appeared, he walked over and rattled the gate. He waited a moment, then opened it and moved along the side of the house.

I checked the windows in front, but the curtains were drawn. I moved to the front step and tried the locked doorknob. If the door had been a stout, solid unit, I would have knocked, but this one was moisture warped and maybe just flimsy enough. "Decisions, decisions," I sighed. Then I reared my leg back and kicked as hard as I could, my heel slamming into the jamb. The wood splintered with a loud crack and the door flew open so fast it bounced off the interior wall and slapped shut before I could react. I hit it with my palm and burst into the house, covering the room with my automatic.

A thump sounded down a dark hallway. I ran over and opened a door to an empty bedroom, then kicked in the locked door across from it, ready to fire. Joe Norton stood shirtless, struggling to pull on a pair of pants. His bed was unmade, and the room smelled stale and foul.

"The fuck is this?" he said, his eyes puffy with sleep.

"Jason Loohan. Where is he?"

"Beats the hell out of me. I'm calling the cops."

"You, call the cops? What, you got some friends on the force? Maybe Nevada PD?"

He sat on the bed and rubbed his eyes, the thick cords of muscle in his shoulders bulging against his white skin. "I was taking a nap, man."

"Tell someone who gives a shit. Where's Loohan?"

"You know what, pal? You're not gonna shoot me, so put your gun away before I get annoyed and stick it up your ass."

"House is clear, Dirt," Cody's voice boomed from behind a wall.

"You know, you're right," I said to Norton, holstering my piece and taking a can of mace from my belt. "I'd be happy to give you a taste of this, though, maybe help you wake up."

Norton laughed, the skin around his bloodshot eyes gray and wrinkled. "You're looking for Loohan, huh?"

"Care to let me in on the joke?"

"What's in it for me?" he said, almost to himself, staring off into space. He grabbed a pack of cigarettes on the nightstand and stuck one in his mouth.

"We can do this the easy way or the hard way." I pointed the spray nozzle at him. He took a deep drag off his smoke and looked up at me, his eyes crinkling with mirth.

"Sure, Mr. Badass Bounty Hunter. You want to hook up with Loohan? I ain't gonna stand in your way. Problem is, he never stays in any place for long, like one night is the max, the dude is seriously mobile. And don't look at me that way. I ain't shittin' you, jack."

"Is he still in the area?"

"Yes, sir, he sure is. He mentioned he plans to stick around until he takes care of some unfinished business."

I felt Cody's shadow from the doorway fall over me. "He told you that, huh?" Cody said.

"That's right."

"Where can I find him?" I said.

Norton's smirk broadened into a grin. "Why don't you just hang loose, man? He ain't gonna be found unless he's good and ready. Then he'll find *you.*"

Cody stepped past me and leveled the shotgun at Norton's face. "How about some free dental work, asswipe?"

"Wow, this is like a bad scene out of *Starsky and Hutch*. I'm really pissin' my pants. Tell you what—why don't I call the cops and you can talk to them about your problems." Norton picked up his cell phone from the nightstand and began punching numbers. Cody knocked it from his hand with the barrel and slammed the stock down, crushing the phone against the floor.

Norton's face reddened, and he lost his buck tooth smile. "I'll send you the bill for that," he said. "And for the door, too. You don't like it, we'll sort it out in court."

"You're full of all kinds of scary threats," I said. "Here's something to keep in mind. Any trouble we have with Loohan, I'll consider you responsible, and then we'll settle it."

"If you're done spewing bullshit, get the fuck out of my house."

I took a deep breath and decided further conversation was pointless. Cody and I left Norton sitting on his bed in his depressing rental home and drove back across the border into California. It was raining lightly, not quite a drizzle, more like spit coming down from the skies. I suddenly felt like a drink, like chugging a fifty-fifty CC Seven. But instead of heading to Whiskey Dick's, I turned at the street leading to Marcus Grier's office.

"You think Norton knows where Loohan is?" Cody said.

"Maybe. I doubt it. I don't know."

"We could always go back and beat it out of him. Maybe zap him with your Taser until he talks."

"It's tempting, but it's also illegal."

"You worried he'd bring the heat down on you? Like maybe he's paying off those plainclothes cops in Douglas County?"

"I think it's likely. How often do ex-con shitbirds threaten to call the police?"

"Never." Cody shifted in his seat and adjusted his injured shoulder.

"He's probably got a couple in his pocket, probably those two we saw at the apartments," I said.

"Should we tattle to Grier?"

"He already knows, or at least suspects. Don't know there's much he can do about it."

"He needs to grow a pair, then."

"Give him a break."

"Why?"

"Cody, you were fired for making your own rules, ignoring politics, and basically pissing off everybody at SJPD."

"That's because half the force was corrupt and I wasn't buying into it."

"Well, Grier's situation is different. He's got a wife and two daughters to support."

"And that gives him reason to not report a scumbag like Norton is paying off a couple local detectives?"

"I don't know he *hasn't* said something. But we're talking about a California sheriff messing with the Nevada PD, so it's complicated."

"You think I was wrong for quitting the force?"

"Quitting?" I looked over at him.

"That's right. I knew I was going to get fired for taking a stand, so it was like quitting."

"What is this, a trick question?" He stared back at me, his face impassive. "No, I don't blame you. Christ, the whole world's for sale. We all have to draw the line somewhere."

"Spoken like a great philosopher," Cody said, now smiling broadly.

"I don't disagree with anything you did at San Jose PD," I said. "Not even shoveling the coals to your boss's wife."

Cody laughed out loud. "God, she loved it, screaming orgasms, the whole bit. I think cheating on the son of a bitch really got her off."

"Let's go talk to Grier then head to a bar."

"Amen, brother."

• • •

Grier sat behind his desk, listening as I told him about the confrontation with Tom at the Switton house.

"You want to press charges?"

"No, I believe I'm square with him."

"All right." Grier looked at his watch.

"About quitting time?" Cody said.

"Yes. My shift's over at five." Grier passed me a folder. "Jason Loohan's jacket."

"Thanks, Marcus."

"Loohan sounds like real trouble," he said, nodding at the file.

"Don't they all?"

"I'm serious. Read it and you'll see what I mean." Grier stood, his thick leather belt tight and shiny across his midsection, his revolver holstered at the hip. "I've put out an APB on him for South Lake, Truckee, Tahoe City, Carson, and Reno. I listed him as armed and dangerous."

Cody raised his eyebrows. "We'll find him."

A flicker of apprehension crossed Grier's face, his eyes widening and his mouth falling open for a moment. Then he recovered, his features clenched, his expression resolute. "I hope so. Good luck, men."

The sun had reappeared when we walked outside, the moisture on the streets steaming, the pines glistening with droplets of rain. We swung over to Whiskey Dick's, where we took a table in a shaft of sunlight near the front window. I drained a whiskey highball, then settled in and began reading the thick contents of Jason Loohan's police record.

A New Jersey detective named Sam Nguyen had taken a particular interest in Loohan after arresting him twice, resulting in no convictions, for homicides that were never solved. Nguyen traced Loohan's record back to his childhood in the fields of Cambodia, where Loohan reportedly was forced to watch Khmer Rouge exterminators dismember his dissident father and feed the pieces to starving dogs. As for Loohan's mother, little was known of her, other than she was suspected to be a white prostitute who was in Asia during the Vietnam War and disappeared shortly after his birth in 1974.

A fourteen-year-old orphan starving on the streets of Phnom Penh, Loohan was arrested for stealing food and sentenced to a three-year term at Kompong Thom, an overcrowded Cambodian prison teaming with infectious disease. Upon his release, the teenage refugee made his way to the United States and soon joined a Vietnamese gang. He did a couple short stints for petty crimes, before pulling fifteen months for grand theft auto. Within a year of his release, he was back in prison on a forgery charge, this time for twenty-two months. For an eleven-year period afterward, he avoided arrest, though he was often a person of interest, until his recent bust for the home invasion job with Billy Morrison. The DA was pushing a three strikes rap, but when Loohan's bail was set at $300,000, he surprised everyone by coming up with thirty grand to post bond.

The detective added notes to the file over the years, documenting instances where Loohan was suspected of violent crimes but never charged, and commenting on two more cases where he was charged but found not guilty. The first dealt with the alleged poisoning of his supervisor at a department store job. The second was considerably more insidious, and was in the newspapers for weeks before it faded from public scrutiny. It had to do with the murder of an infant, to be used as a human sacrifice in a satanic ritual. The case had gone to court, but since the body could not be found and the mother committed suicide while being held, Loohan walked. The mother was suspected of being his girlfriend and cohort, and the child his son, but without DNA evidence, the case fell apart.

Sam Nguyen offered his perspective in a closing paragraph: "Loohan is no doubt a psychopath, and as such poses a significant risk to society. The horrors of his childhood, in conjunction with his natural inclinations, have created a man with no conscience. Though I don't believe he fits the profile of a typical serial killer, i.e., killing to satisfy a psychological urge, he will not hesitate to kill if he feels it suits his needs. His criminal behavior seems calculated, not the result of emotion but instead cunning and well planned. He thrives on the element of surprise, the unexpected, and considers himself more intelligent and capable than US law enforcement agencies. The fact that he is, as of this writing, a free man, seems to validate his opinion."

"Lovely," I muttered, closing the folder and joining Cody where he was watching TV at the bar.

"What'd you learn?" he said.

"Jason Loohan is a little beyond your typical career criminal."

"How so?"

"You read it." I handed him the papers and ordered a double in a tall glass.

Cody lit a cigarette and I took one from his pack. "Any clues where he might be hanging out?" he asked.

"Not really. There's a cop out in Jersey who seems to have an obsession with him, though. Maybe he could give some direction."

"It's nine P.M. out there. Why don't you give him a call?"

I went back to the table, hitting off my drink, watching the cars pass by on 50 until there was a break in the traffic and I could see a radiant stripe of silver splitting the lake and stretching all the way to the north shore, where the sun rested just above the sharp edges of the gray peaks. When the flow of cars resumed, I opened the file and found the number for Sam Nguyen. He answered after two rings.

"A bounty hunter from where?"

"South Lake Tahoe," I said. "It's four hours east of San Francisco, in the Sierra Nevada."

"Oh. I've never been out there."

"It's a nice place to live, for the most part. Except recently I've been having some trouble with a man I think you know well—Jason Loohan."

"*Loohan?* He's there?"

"Yes. He skipped bail a couple months back—"

"I know he did. I've been looking for him here."

"You can stop. He took a shot at me and winged my partner two days ago. I think he's still in the area."

"I'd say you're fortunate to be alive, then. How long have you been a bounty hunter?"

"What's it matter?"

"I've been a cop for thirty years. I've been trying to put away Loohan for almost half that long."

"So?"

"You want my advice or don't you?"

"I'm listening."

"I traveled to Southeast Asia to research him. I talked to convicts who served time with him in prisons that make Attica look like a country club. I met friends of his father who told me stories I still sometimes wake up at night and wish I'd never heard."

"Yes, I've read his police report. I understand his background."

"You do, huh? I doubt it. I'm convinced Loohan has killed at least a dozen people. Does that make him special? Not really. But I think he crossed the line from a murderous thug to a full-blown psycho about three years ago. You read about the baby killing?"

"Yeah."

"Of all the criminals you've dealt with in your career, how many have murdered an infant?"

"None that I know of."

"Let me rephrase that. How many have killed a newborn baby that was their own offspring?"

"I get your point."

"Good. Now I'm going to give you the best advice I can about how to find him." Nguyen paused and the scratchy flick of a lighter sounded over the line. "Loohan became active in a devil worship cult prior to the infanticide case. Most Satanists talk the talk and that's about it. But Loohan's group was the real thing—they were into voodoo spells, animal sacrifices, vampirism, *human* sacrifices, all culminating in a thing they call the black mass."

"Which is?"

"It's considered the grand event of Satanism. Imagine this—a blood-splattered virgin on the alter with a cross stuck in her vagina, a dead child at her feet, a bunch of psychotic meth heads chanting homage to the devil, before the virgin is gang raped, sodomized, subjected to bestiality, then finally killed."

"This is what Loohan was involved in?"

"Not just involved. He was a leader."

"You say he went off the deep end three years ago. Is he still into this stuff?"

"I have no doubt he is. He was active here recently."

"You're talking a cult that practices rape and murder. How do they get away with it?"

"The full-blown black mass is not something that happens often. The daily practices of these people are not necessarily illegal, and they stay underground for the most part."

"All right. So, back to your advice on how to find him."

"Loohan is a loner, but Satanism is usually a group activity. Fortunately there's not many people deranged enough to go there. My recommendation is to track down local devil worship groups. It's possible Loohan has already done so."

"Thanks. Mind if I ask you a question?" I heard him exhale a lungful of cigarette smoke. "Go ahead."

"Why have you taken such an interest in Loohan?"

He was silent for a second. "My daughter went missing ten years ago. She had been dating him."

14

BACK BEFORE THE INTERNET became ubiquitous, a detective's job was a matter of phone work and face-to-face encounters. Get a lead and follow up in person, and if the answers aren't forthcoming, apply a little physical pressure. The old tried and true. What's changed now that it's possible to log on to a PC and access vast stores of information? Maybe a few shortcuts, a quicker route to clues, but not much more. While the digital age may have revolutionized many industries, its benefit to the art of people finding has been modest for the most part.

But that didn't stop me from spending all night scouring the web, reading up on the varieties of Satanism and incidents involving devil worship cults over the last five years. I read the contents of a few sites from start to finish, then skimmed dozens more, looking unsuccessfully for anything indicating the existence of Satanists in Reno, Carson, or the communities on the shores of Lake Tahoe. I was considering posting a bogus profile on Facebook, when around midnight I came across an article buried deep in the search engine. A pair of young men had been arrested two years ago for spray painting pentagrams on two churches and a synagogue in Reno. The names of the accused and the arresting officers were listed.

"Find anything?" Cody said, his feet on my coffee table. He knocked back a beer and crushed the can in his fist.

"Get some sleep," I said. "I want to drive to Reno in the morning."

• • •

The covered parking stalls at the Pine Mountain Apartments were shrouded in the predawn darkness, the cement floor and walls musty with decay from years of snowmelt. Pedro fumbled his keys from his jacket pocket and eased into the Impala, his mind on picking up a breakfast burrito and more pain pills from the nearby convenience store. Fastening his seatbelt, he started the motor and dropped the transmission into reverse. He raised his eyes to check the rearview mirror, and froze, his breath caught in his throat, his skin buzzing as if he'd stepped on a downed power line. A pair of eyes in the backseat stared back at him silently, the face indecipherable save for the silhouetted sheen of black hair hanging straight over the ears. Pedro knew immediately who it was. The Angel had come.

"Turn off the engine," the voice said. "Do not look in the mirror again."

Pedro stared out the windshield, blood pounding in his ears. The garage's gray, tomblike walls felt like they were closing in on him. His mind raced, as if a day's worth of thoughts were crammed into a few seconds. Then a key ring fell into his lap, the sudden motion and sound causing him to jerk, his eyeballs bouncing in their sockets.

"On the street is a tan Dodge SUV. Wait five minutes, then drive it to the police station where you were taken."

"I'm not sure..." Pedro started, then he heard the clunk of the door closing.

Pedro held the keys in his fingers and told himself he would not speak unless spoken to. If he portrayed himself as one who knew how to keep his mouth shut, maybe it would improve his chances of survival. Clinging to the thought, he walked out to the street and drove away in the Dodge, the face of the man in the backseat hidden by a newspaper.

When they reached the Douglas County complex, the man told Pedro to turn onto a road that ran past the parking lot and climbed into the forest. They drove for a few minutes, the road twisting, the pines and fir obscuring the police station, until the woods fell away beneath a sharp corner, affording a clear view of the buildings a thousand feet below.

Pedro parked on the shoulder and a gloved hand passed him a set of binoculars. A tiny spark of sun flickered atop the ridgeline above them, and blue-green tapestry of the valley floor emerged from the darkness. But the police complex had not yet awakened—save for two neat rows of squad cars, the parking lot was empty and still.

For the next two hours, Pedro trained the binoculars on the complex, hoping to spot and identify the two plainclothesmen who had arrested him and beat Rodrigo bloody. He hoped it wouldn't take long—he did not wish the man sitting behind him to become impatient. That The Angel intended to kill both the policemen, Pedro had no doubt. He still had not glimpsed him, except for the initial startled glance in the rearview mirror. Pedro wondered fleetingly if he might venture a bit of small talk to break the dreadful silence in the vehicle, but he rejected the notion as soon as it crossed his mind. The less contact between them, the better.

"Tell me about the men who beat you," the voice said. Strange, Pedro thought. The man's English was nearly perfect, just a hint of accent.

In a halting voice, Pedro described the men in white shirts and black pants. The Angel grunted in satisfaction and asked no questions when Pedro finished talking. It seemed like The Angel was already familiar with the white trash thugs who were connected to the bad cops. Good, Pedro thought, touching his ribs and wincing.

Another hour stretched by. Pedro tried thinking positive thoughts, reminding himself he had four thousand in cash stashed away, and more would be coming once they could resume business. The cops trying to force them out of town were standing between him and his plans to reinvent his life, to open a cantina in Cabo. He had never seen the ocean, had never seen waves crashing on a beach. He knew nothing but the gritty slums of Juarez. How much more of the world might he see one day? The answer depended on one thing—money.

A shiver of panic swept through Pedro when he considered the money meant nothing if he was dead. The Angel was rumored to be responsible for the murders of entire families in Juarez. It was said he operated in the shadows, a ghostly presence briefly presenting himself to his victims before the soft sputter of his silenced TEC-9 splattered the walls with chunks of bone and gore. Might Pedro wake in the morning, maybe as soon as tomorrow, to see the grim face of The Angel, in the last moment before his life was ended by a few well-placed bullets?

Pedro squeezed his eyes tightly, pushing the fear away. The events of his life had already been set in motion, and if his death was to be, then it would be. All he could do was stay alert, use his intelligence and instinct, and above all, do nothing stupid, nothing that would give The Angel more of a reason to kill him than he might already have.

Setting his jaw, Pedro resolved to stay focused on the task at hand. The thought had no sooner entered his head when a white van pulled into the lot, the doors swinging open to reveal Pete Saxton and Dave Boyce.

"There, the white van, those two." Pedro pointed and watched the two men conversing as they walked to the main entrance and disappeared behind the glass doors.

Taking the binoculars from his eyes, Pedro waited, the seconds ticking by, the presence in the backseat like a random hand of fate that could strike him down or set him free on a whim.

"You can go now," the voice said finally.

Pedro slid out the door and didn't look back.

·   ·   ·

I woke early and when the sun rose I left my house wearing a fifty-pound pack. I jogged a mile through the meadow behind my backyard, until the terrain turned steep and the trail narrowed, forcing me to slow to a walk. The mountainside was covered in buttercups and wild grass, the spring air crisp and sweet with their fragrance. Far above me, a wide ledge of snow clung to a rock face, the smooth granite streaked dark with runoff. Now hiking up a difficult grade, I reached a section where a landslide had washed out the path, leaving a sheer dirt cliff falling to a river hundreds of feet below. I kicked a few pebbles over the edge, watching the rocks spiral downward. Then I turned back, and two hours later was showered and sitting at my desk, dialing Reno PD.

"Detective Frank Swaney, please."

"Detective Swaney no longer works here," said a gravelly female voice. I asked if she knew how I could reach him.

"Try Carson City PD. I believe he took a job there."

"How about Detective Jacob Booker?"

"He's not in yet. May I take a message?"

"Do you expect him today?"

"I don't know. I suggest leaving a message."

"All right. Tell him I'd like to get his feedback on a case from a couple years ago. Two men were arrested for spray painting pentagrams on a church." I left my number and heard Cody shuffling around in my guest room. He came out shirtless, his chest a massive pale slab, his shoulders wider than the doorway.

"Lookee here," he said, bending down and showing me the four inches of stitches across his left deltoid, the black sutures like the legs of an upended centipede.

"How's it feel?"

"Itches a little, but the pain's mostly gone." He pulled a T-shirt over his head and walked to my coffee pot.

"Listen," I said, "If we catch Loohan, I'll split the bounty with you."

"If? What happened to *when*? What about your leads?"

"I left a message for one cop in Reno. The other is supposed to now be working in Carson. I haven't made any calls on the vandals yet."

"Tell you what—make your calls on the road. I'm ready to hit it."

"What's the hurry?"

He raised his eyebrows at me, a smile on the corner of his mouth. Then he yanked on his body armor, secured the straps, and spun the cylinder on his big pistol.

"Gear up, partner. Time's a wastin'."

"You're not hungry?" I asked.

"I'll eat later."

Five minutes later we gunned it out of town under a cobalt blue sky, Cody's tires spitting dirt on the sun-warmed road, the radio blasting "Beer Drinkers and Hell Raisers" by ZZ Top.

"God, I love this song," Cody said, cranking the volume, his palms pounding on the steering wheel, his green eyes charged with a secret energy, as if he were anticipating a salvation known only to him.

For as long as I'd known Cody, he'd avoided a static lifestyle. Downtime and boredom were his worst enemies. I imagined that in his quiet, solitary moments, perhaps when he was alone in his apartment at night, straight booze might not be adequate to soothe the wounds of his past. His pain could only be extinguished by action, by confronting his demons, by violence. This was his defense mechanism, how he dealt with the grief of a father who abandoned him and an uncaring mother. Crazy as it sounds, living on the edge provided the balm for his unhealed scars. I'm sure psychology professionals would have a field day with this one, but his method for dealing with his pain was keeping him sane. Hell, in a world where criminally demented acts are routine, Cody was probably saner than most.

As we climbed Spooner Pass, I called the numbers I'd found for the two men charged with hate crimes for defiling places of worship. The first number, for a Greg Ruehr, was disconnected. I dialed the second number and almost gave up before a woman finally answered.

"Hi, Eric Wenhert, please."

There was a pause. "Who's calling?"

"This is Pete Johnson. We went to high school together."

"Well, he's not here."

"Does he still live there?"

"I'm sorry, he doesn't," the monotone voice said, then the line went dead.

"How rude," I said. "I believe we'll have to pay her a visit."

"Where?"

"Address is in Reno, out toward Sparks."

"You want to drive straight there?"

"No. Let's stop at Carson City PD first. I want to see if my old buddy DeHart is around."

"Your old buddy? The same one who locked you up for two days last year without arresting you?"

"Yeah. Maybe he can hook us up with this cop, Swaney. DeHart owes me."

"I'm sure you feel he does."

"Always the skeptic."

Cody smiled, downshifting as we came off the grade and out of the rolling hills. When we reached Carson Valley, the cloudless sky and patches of green on the far slopes almost made the city look pleasant. We drove through town and made our way to the sheriff's office, a white colonial style structure with huge oaks out front, neatly trimmed hedges, and scrolled iron banisters lining the walkway to the main entrance. In a city sprawled on a forgettable plot of desert land and defined by a decaying downtown surrounded by car lots and convenience stores, the elegant police head-quarters almost seemed like someone's idea of an ironic joke.

But inside it looked a lot like any other cop shop, drab and colorless, as if the designers conceded any attempt at cheerful décor would be wasted on most visitors. Two uniformed women sat behind bulletproof glass, talking through round speakers to citizens in varying stages of distress. The line was three deep. Cody and I stood waiting, watching patrolmen and detectives come and go out a steel side door that buzzed and clanged like those in a prison.

Ten minutes later we reached the counter and I asked a gray-haired lady if Lieutenant DeHart was available. Before she could answer, I heard a familiar voice from behind.

"Reno, Gibbons, I figured I'd see you soon enough."

I turned. "Lieutenant."

Gordon DeHart was portly and mostly bald, and if not for the .38 on his side, he could have been mistaken for a neighborhood grocer. He wore an out-of-style pair of wire-rim glasses on his nose, the skin porous and reddened around the nostrils, as if he suffered from chronic allergies. The size of his stomach caused his slacks to curl over at the waistline, his belt buckle hidden under the mass. His hands looked soft, almost puffy, but when we shook, his grip was like a vice. He looked over his glasses at me, his eyes blunt and hard, a reminder that appearances could be deceiving, and he was not a man to be taken lightly.

"Do you have a minute, Lieutenant?"

"Is this regarding Jason Loohan?"

"How'd you know?"

"I spoke with Marcus Grier."

We followed him through the steel door into the squad room, around metal desks and into his office. He hiked a haunch onto his credenza and crossed his fingers in his lap.

"I'm glad you saw fit to stop by and keep me advised of your activities in my town," he said.

Out of the corner of my eye, I saw Cody begin to smile. I spoke quickly, before he could.

"You know I always cooperate with the authorities, Lieutenant. Do you—"

"Then why didn't you report being shot at last week?"

"An oversight."

"Don't let it happen again. I can always have your cot made up."

"Yeah, I suppose you could."

"I advise you keep that in mind." I nodded, and apparently that was good enough for him. He took off his glasses and rubbed his eyes, then walked behind his desk and sat in a leather chair.

"Loohan is apparently into devil worship," I said. "I'm trying to track down fellow Satanists or cults in the area. Any ideas?"

His eyes staring off, Dehart thought for a moment, then said, "Yeah. Maybe. A local character name Luther Conway. A couple years back he got noticed when he proclaimed himself the son of Lucifer."

"That's a new one," Cody said.

"He was generally considered a harmless whack job, until he started hosting weekly services at his house. He sucked in a few misguided high school kids, and then there was a rash of cat killings near his home. We shut him down after that, locked him up for a week on a contributing charge. From what I understand, he was taught some religion by a couple of his cellmates.

"Chuga-chuga-choo-choo," Cody chuckled. When I looked at him, he shrugged. "Hey, I like cats."

"Is Luther still in town?" I asked.

"Not sure." DeHart punched his keyboard and a printer behind him clattered. He handed me a sheet of paper with an address. "Maybe he still lives there."

"How about a cop named Frank Swaney? Does he work for you?"

"Swaney? Yeah, why?"

"When he was with Reno PD, he busted a couple punks for vandalizing churches and a synagogue. I'd like to talk with him about the case."

"He's on patrol. I'll have him call you."

Dehart took a call after that and a deputy escorted us out. In the parking lot, I opened a map and found the street address for Luther Conway.

"I can just imagine the newspaper headline," Cody said, leaning on his elbows over the hood. "Son of Satan gets ass reamed in Carson City jail, vows to possess souls of tormentors."

"What newspaper, the *National Enquirer?*"

We drove north out of town. A desolate stretch of high desert lay before us, the barren flatlands split by the pavement and banked by ridgelines distant and nameless. After fifteen minutes we came off a small rise and Reno lay before us, the casinos and hotels clustered against the jaded sky, a mute testimony that twenty buildings of more than twenty stories surely justified Reno's claim that it was the biggest little city in the world.

Say your luck's run out, the last steady job you had was months back, and you've become a denizen of the streets. Winter comes around and the cold rain in Seattle convinces you it's time to head south for warmer climes. So you set out for Phoenix, visions of warm, dry weather dancing in your head. You hop a train, full of drunken adventure and optimism, fueled by the quart bottle of malt liquor hidden inside your pea coat. But when you wake in the morning, you're bleary, flat busted, and hungry. The only problem, you ain't in Arizona, not by a long shot. Your train has stopped in Reno, and out you go, to join the ragtag family of winos that inhabit the crumbling downtown boulevards.

While it's true downtown Reno is the dingy home to a high population of transients, upscale communities on the city's outskirts were thriving, mostly new developments catering to retired California baby boomers. Fancy shopping malls had sprung up to accommodate the influx of new residents, countering a decade of economic deterioration. In the last ten years, Reno had evolved from a second-rate gambling destination into something more complex, a patchwork of squalor, middle class, and the newly arrived affluent.

I didn't know quite what to make of the neighborhood where Dehart said Luther Conway might still be living. A single-story apartment complex stretched along one side of the avenue, its cracked stucco sun-bleached and colorless. Across from the apartments was a ranch that appeared deserted, the barn collapsed, a rusted tractor listing to one side, as if being slowly consumed by the overgrown fields. Next door was a small factory of some kind, its dirt parking lot scattered with cars, a gray plume spewing from a single smoke stack. A row of small cookie-cutter houses opposite the factory led to the end of the road, where a larger home, an old Victorian, sat near a fenced-off concrete aqueduct.

Cody stopped in front of the house and shut off the motor. The Victorian was beige in color, its woodwork ornate, the windows hidden behind gray shutters. A purple 1960s Lincoln Continental with suicide doors sat gleaming in a gravel driveway leading to a flat-roofed garage behind the property. We stepped up to the porch and banged on the door with a brass knocker shaped like a goat's head.

The man who answered was six-feet tall and scarecrow lean. He was perhaps fifty years old, and wore an old-fashioned frock coat, a western bolo tie over a white dress shirt, dark slacks, and black lizard skin cowboy boots. His face was pasty white and his steel-gray hair was slicked back, the ends curling behind the ears and falling below his collar.

"Ah, visitors," he said.

"Are you Luther Conway?" I said.

"I am he, sir."

"My partner and I are doing some research on local satanic groups. We understand you're somewhat of an expert."

He laughed as if delighted, his tongue red against his teeth. "Indeed, I am. Would you like to come in?" He held the door wide for us. "Welcome to my humble abode."

We followed him through the marble-floored foyer into the gloom of the interior. Some of the walls were painted black, others red, and all were adorned with various images of the occult. The feel was not unlike a museum.

"Sit, be comfortable, gentlemen, please," Luther Conway said once we reached his living room. We sat on an antique parlor sofa, which creaked uncertainly under Cody's weight. A black rug lay beneath our feet, a red pentagram embroidered in its center. In the corner a Ouija board rested on a small table, illuminated from above by a pair of flickering silver candles. Between the candles was a poster of a green-faced Linda Blair from the movie *The Exorcist*.

"Let me guess," Cody said. "Your favorite movie."

"Oh, no, certainly not. Entertaining, yes, but a rather trite film."

"I must have been eight years old when I saw it," I said. "Scared the shit out of me, to be honest."

"For the masses, yes, I suppose it was terrifying. The idea of Lucifer possessing the body of an innocent child." Conway smiled wetly and gave a tiny shiver, the thought apparently bringing him great pleasure.

"Mr. Conway, I've heard you portray yourself as the son of Lucifer. Is this true?"

He winced, his face darkening, the skin shrinking against the bone and flaring with wrinkles. "That foolish notion was a rumor, propagated to harm me. You see, people fear what they do not understand."

"What brand of Satanism do you practice?" I asked. "Church of Satan?"

"I did once. I consider myself nondenominational now."

"The Church of Satan is pretty watered down, right?" Cody said.

Conway crossed his legs and brought his fingertips together. "The Church of Satan does not believe in the Prince of Darkness as an individual entity," he lectured. "Its dogma revolves around the idea that modern society has a brainwashing effect, repressing individualism, forcing humanity to conform to values that render us irresponsible to our true selves."

Cody and I shared a glance, and Conway eyed us dourly. "But I take it you're not here to discuss the various philosophies of Satanism," he said.

I leaned forward, my eyes fixed on Conway's. "If a man new to the region, a devoted Satanist, was looking for fellow members, where would he go?"

"Well," he said, a touch of pride etched across his features, "I may well be the only one left here who doesn't hide his beliefs. Others as open as me have departed for larger cities where freedom of religion is upheld by the law."

"I'm sure you're not the only Satanist in the area," I said.

"It's a lonely endeavor, to be sure."

"But not one entirely solitary, right, Mr. Conway?"

"I suppose..." he started, then his eyes pinched at the corners. "You know, you've not yet introduced yourself."

"Dan Reno. Private investigations."

"Ahh." His eyes receded into his flesh, his thoughts turned inward.

I pulled a picture of Jason Loohan from my back pocket and handed it to Conway.

"Do you know him?"

He studied the sheet of paper for a long moment. "I've never seen him," he said.

"Mr. Conway, this man is a known murderer who jumped bail. I believe he has likely sought out local Satanists. What I'd like to get is the names and contact information for every Satanist you know in Reno, Carson City, or the Lake Tahoe area."

"And this is the purpose of your visit?"

"That's right."

"I highly doubt that would be ethical," he said, his brow furrowed. "I will not be party to harassment or invasion of privacy."

"You got any brewskis around this mausoleum?" Cody said.

"I beg your pardon?"

"'Cause we ain't leaving until we get the names and numbers. And I'm getting thirsty." Cody stood and walked to where the Ouija board was displayed. He grabbed it and held it up near a lit candle. "These things are a crock of shit, right?"

Conway shot Cody a withering glare, then turned his eyes back to me.

"Sorry about my partner. He's not a patient man."

"I fail to see—"

Conway stopped short as Cody stepped to him and leaned down, pulling up his shirtsleeve to reveal his shoulder.

"You see these stitches, my friend?" Conway stared at the mass of muscle, his lips pursed as if a bad odor had invaded his nostrils. "They were made by a bullet meant to blow my brains out. The man who shot me happens to share your asinine religious beliefs. And being that there ain't many of you devil-worshipping nutcases out there, we figure you probably know who did it."

"That's preposterous!"

"Which way's your fridge?" Cody said, strolling out of the room, his hip grazing a blown glass skull on a thin, almost invisible plastic stand. The skull teetered and would have fallen if not for Cody steadying it with his fingertips.

Conway leapt from his chair. "Do you have any idea how expensive that piece is?"

"I'm sure you have many priceless treasures here," I said, a smile on my lips.

Conway huffed, his hands on his hips, his pale complexion turning an unnatural pink.

"So this is how you do business? Invade innocent people's homes and intimidate them into giving you what you want?"

"Sometimes, if that's what it takes," I said. "But we haven't even got out of first gear yet."

Conway sat back down as Cody reentered the room, a bottle of imported beer in his hand. He guzzled half of it and let out a tremendous belch.

"How utterly charming," Conway muttered. "Fine. If it's names you want, it's names you'll get." I handed him my notepad and he began writing.

"Hey, Luther," I said. "Don't even think about bullshitting us. I'd hate to have to come back here."

"And in return, I'd like your promise to not mention I'm your source for these names."

"All right."

We left Luther Conway after that. He glowered at us from the doorway as we drove off, his carriage gaunt, his stare rueful and menacing. Probably trying to save face, maybe a pathetic attempt to let us know we were lucky he cooperated. Like maybe we wouldn't be as fortunate if we returned. I sat in the passenger seat studying the four names he'd written in sharp, precise penmanship, wondering if he'd made them up out of whole cloth, or if one might actually lead to Jason Loohan. One of the names was Greg Ruehr, the convicted vandal. But the name for his partner, Eric Wenhert, was absent. I put the list aside and decided to start with the address I'd found earlier for Wenhert.

"Get on 80 heading east," I said. Cody hit the gas and soon we were on the freeway circling downtown Reno, the casino hotels jutting from the desert floor on our right, the distant flanks of the Sierras to our left. The mountain pass that doomed the Donner party faded from view as we left downtown behind, heading toward Sparks. Ten minutes later we exited the freeway and within a mile found the street we were looking for.

All the houses in the neighborhood were sprawling single story homes, the lawns green and mowed, the landscaping splendid, each dwelling an example of subtle but expensive suburban taste. A group of grade school kids were playing touch football in the street, and they politely moved to the sidewalk as we drove past. The Wenhert residence occupied at least half an acre on the broad avenue, its expansive yard shaded by giant maple and elm trees.

We parked and followed a curved brick path to the front door. I rang the doorbell on the frame of the stained oak door twice. No one answered. It was noon.

"Maybe out to lunch," Cody said, but then the doorknob clicked. A blond woman, perhaps forty, peered out from the doorway. She wore no makeup, her face drawn, dark circles under her eyes. Her sweatshirt and baggy pants hid her figure for the most part, except for her breasts, which looked firm and large. Definitely fake, I thought. A small, fluffy white dog at her ankle looked up at us and wagged its tail.

"Mrs. Wenhert?" I ventured.

"Yes?"

"My name's Dan Reno, and this is Cody Gibbons. We're private investigators."

Her eyes brightened a little and a small smile began at the corner of her mouth. "A couple private eyes, huh? Are you the hard-drinking variety?"

I said no and Cody said yes simultaneously.

"Looks like you're outvoted, cutie-pie," she said to me. "Y'all come on in."

The interior of the house was spacious and decorated in earthy tones. A bouquet of purple flowers sat on a glass table in the entry, and watercolors of mountain scenery hung from the walls of the hallway. She led us into a large room where a muted television was tuned to a reality show. A bottle of Absolut vodka was on the coffee table, next to a half-full water glass.

"Please excuse me for a few minutes, you two. I wasn't expecting company." With that she walked out of the room and left us sitting on a crème-colored circular couch. I looked at Cody and shrugged. "I guess she's the trusting type," he said, then grabbed the remote control and began surfing the channels. I picked up her glass and tasted the clear contents. Straight booze.

"Barely noon, and I'd say she's half lit. Come here, pooch." I patted my leg and the little dog jumped up to my lap and rolled onto his back.

"That would make a nice picture," Cody said, smiling as he watched me scratch the dog's stomach. "The bounty hunter and his lap dog."

Ten minutes passed. Then the rattle of ice cubes sounded from the kitchen, and a moment later the woman walked in and set a tray with glasses and a bottle of orange juice on the table. She'd done her face, lips red, eyes highlighted with liner and mascara, her hair combed out and falling around her shoulders. Now wearing tight jeans, high heels, and a clinging T-shirt.

"Help yourself," she said, motioning at the bottle. She fell into an easy chair, sipped her drink, and batted her eyelashes.

"Well, don't mind if I do," Cody said, pouring himself a stout screwdriver.

"Mrs. Wenhert," I started.

"You can call me Miss. I'm divorced."

"Right. The reason—"

"You see, my ex-husband, *Doctor* Wenhert, saw fit to be banging his twenty-two-year-old secretary. So now he's living with her, and I got the house." She waved her arm and giggled.

"I see. Actually—"

"I mean, I'm not half bad myself, you know? At least the bastard did my boobs before he left me. Want to check these babies out?"

"If we must," Cody said.

"Mrs. Wenhert," I said again, but she ignored me and yanked up her shirt to reveal a pair of cantaloupe-sized breasts in a skimpy red bra.

"Not bad, huh? My husband had a thing for Pamela Lee Anderson."

I tried not to stare too hard, but it was true Doctor Wenhert had done an excellent job.

"I'd say those are even nicer than Anderson's," Cody said.

She grinned drunkenly and took a healthy slug from her glass before pulling her shirt down.

"Ma'am, we're here because we'd like to speak with Eric Wenhert," I said.

Her smile vanished. "You sure know how to kill a buzz."

"Sorry about that."

"Eric was my son."

"Was?"

"Yes." She took a breath, then rested her eyes flatly on mine. "Eric hung himself three months ago. He's dead."

The words hung in the air like a toxic odor. "I'm sorry," I said after a moment.

"I'm sorry for your loss, Miss Wenhert," Cody added. Right out of the police training manual.

"Thank you," she said, trying to smile, but I saw her lower lip start to tremble. I waited while she took another long sip from her vodka. She blew out a breath and blinked tears from her eyes.

"I know this must be very difficult, ma'am, but do you mind if we ask a few questions about your son?"

She shrugged. "I suppose."

"I'm aware he was arrested a couple years ago for vandalizing churches. Was he involved in any other anti-Christian activities?"

She reached down and brought the dog onto her lap. "He was obsessed with the occult, with devil worship, for a time. But he had got away from that in his last few months. I really thought he might turn his life around."

"Did he have friends, or associates, that were into Satanism?" Cody said.

"His best friend was Greg Ruehr. He was a real prize. He moved out of town about a year ago."

"Anyone else?" I asked.

"Associated with Satanism? The only other one would be that sicko, Luther Conway."

"Why do you call him a 'sicko'?"

"Besides the fact he claims he's the son of the devil? He's also a pedophile."

"Really? Has he been charged with molesting anyone?"

"I don't think so, but when Eric was a teenager…"

"Yes?"

"Do I have to spell it out for you?"

"I'm sorry, I know this is painful," I said.

"Painful? You want to know what painful is? Have you ever had children?"

"No, ma'am."

"I didn't think so," she sneered. "You don't look complex enough to handle it."

"Okay," I said.

"Try raising a child, giving him your unconditional love, giving him *everything,* then watching his life turn into an abomination, and there's not a goddamn thing you can do about it. But you never give up trying, do you hear me, *never.* Not even when he chooses to have sex with an older man. Not even when he's so messed up in the mind he embraces the devil as his god. Do you think you could handle that?"

Cody and I sat quietly, listening as her voice rose in intensity.

"Then I come home one day, into this big, silent house, and find him hanging from a rope in his room, his face bloated and white, and I touched him and he was cold, so cold…"

She tried to continue but her voice cracked and she began sobbing into her hands. Cody stood and placed his hand on her shoulder, and we waited for her to cry herself out. But just when her sobs faded to whimpers, she jumped to her feet, her face wild with rage.

"So that's been my experience with parenthood!" she screamed. "And you know what? It sucks! It fucking sucks! Get it? Do you get it?"

I pulled a picture of Loohan from my pocket.

"Have you ever seen this man?"

She looked at the paper, then guzzled the rest of her drink.

"No, I've never seen him." Her face no longer livid, she dropped back into her chair, her head lolling on her neck.

"I think I'll pass out now," she said. "Please show yourselves out."

We didn't hesitate.

• • •

As we drove out of the neighborhood, I wondered about the lives behind the facades of those homes, about how the wealthy inhabitants were not immune from the most sordid, desperate circumstances. Knock on the door to the Wenhert house, and welcome to a private hell.

"Money sure doesn't buy happiness, huh, Dirt?"

"You got that right. Christ, I think she even scared you off."

"That she did, old buddy. I'm starving. Hysterical women always make me hungry. And thirsty too. Let's get lunch."

We drifted back toward downtown Reno and found a hofbrau with chicken and sides of beef roasting on spits in the front window. The chill of the morning hours had succumbed to the afternoon sun, and the promise of cold beer and real food drew us into the place like a magnet.

The dining room was crowded and noisy, but the bar, done in stained and lacquered pine, was mostly empty. Hunched over at the bar, I scribbled in my notebook, while we waited for our lunch order.

"No wonder Luther Conway didn't give us Eric Wenhert's name," I said.

"Obviously he didn't want us to find out he'd had sex with the kid. Fuckin' pervert."

"I bet that's part of the reason the kid croaked himself. Not only is he gay, but getting it on with an old creep like Conway?"

Cody swigged off his beer. "You told me Loohan is supposedly a poon hound. And now we find out Conway is a sexual degenerate. Think there's a connection?"

"I don't know. I think these Satanists are all sexual deviants to some extent."

"Yeah? Let me tell you something. If none of these names old Luther gave us pan out, I want to go back and nail his nuts to the wall."

"We already know one is bogus—Greg Ruehr. Wenhert's mother said he moved away a year ago."

Before Cody could respond, my cell rang.

"Yeah, Frank Swaney," the voice said.

"Dan Reno. Thanks for calling, Detective."

"DeHart called me, said you're looking for a bail jump named Jason Loohan."

"That's right.

"I saw the APB on Loohan. He hasn't turned up yet, but we'll keep our eyes open."

"Right. I wanted to ask you about a case from a couple years ago. Two men arrested for spray painting pentagrams."

"Sure, I remember it. What's your interest?"

"Loohan's into devil worship. I'm trying to locate people into the same."

"Ah. Sorry this is not gonna help you. One of them moved away months ago. The other committed suicide recently."

"How about Luther Conway, Detective? What's your take on him?"

"Conway? He's a strange one, no doubt, but he's stayed off the radar since doing a week in the county slam a while back."

"Anybody else you can think of that's into Satanism or the occult?"

He paused. "Hmm. Not really, no."

Cody looked at me after we hung up. "Nothing," I said.

The bartender brought our lunch orders, and my barbeque beef sandwich was so messy I had to eat it with a knife and fork. Not that I was complaining. I washed it down with a cold brew while I studied the three remaining names Luther Conway had provided. After we finished eating, Cody ambled off to take a leak, and my cell rang again. It was Candi, my sometimes girlfriend from Elko. We hadn't spoken in a week, and in the back of my mind, I was a bit concerned. I should have called her.

"Hello, doll," I said.

"Hey, you. Staying busy?"

"Yeah, I'm in the middle of a new case. I'm sorry for not calling."

"It's okay, Dan. I've been up to my eyeballs myself. I can always pick up the phone too, you know."

"I know," I said, smiling. Candi always put me at ease when I thought she might be unhappy with me.

"Listen," she said. "Remember I told you about that job opportunity at the community college out there?"

"Yeah?"

"I have an interview scheduled for next Wednesday."

"Really? Hey, that's great."

"Are you just saying that?"

"Huh? No, of course not."

"They're considering me for art director. They were very impressed with my work."

"They should be. You're stuff is great, Candi."

"Thank you, Dan."

"You're welcome, doll."

"Are you still staying in shape, jogging with that fifty-pound pack?"

"Every chance I get."

"Good," she said, a sly edge to her voice. "I want to spend the night with you Wednesday and test your stamina."

"Oh, god."

"So, I'll be hitting the road Wednesday morning, probably be in South Lake Tahoe midafternoon. Will you be at home?"

"Yeah, I should be."

"Oh, well if—"

"No, I'll make sure I'm home, Candi. It's just this case I'm working has me on the run."

"What kind of case?"

"An elusive bail jumper."

"Well, I won't be there for three days. Do you think you can find him by then?"

"I'll be doubly motivated to."

"Good," she said, the suggestive tone back. In my mind's eye, I saw her tongue curl as she spoke, her eyes sparkling beneath the bangs of her brown hair.

We hung up, and Cody, who returned to hear the last half of the conversation, toasted me with his mug.

"Your brunette from Elko?"

"Yeah."

"Getting serious?"

"You never know."

"I think I see a second marriage in your future."

"I think that's just the vodka talking."

He guffawed at that, his meaty paw massaging my neck, his fingers rough as raw leather.

"Maybe so, Dirt. Maybe so."

. . .

We spent the rest of the afternoon driving from one side of Reno to the other, then south of Carson City to Minden. None of the names provided by Luther Conway amounted to anything. The phone numbers were either disconnected or wrong numbers, the addresses vacant, nonexistent, and, at our final stop, to a closed machine shop.

The sun had dropped behind a swath of hazy clouds. I sat on Cody's hood, my feet on his bumper, while he stood and stared at the steep, craggy mountainside behind us. We were now well south of Spooner Pass and would have to drive up the sharp, narrow road leading up Kingsbury Grade back to Tahoe.

"Give me a cigarette, would you?" I said.

He tossed me his pack. "You want to go back and do a prayer session with Conway?"

I shook my head. "Not today. I think it might be a waste of time."

"You got any better ideas?"

I took a couple drags, then flicked the cigarette into the gravel. "Yeah," I said. "It's time for round two with Joe Norton."

"Mmm-hmm," Cody said, his eyes lighted with a knowing gleam, as if he'd been waiting patiently all day for me to reach that conclusion.

15

FOR THE FIRST TIME since he'd arrived in Lake Tahoe, John Switton felt truly at peace with the world. It was an odd sensation, he thought, as he drove along the highway and watched the blue waters of the lake sparkle in the morning sun. Life doesn't always have to be a battle. Sometimes it's best not to sweat the little things. So what if Vinnie Tuma was procuring the services of his whore? She was a prostitute, after all. If John wanted something more, a real girlfriend, he could always go down that road. Maybe one day.

More importantly, his bigger concerns, those revolving around his son, seemed to be in control. After his little powwow with Tom, John showed up at the gig at Zeke's. The freak show was in full force, but the music was almost tolerable, since John borrowed some of Robert's industrial-strength earplugs. And his son's performance on the drums was nothing short of amazing. Where he'd acquired the talent, John didn't know. Probably some random recessive gene from who knows how many generations ago.

Even the bizarre show in the mosh pit was entertaining. John enjoyed watching the fools stomp around like raving lunatics in their strange celebration of violence. Every so often one of them would take an elbow to the face or a knee to the groin, and then the swarm would gain in intensity, like a school of hungry piranhas smelling blood in the water.

During the band's break, Robert came to where John stood near the bar.

"Hey, Dad. What do you think?"

"You did great, son. I'm very proud."

Robert beamed, at a loss for words as he often was, but his affection for his father was clear in his eyes.

The other band members approached. "Hello, Mr. Switton," the bearded guitar player said. The bassist said the same and shook hands. Then Tom stepped forward and made eye contact, bowing slightly, showing respect. They left quickly afterward, leaving John alone to consider whether their reconciliatory gestures were authentic or not. He decided they were—his roughing up of Tom had apparently gotten through to them.

When John reached his office, he read the *Tahoe Daily Tribune* while drinking a cup of coffee. Maybe it wouldn't be so hard getting used to this town. Sure, he still missed some things about the East Coast, but the clean mountain air, the breathtaking scenery, and some of the funky local restaurants were starting to grow on him. Just the night before last, he and Robert had eaten at a place called The Redwood Tavern, and John couldn't deny their twenty-two-ounce T-bone was the best he'd ever had.

After finishing some paperwork, John walked out to the casino floor. When he passed by the sports book, he saw Vic Severino come out of the "Employees Only" doorway. It struck John as unusual; Severino rarely showed his face in the casino.

"John, I was looking for you," Severino said, waving John toward him and retreating to the hallway leading to his office.

"You found me," John said, following him. "What's up?"

Severino didn't reply until they reached his office, a large, carpeted room. One wall was lined with file cabinets, the others with cheap framed posters of motivational messages. The phrases might have been appropriate for the halls of a high school, or maybe even a corporate boardroom, but in this office, John thought they were ludicrous. Severino sat behind his desk, a large, glass-top unit.

"Sit," Severino said, motioning at the single chair facing the desk.

A tiny buzz coursed through John's viscera. He studied Severino: his long fingers curled around a pen, the stiff posture, the downturned lips. John lowered himself into the chair.

"Have you seen Vinnie Tuma?" Severino said, staring straight into John's eyes.

John relaxed a bit and allowed himself a small smile.

"No, I haven't seen the kid. What, I'm his babysitter?"

"When was the last time you saw him?"

"I don't know—two, three nights ago. Why?"

"He's missing," Severino said. Still staring, his pupils like black marbles.

"He is, huh? I'm sure he'll turn up. Maybe he's out on a binge somewhere."

"What were you doing Saturday morning?"

"What? What is this, an interrogation?" John stopped himself. An odd glow had taken hold on Severino's face, his eyes shining with an intensity that seemed almost carnal. It occurred to John he'd never known Severino to be with a woman, and maybe it was because the creepy prick was the type who got his rocks off on snuff films.

"I was enjoying my day off. Eating breakfast and relaxing at home."

Severino was quiet for a moment. He put his fists together in front of his mouth, his elbow resting on the desktop.

"Everyone knows you can't stand the kid."

"So what? He's a jerkoff. Nobody likes him."

"He told me you threatened him, and he was going to talk to Sal about replacing you."

"That's ridiculous. I never threatened Vinnie Tuma."

"He claimed you did. And now he's vanished."

"He's probably shacked up with a hooker or two and frying his brain on crack. The kid's got a drug problem. He'll probably show up sometime today."

"Let's hope so," Severino said, his eyebrows creased low, the grainy skin on his forehead shining in the light, his gaze fixed on Irish John.

Standing to leave, John looked at Severino one last time. Perhaps Severino had been seething all these years because John whacked Severino's old friend. If so, was this the opportunity Severino had been waiting for, a chance to settle the score?

• • •

The desert floor fell behind us as we climbed the two-lane through the foothills and into the deep forest. The road wound up the grade through a sea of pine and fir, the trees towering above us, their tips touching the darkening sky. The last of the twilight had given way to a starless night by the time we reached the summit and started descending toward Lake Tahoe. When we reached Highway 50, it was pitch black outside. We turned right, heading toward Joe Norton's rental home.

There were no streetlamps on Norton's street, and the light emitting from the neighboring houses was almost nonexistent. Norton's blue Chevy was not in the driveway, as it had been on our previous visit. We parked and watched the dark house for a few minutes.

"Looks empty," Cody said.

"Maybe he's taking another nap."

"Let's go see."

We crept across the front yard. Cody went to the side yard while I approached the front door. The dead bolt that had been there before was replaced with a cheap bedroom-style lockset, and the splintered doorjamb looked like it had been glued together. I turned the knob and gave the door a quick bump with my shoulder. A cracking sound, and the latch snapped free of the jamb. I slid into the entryway, past a small kitchen, and into the main room, where through the sliding glass door I could see Cody's silhouette move silently in the backyard.

It was dead quiet inside. I felt my way down the hallway to the two bedrooms. My Beretta in my hand, I pushed open Norton's bedroom door and flicked on the light. I let out my breath. The room was empty.

So was the other bedroom, but a rumpled green blanket and a grayish pillow lay on the bed. I was sure they hadn't been there when I was here before. I ran my finger over the pillow and came away with two long, black hairs. I paused for a second, then checked the closet—nothing, not even a hanger.

I moved to the family room and hit the light switch. A couch, coffee table, and a TV, all dated and probably bought used. Some jackoff mags on the coffee table. *Hustler* and a few others I'd never heard of.

Cody knocked on the window, and I opened the slider. In one hand was his flashlight, in the other an empty quart container of Castrol 4-stroke motorcycle oil.

"This was in the garbage can," he said. "Let's go check the garage."

We went through the dingy kitchen to a door leading to a vacant two-car garage. Spider webs hung thickly from the two-by-fours, and dust floated under the fluorescent light overhead.

"Look," Cody said, pointing downward, to where the distinct tread pattern of an off-road motorcycle tire tracked the concrete floor.

"Question is," I said, "assuming Loohan was here, when was it?"

"Better question is, when will he be back?"

Before leaving we turned out the lights, and I pressed the splintered doorframe back in place, hoping Norton wouldn't notice it had been re-broken. Unless he was brain-dead, he'd probably see it had been. But at this point, I didn't really give a shit. I planned on kicking the door in again first thing in the morning, and then we'd see how Norton liked my personal version of heavy metal.

•   •   •

We drove away into the moonless night and were almost to 50 when a sedan pulled up close behind us. A moment later a single red light atop its roof flashed, followed by the long piercing note of a siren. As Cody pulled over onto the dirt shoulder, I turned and looked behind us, but the spotlight attached to the driver's door was blinding.

"Routine traffic stop?" Cody said.

"Doubt it."

They approached from either side, the two men shining flashlights.

"Driver's license and registration," the voice on the left said.

A dark night. An unmarked car. An anonymous voice. I looked at Cody. He hadn't yet switched off the ignition key. I could tell by his grimace he was thinking along the lines I was: maybe best to punch the gas and barrel into California. The state line was less than half a mile away.

But then the man on Cody's side leaned down and showed his face. It was the plainclothesman from Douglas County, the tall man whose patch-like complexion and thick eyelids made me think of a grouper. The same cop who came into California and busted the Mexican drug dealers, the same one who evidently played by rules that stretched both legality and convention.

I found the registration in the glove box and handed it to Cody. "What's happening, Detective?" I said.

The man took the document from Cody's hand and studied it, and after a minute he leaned his face back into the window.

"You Dan Reno?"

"That's right."

"A complaint's been filed against you both for breaking and entering and destruction of property. Step out of the car so I can read you your rights."

"We're licensed fugitive recovery agents," I said. "Anything we've done is within our legal rights."

"Really? Interesting stuff. Step out of the car, please."

Cody and I climbed out. The man on my side of the truck was of average height and had well-shaped facial features compromised by bumpy and pitted skin. As he began reading us our Miranda rights, an odor like spoiled cologne wafted from his body. When he finished he said, "Assume the position. Hands on the hood, legs spread."

While the man patted me down, I fixed my eyes on the big cop.

"Joe Norton has a rap sheet that includes a charge of murder. I suspected he was harboring a bail skip from New Jersey. The bail skip is a guy who makes Norton look like a boy scout."

The policeman clicked a cuff around one of my wrists and pulled my arms together behind me. "Tell it to the judge," he said.

"Hey, guys," Cody said, as he was cuffed, "I spent five years on the force in San Jose. I worked for one of the most corrupt squads in the western US. When it all came crashing down, two of my ex-partners were sent to San Quentin. They're still there."

"And I give a shit, why?" said the smaller cop.

"Just something to think about, know what I mean?"

"Nope," the cop said, and cinched the cuffs tight enough to cut off my circulation. Then they escorted us to the back of their car, and fifteen minutes later we were booked into the Douglas County jail.

• • •

I imagine after a certain length of incarceration, you reach a point where getting a decent night's sleep is not impossible. The olfactory system tends to desensitize quickly, so maybe the thick odor of stale sweat, unwashed clothes, and low-grade institutional food becomes tolerable. As for the constant assault on the ears, the answer is less clear. During the quietest moments in a holding cell, the noise level is a cacophony of snores, groans, sighs, and gaseous eruptions. Dozing through it might be feasible for a deep sleeper. But on a regular basis, perhaps every hour or so, the night is disrupted by the heavy clang of cell doors, or loud, angry voices, or the wretched coughing and convulsions of a drunk heaving his guts out.

At dawn I sat up on my cot and surveyed the dozen or so men sharing the pen with Cody and me. A gray-bearded schizophrenic lay sleeping across the room, his hands black with grime, his body encased in layers of clothes. On the cot above him a skinny black man snuffled continuously, dealing with some private grief. In the next bunk, a young white kid was curled beneath his blanket, while the mattress over him sagged low with the weight of a snoring Mexican. Two cots over, a pair of bikers sat whispering, their eyes lit as if hatching some grand scheme, probably wired out of their gourds on crank.

An hour later not much had changed, except the grayness in the room had lessened as daylight ebbed through a pair of small, barred windows. One of the bikers, a stout, greasy man, shorter than me but just as heavy, walked to where the white youth lay, and stripped his blanket from him, revealing the kid huddled in a blue ski coat.

"I like your jacket," the biker said. "Take it off."

His eyes round with fear, the kid sat up and began pushing his arms out of the sleeves.

"Hey, buddy," I said from where I sat. "What's the matter, don't you like my coat?"

The biker shot his eyes at me, his face at first surprised, then he put on his best deadeye stare.

"Mind your own fuckin' business," he said.

I stood and walked toward him. "I'm serious, man." I said. "I think my coat would fit you better. His is too small. Are you telling me you think different?"

He shook his head, one side of his mouth opening in an incredulous sneer that exposed blackened gums and a missing tooth. I could see his hostility recede as he sized me up.

"What's your problem, bro?" he said.

"I ain't your brother, asshole."

"Hey, man—"

I felt an icy blast of adrenaline course through my veins, as if the frustrations of the last twenty-four hours were encased in a crystal sphere held together only by the glue of my patience, and now that the first cracks in the shell had manifested, its shattering was imminent and outside my control. I smiled, my mouth cold and suddenly flooded with a taste like raw copper. The biker backed up a step.

"Tell me if I'm right, here," I said. "You're a chickenshit cocksucker who preys on those who can't defend themselves. You hang around with other so-called badasses because left alone you wet your pants when someone gets in your face."

The other biker, a bald-headed dude with a Fu Manchu mustache, scrambled down from the upper bunk.

"Back off now, man," he said. "We're cool here."

"Bullshit we are," said the stocky biker, his voice coming from the gut. He rushed forward and feigned a left hook, then tried to tackle me. I grabbed him by the back of the neck with both hands and brought my knee into his face, the crunch of bone on bone loud in the dank room, the impact like a sledge hammer busting through a piece of rotted wood. The man fell back unconscious, but before he hit the ground, his partner threw a fast right aimed at my ear. I ducked the punch, felt his fist graze my hair, and came up swinging, landing a hard shot to his ribs. His mouth went round as he tried to suck air, one eye clamped shut against the pain. Bent at the waist and backing up, he jabbed ineffectually until his heel caught the metal leg of a bed frame, and he fell onto his back. He tried to scramble to his feet, but I kicked him in the midsection, the toe of my boot ramming deep into his stomach. He collapsed gasping onto the dirty concrete floor. Curled in the fetal position, he raised his hand in surrender.

"Bravo," Cody said, clapping twice, his legs hanging down from the top bunk. After a long moment, I said, "Fuck it," and returned to my cot.

A few minutes later the jailer came by, a crusty, bow-legged man of indeterminate years who briefly cast his opaque blue eyes on the unconscious and bleeding biker, and seemingly discounted the situation as if it were no more a nuisance than a tipped-over trash can.

"What happened to him?" the jailer croaked.

"He fell out of bed," said the other biker, who'd slithered back up to his bunk.

The jailer left without reply and within a few minutes, two men with a stretcher came and took the injured man away.

Breakfast came and went, and around ten in the morning, my lawyer, Sam Ruby, an ex-San Jose defense attorney who now worked out of Tahoe City, arrived. By noon we were kicked free on our own recognizance, Norton's complaint still pending.

"You think they'll proceed with the case?" I asked Ruby.

"I doubt it. The DA here is a woman I've known for years. She seemed to think the charges probably don't have much merit."

"They don't, especially considering the source."

"Be careful. Joe Norton may be an ex-con, but he has rights like anyone else."

I considered his remarks as he drove us the five minutes to where Cody's truck was parked on the side of the road near the Horizon Casino. "The cops who arrested us," I said. "Did you get their names?"

Ruby pulled a pad of paper from his briefcase. "Pete Saxton and Dave Boyce."

"Thanks for everything, Sam."

Cody and I climbed into Cody's truck as Ruby drove away. He would send me a bill later for his services. It would probably be at least a thousand dollars. Shit, I thought. My flush financial situation wouldn't last long at this rate. Other issues aside, going after Jason Loohan was turning out to be a bad business decision.

But I had another, more pressing concern, one that had been gnawing at me since Candi called yesterday. She was the only woman I'd had serious thoughts about in three years. Every time I reminded myself she'd be here in a few days, I felt a warm buzz of anticipation in my heart, followed by a lump of unease. Her timing couldn't have been worse. To say it would be awkward if Cody and I were running around trying to find Loohan while she was here would be an understatement. Worse, having her stay at my house potentially gave Loohan a target for a hostage. I felt my teeth grinding and opened my jaw, trying to relax the muscles.

I had fried my first and only marriage, the result of my inability to deal with the fallout from my career. My ex-wife was a good woman, and I suppose she had wanted what I thought most women want—a reasonably sober man with a steady job and positive prospects for the future, a man who could be a good husband and father. Given what I was going through at the time, it was too much to ask. I remember telling myself that my downward spiral into the world of 2 A.M. dive bars was normal, just a way to wash the taste of death out of my system. By the time I realized my rationale was bullshit, my wife was long gone.

"Goddammit, Cody," I said. "We could be just spinning our wheels here. We have no evidence Loohan is still around."

"We saw tire tracks in Norton's garage," Cody said. "My gut tells me he's out there. I don't think Norton was lying when he said Loohan would find us."

I sighed. It had been three days since our run-in with Loohan, and besides Norton's comments, we'd turned up no solid evidence he was still in the area. I was beginning to think that if he wanted to come after us, he would have already done so.

"I guess we could politely knock on the door and inquire if Mr. Norton could direct us to Loohan," Cody said, steering off the shoulder onto the road.

"I suppose there's no law against that."

"His house is only five minutes away."

We didn't say much on the way there. I was tired from the lousy night's sleep, hungry after missing dinner and skipping the lousy jailhouse breakfast, and feeling lousy about the fact that an ex-con lowlife like Norton had not only arranged to have us arrested, but was also the only lead we had in the search for a man who was either long gone or possibly nearby, waiting for the right moment to take us out of the equation permanently.

I rubbed the fatigue from my eyes as Cody turned onto the street where Norton lived. We could see his blue Chevelle in the driveway from a dozen houses away.

"Looks like he's home this time," I said, while we parked across the street.

"Just to be on the safe side, I think I'll bring your shotgun," Cody said.

"Better safe than sorry, my mother always told me."

We walked up to the front door and when I knocked, the door swung open a few inches. The jamb had not been repaired from the night before.

"Hello? Tahoe Gas and Electric here," Cody said loudly.

No one replied. I pushed the door open all the way.

"Gas and Electric," Cody repeated, louder. No reply.

We looked at each other. "Maybe he's asleep," I said. "He seems to keep late hours."

"Wait here," Cody said. "I'll go see if I can look in his bedroom window." While Cody walked to the side yard, I stepped inside the house and took a quick look. Not a light was on; the place was still—too still. I retreated to the porch and stood motionless, straining my ears for the slightest sound. It was warm in the shade, the sky almost cloud free, the afternoon turning unseasonably hot.

"Ah, shit," Cody said, coming around the corner of the house. Trouble, his eyes said.

"What?"

"Norton ain't gonna help us find Loohan. Someone painted the walls with his brains."

• • •

Through the bedroom window, I could see Norton's body sprawled on his blood-soaked mattress. He wore only boxer shorts, his muscular torso bare, the pale, tattooed skin coated in congealed blood. By my count he'd taken at least a half-dozen bullets to the chest, and one to the head, a kill shot above his left eye that had indeed blown bits of his gray matter onto the wall above the headboard.

I started dialing 911, then cancelled the call and punched in the numbers for Marcus Grier's mobile phone.

"Hello, Dan," he said. He sounded like he was in an upbeat mood. I wondered what effect my next words would have on his emotional state.

"Hi, Marcus. Listen, I need to update you on a couple things. Cody and I got a tip Jason Loohan was hanging with Joe Norton, who lives at a house on Zane Avenue, right across the state line."

"Yeah, I know where it is."

"Anyway, we met with Norton yesterday, and he was less than cooperative. Things got a little rough, nothing major, but he filed charges against us with Nevada PD. We were brought in last night by the two cops who were hassling the Mexican gangbangers at the Pinewood Apartments. Pete Saxton and Dave Boyce are their names."

"Those two, huh?"

"Yeah. So, after spending the night in the Douglas County holding tank, we decided to talk with Norton again. But when we got here, we found him dead. Shot to death."

"What? Are you there now?"

"Yeah."

"Have you called 911?"

"I wanted to let you know first, Marcus. I'd appreciate it if you could drive over here and be present. I'm not sure what to expect if Saxton and Boyce come out."

Grier didn't say anything for a long moment. I knew he was wrestling with the fact that Nevada was out of his jurisdiction, but the two Douglas County plainclothesmen had trampled over Grier's turf previously, on their own volition and without the slightest courtesy.

"Call 911 now," Grier said. "I'll be there in a few minutes."

16

TWO SQUAD CARS ARRIVED first, bubble lights on, their engines revving as they came down the street. Cody and I stood on the sidewalk as four uniforms poured out of the vehicles.

"In the bedroom," I said, jerking my thumb at the house. Three of them began scouting around the outside of the structure, probably hoping to find evidence and score points without disturbing the crime scene. A young patrolman stayed by our side, removing his sunglasses and squinting at us as if we were an alien species.

"Which one of you called this in?" he said, pen poised over his call book.

"Me," I said. My eyes were focused down the street, from which direction I could hear the whine of a siren.

"Can I see your ID, please?" he said.

"Yeah," I said, as an ambulance followed by a white van turned onto the street and bore down on us. The vehicles stopped and two paramedics in blue coveralls wheeled a gurney to the front porch. A slender man in a brown sport coat walked around them and into the house, his pace steady and measured.

"Your ID?" the patrolman asked again.

"It's in the truck," I said, and then we were distracted by the sound of rubber squealing on pavement. An unmarked car fishtailed around the corner and hammered down the lane, its tires raising a plume of brown dust.

The passenger braced his hands on the dashboard as the driver jammed the brakes, and the sedan screeched to a stop at the curb. Their side arms were leveled at us when they jumped out of the car.

"On your knees, hands on top of your head," Dave Boyce yelled.

"Hey," Cody said. "We're the ones who called it in."

"Do it now!"

I shook my head in exasperation. "A couple of real cowboys," Cody muttered.

Boyce cuffed us while Saxton began reading us our rights.

"Excuse me, Officer Saxton, but what are the charges?" I said.

"You show up at Norton's house, and he ends up dead, and you gotta ask?"

"How about murder one, tough guy?" Boyce said, cranking the cuffs down on my wrists.

"Yeah, that makes a lot of sense," I replied. "We killed him, then called 911."

"I never did think you were too bright." Boyce said.

"Your ME is in there looking at the body," Cody said. "He's probably already determined Norton was shot while we were enjoying your hospitality."

"It's an honor to be around such experts," Saxton said. He and Boyce walked into the house and left us kneeling on the sidewalk. I could feel the hot sun beating on the back of my neck and the steel cuffs digging into my wrists. We sat there for a minute or two, until Marcus Grier pulled up.

Grier stepped out of his cruiser, his eyes shaded under his sheriff's cap, a sheen of sweat on his dark jowls, the skin shining like polished walnut. Mouth downturned, he took in the scene, and said, "Saxton and Boyce?"

I nodded. "They're inside."

"Over here," he said, motioning for us move out of the sun.

Cody and I stood and walked into the shade of the single tree on Norton's lawn, where Grier waited, his hands on his hips below his gun belt.

"Hey, I didn't say you could move," the young patrolman said.

"It's all right," Grier said to him. He started to object but stopped when he saw the look on Grier's face.

"Marcus, this arrest is nothing but harassment," I said. "Could you do me a favor? My cell is in Cody's truck. The number for my attorney is in the address book. Once I talk to him, he'll call the Douglas County DA and shut this bullshit down."

Grier nodded and retrieved my phone. He found and dialed the number for me, and I was cradling the phone and talking to Sam Ruby when the man in the brown sport jacket came out of the house.

"That's the medical examiner," Cody said to Grier. "Ask him how long Norton's been dead."

Grier intercepted the brown-jacketed man and they had a brief conversation. The man then told the paramedics it was okay to go inside, before continuing to his van and driving off.

Grier walked back to where we stood. "He estimates the time of death around two A.M."

"We were in the Douglas County roach hotel from eight last night until noon today. So there's no way we could have killed him," Cody said.

I finished talking to my lawyer. "If they bring us in for this, Ruby says he'll have us out by nightfall."

Grier didn't say anything, waiting with us for the detectives to reappear. The uniformed cops began cordoning the area with yellow crime scene tape, trying to figure a way to cover the perimeter of the driveway and front yard.

By the time the paramedics wheeled Norton's bagged corpse out the front door, we'd been standing under the shade tree for half an hour. A minute later Saxton and Boyce finally stepped out into the yard. Saxton held a brown grocery bag in one hand. He ignored us while he walked to his car and locked the bag in the trunk.

"What are you doing here?" Boyce said to Grier.

"I hear Joe Norton's been murdered," Grier said.

"What's it to you?" Boyce said.

"He was a person of interest in my department's investigation of drug dealing around the Pine Mountain Apartments."

"Norton lived in Nevada and died in Nevada, Sheriff," Saxton said as he walked up, one eye squinted shut against the sun.

"Members of Norton's gang were feuding with a Mexican gang over turf at the apartments, in California," Grier said. "I think Norton's murder is probably connected. What do you think?"

"You let us deal with it," Boyce hissed, his voice charged with a seething energy, as if a cattle prod had been shoved up his ass. But Saxton's demeanor had definitely shifted. The irreverent smirk on his face was gone, replaced with an expression of uncertainty, I thought, or perhaps it was something else. Something not good.

Saxton stepped behind us and unlocked our cuffs. "You're cleared," he said simply. We rubbed our wrists, facing him and Boyce.

"You think Jason Loohan was involved in this?" Saxton said.

"Don't know what his motivation would be," I said. "I'd heard him and Norton had been together, but I don't know what their relationship was."

The five of us stood there looking at each other. Boyce glared at Cody and Grier and me, but no one said a thing. Finally, Saxton handed me his card.

"We'll be on the lookout for Loohan," he said. "You get any ideas where he is, call me."

The Nevada cops left after that, the detectives and uniforms driving away slowly, as if unclear what direction they were heading.

"What the hell, numb-nuts throws us in jail and now he wants to be your asshole buddy?" Cody said, and began walking to his truck.

I shrugged at Grier. "Thanks for coming out, Marcus. Sorry if this screwed up your day."

Grier raised his cap, smiling and letting the sun hit his face. The wrinkles around his eyes and mouth looked less pronounced than I remembered, and his dark skin took on a vibrant glow. He suddenly seemed transformed into a man basking in a newfound serenity.

"No problem, Mr. Reno. Like Saxton said, Norton's murder is Nevada's problem. Look at that, not a cloud in the sky. This weather is something, isn't it?"

• • •

"I'm so hungry I could eat half a horse's ass," Cody declared as we crossed the state line into California.

"As long as you don't eat the ass whole."

"I see a night in jail has done nothing to diminish your wry sense of humor."

"Let's go pound some burgers at the Redwood Tavern. Take a right up here."

"They serve beer by the pitcher?"

Cody parked near the front door. The place was nearly empty at three in the afternoon. The building was just off the beach, and offered a wide view of the lake from the windows behind the bar. A few patrons sat out on the sundeck under umbrellas, sipping drinks and enjoying the weather. Previous to becoming the Redwood Tavern, the restaurant was called the Tahoe Mining Company, or something similar, and the new management had kept the wood plank décor, the yellow lanterns, even the mining paraphernalia mounted on the walls.

We sat at the bar and ordered half-pound burgers and a pitcher of Bud. Cody downed his first beer in one long swallow.

"That's better," he said, wiping his mouth and pouring another. "Any ideas on what happened to Norton?"

I drank from my beer and studied the lake. "Looked like a professional hit. Someone must have caught him asleep and emptied a clip into him."

"Yeah, but why?"

"A guy like Norton…could be any number of things."

"True, but let's get specific here, Dirt. You saw some of Norton's boys at the table where the Mexican gangbangers were dealing. That means HCU is in the drug trade. More than that, to be blatantly encroaching on another gang's turf, it means they're into it in a serious way."

I nodded, though I didn't see how HCU's activities might be connected to Jason Loohan.

"So, let's assume, for the sake of argument, Norton's death is drug related. Who would want him dead? The Mexican gang, for one, right?"

"Sure," I said. "Seems like they would have motive."

Cody fell silent. "Okay, then," he said after a long pause, "let's assume Loohan's relationship with Norton was business related, to some degree. So Loohan's involved in the drug aspect."

"It's possible."

"Maybe Loohan killed Norton for drug money."

"Hell," I said, "maybe Loohan killed him so he could take Norton's spot as the leader of HCU."

Cody started to smile, but it was more like a grimace. "That's a stretch," he said. "Loohan's more of a loner, don't you think?"

"He seems to be." A wave of weariness swept over me, and I remembered I'd not slept much the night prior. I rubbed at my unshaven face, the skin oily to the touch.

"What about the Douglas County detectives?" I said. "Did you catch Saxton's attitude when he came out of the house?"

"Yeah. Like he'd been bitch-slapped. My guess is Norton was paying him off."

"I think we need to go have a talk with the remaining HCU boys," I said. "Without their leader around, we probably have a better chance at learning whatever they know about Loohan."

"Your friend, the guitar hero? What's his name?"

"Tom."

"Right. I'm sure he'll be happy to see us again."

"I don't give a shit whether he's happy or not."

A waitress came out of the kitchen and served us our late lunch, the first food I'd had in twenty-four hours. The salty flavor of the ground beef and onions was a blessing, and with each bite I felt my energy return. Cody and I devoured our meals without conversation, and when we were finished, he ordered another pitcher.

"If we don't find Loohan by Wednesday morning, I say we call it quits," I said.

"Yeah, I know. Your broad is coming to town."

"I'd like to get this shit behind us before she does. Cancel the beer and let's get back to work."

I excused myself to use the head, and when I came out, two patrons had just arrived, sitting at a table in the barroom and talking to a waitress. They were facing toward the windows and I couldn't see their faces, but I recognized them from behind: Rabbit Switton and his father, John.

I waited until the waitress left, then walked to where they sat.

"Gentlemen," I said. John Switton's face registered mild surprise, while Rabbit's disjointed expression was impossible to read. I shook hands with John and introduced myself.

"Take a seat," he said.

I sat opposite them, and something in Switton's neutral manner made me feel he could be an ally, if I played it right.

"I'm sorry for causing a scene at your home," I said.

"Don't worry about it," Switton replied.

"Okay." I waited for a moment, measuring my words. "I want to let you both know about this—you know Joe Norton, right?"

Switton stared at me, unblinking.

"He was shot last night, in his home. He's dead."

"Big Joe?" Rabbit said.

One side of Switton's face twitched. "How do you know this?" I wasn't certain before, but now his East Coast accent was unmistakable.

"I'm a licensed bounty hunter. I'm looking for a known associate of Norton's, a rapist named Jason Loohan. I went to Norton's house this morning to speak with him about Loohan."

"And you found him dead?"

"Yes. It appeared to be a professional execution."

"Big Joe was electrocuted?" Rabbit said.

"No, son," Switton said. "Do you know who killed him? Or why?"

"Norton and his boys are involved in drug dealing. I suspect Jason Loohan is also involved. I consider it likely Norton's death is drug related."

Switton turned his eyes from me and stared out at the lake. The crow's feet around his eyes looked etched in stone, and I could see his thick fingers flex around his water glass.

His eyes returned to mine briefly. "I appreciate you sharing this."

"Mr. Switton, do you know Jason Loohan?"

"No. I've never heard the name."

I handed him a rumpled picture. "Ever seen him?"

He dropped his eyes to the sheet of paper. "No."

"Would you call me if you do?"

"Yeah," Switton said. His voice was a hoarse whisper.

"I'm sorry if I've disrupted your day. Are you new in town? Retired?"

"I look old enough to retire?"

"A lot of people move here once they don't have to work."

"That doesn't apply to me. I'm a manager at Pistol Pete's."

"I see." I wrote my phone number on Loohan's picture. "Please don't hesitate to call if you have any information as to his whereabouts."

Switton didn't reply, seemingly lost in his thoughts. I went back to the bar, where Cody sat watching, his eyes raised in question. He'd filled my beer mug, but when I took a swig, it tasted stale and flat.

"Come on, let's hit it," I said.

We went outside into the heat of the day, the sun glaring in our faces. I squinted and saw Juan Perez pedal into the parking lot on his bicycle, his black hair windblown, his face shiny with perspiration.

"Hi, Mr. Reno and Cody," he said, hopping off the bike. We walked over to where he'd stopped in the deeply shaded grass by the side of the restaurant.

"How's things at the homestead?" Cody said.

"The what?"

"At home, Juan," I said. "Anyone causing trouble at the picnic table?"

"Not recently, no."

"How about those white guys we saw a few nights ago?"

"Two were there for a little while yesterday."

"How about the Diablos Sierra?"

"They haven't been out there since Rodrigo was injured. Why, what's going on?"

I slid my last picture of Jason Loohan from the back pocket of my jeans.

"Ever see this guy hanging around?"

Juan's eyes roamed over the photocopy. "Yes, I've seen him."

"*You have?*"

"Three of four days ago. He was at the apartments."

"What was he doing there?"

"I remember him because Teresa said some creepy man was staring at her."

"This man," Cody said, his finger jabbing at the paper, "was staring at Teresa?"

"Yes. He was in the common, with another man."

"Can you describe the other man, Juan?" I said.

"Well, he was about your size. A white guy, tattoos on his arms."

"What color hair?"

"Short, brown hair. And his teeth—very crooked, I remember."

"What were they doing there?" Cody said.

"Nothing. Just standing around talking. They were only around for maybe fifteen minutes that I saw."

"Shit," Cody said.

"I better go. I don't want to be late for my shift."

We watched him push his bike through the restaurant's back door. Up the street I could see a line of vehicles waiting at a signal light on 50. The cars began moving forward, the sun reflecting off the chrome in bursts of silver. A group of shirtless teenagers in a convertible were laughing and yelling, followed by a family in a station wagon weighted with luggage tied to the roof. Behind them, a pack of motorcyclists on big touring bikes rolled forward in rows of two.

"Let's go rest up," I said. Cody didn't reply, his huge frame still as a statue, eyes squinted and jaw set, staring past the traffic in the direction of the Pine Mountain Apartments.

• • •

Irish John tried to shove the churning thoughts from his mind while he cut into the steak the waitress had brought. But the meat seemed tasteless, the green salad soggy, his scotch rocks a watery blur.

"Aren't you hungry, Pop?" Robert said.

John shoved his plate aside. "I think I'll get a go box."

Sitting back while Robert ate noisily, John finished his drink and motioned for a refill. Two days ago he thought his problems were behind him, as if he'd reached the end of a rutted road, and was finally cruising the open freeway. He felt like a fool for his gullibility. Hadn't he been around long enough to know that tranquility is nothing more than a temporary state?

When he'd agreed to the arrangement in Tahoe, John had pointedly sought to stay outside the inner workings of the Tuma family. This in itself wasn't hard, because that's the way Sal Tuma wanted it. But John had also done his best to remain completely uninformed and oblivious to the Tuma's criminal activities. When Sal told John to house the HCU gang, John had asked no questions. When on occasion he'd overheard snippets of conversation hinting at drug business, he'd left the room. The less known the better.

But now things were unraveling, and the recent sequence of events pointed to a situation spinning out of control. Vinnie Tuma was still missing, and John no longer believed he was out on a binge somewhere. Severino had not hid his suspicion that John had killed the kid, and actually seemed to take a perverse pleasure in accusing John of it. Severino was one of Sal Tuma's most trusted men. If Vinnie Tuma remained missing, or turned up dead, all it would take was Severino's word, and the Tumas could conclude John was guilty. Despite John's history with the Tuma family, he would not be afforded the slightest benefit of the doubt. They'd find someone else to serve as paper owner of the casino, then his elimination would follow, probably by way of a bullet to the head.

Robert started talking, but John didn't process the words. He was still trying to digest the news of Joe Norton's murder. Was Norton's death linked to Vinnie Tuma's disappearance? It seemed likely, maybe even obvious. Would Severino see it that way? If so, John should be off the hook.

Or not, he mused. Being accused of killing a family member was akin to having one foot in the grave. John had seen fellow mobsters killed for less. In the Mafia, suspicion was often cause enough for execution. Factor in that Severino still likely harbored a grudge, and John's future was about as promising as a death row inmate's.

John widened his eyes and tried to relax the muscles in his face. He looked at his son, who was eating happily. What would become of Robert if the Tumas decided to whack Irish John the Hammer? The possible scenarios made John's head feel like it was in a vice. Left alone, Robert would be unable to fend for himself. He'd probably be sent to an institution for the mentally disabled, a place where lunatics wiped shit on their faces and were put in straitjackets for their own protection.

Maybe it was because Robert was disabled and had the mental capacity of a child that John felt such an overwhelming love for him. His feelings for his son had never evolved past the point when Robert was a cuddly five-year-old sitting on his lap. John doubted his affection was normal, but then again, neither was Robert.

Living with the threat that Vic Severino might put a hit on him was unacceptable. But what were the options? An idea skirting the edges of John's consciousness for the last twenty-four hours propelled itself to the center stage of his thoughts. "Okay, then," he said, whispering the words out loud. "Time for Plan B."

17

I'D PLANNED ON TAKING a long shower the minute I got home, but when I walked inside, I dropped onto the couch and was asleep within seconds. The sun was low in the sky when I woke, and my backyard and the meadow beyond were deep in shadow. I poured myself a cup of two-day-old coffee and heated it in the microwave.

"Hey, Cody," I said, once the cobwebs began to clear. When he didn't answer, I checked the house, then saw his truck was no longer in the driveway. Maybe he'd gone out to get food, I thought. He was probably still hungry, and we were low on provisions.

I tossed my clothes in the washing machine and showered with the water as hot as I could stand it, scrubbing the jailhouse stench off my skin. I was standing in my living room in my boxers, drying my hair with a towel, when Cody burst in.

"Throw your duds on, man. Let's head out to Pistol Pete's."

"What for?"

"I swung by the apartments, and no one's home."

"So what?"

"According to her brother, Teresa said Loohan was scoping her. We should talk to her, don't you think?"

"Probably a good idea."

"Come on, let's ramble."

"Anyone in the common when you were there?"

"No. It was quiet."

"Let me print out some more pictures of Loohan first."

Ten minutes later we parked in the lot outside Pistol Pete's and hiked toward the casino. Above the thirty-foot-tall neon cowboy at the entrance, the black glass of the upper story hotel rooms shimmered in the last of the day's sun. The air was still warm and no breeze blew off the lake. Some folks were getting stoned in a nearby car, their voices and laughter drifting out the open windows. A drowsy haze of pot smoke engulfed us as we walked by.

"You got any ganja at home?" Cody asked me.

"I've got half a joint somewhere, from the last time Candi was in town."

"I think I could use a few hits."

In the final row of parking spots, a dark blue Ford sedan with exempt plates was parked in a handicapped spot. I stopped at the car.

"Look familiar?' I said.

"Maybe."

"It's Saxton and Boyce's car," I said.

"It could be some other cop's ride."

"No, it's theirs. I memorized the license when they hauled us in."

"I admire your attention to detail," Cody said. "Any idea why they're here?"

We continued walking to the front doors, but I paused before going in.

"Not yet."

We went onto the casino floor, past the theatre, and into a maze of slot machines. Did I think it was coincidental Saxton and Boyce were here? One of the first dictums of investigative work is coincidences don't happen. John Switton, whose son was in a band with Joe Norton's buddies, worked at Pistol Pete's. So did Teresa Perez, who reportedly said Jason Loohan had stared at her. And now Saxton and Boyce show up, a few hours after

Norton's death. The confluence of these four individuals was too much to ignore, especially given the history of Pistol Pete's.

It had only been a year since the casino's previous owner, Sal Tuma, had quietly fled town, one step ahead of federal accusations of racketeering. Word on the street was he left the country to avoid being indicted along with his son, Jake, who today was enjoying twenty years in Folsom for dealing serious quantities of coke, meth, and pot. Shortly after Jake Tuma was sentenced, the Nevada gaming commission forced the Tuma family to liquidate their interest in Pistol Pete's. But did the mob ever really leave? The presence of thickly built middle-aged men with Bronx accents gave me reason to doubt it.

I followed Cody out toward the gaming tables, trying to keep up with his quick stride. So far, the few clues I'd uncovered in my search for Loohan had come up bust. The devil worship angle had gone nowhere, and the only man I thought likely knew where Loohan might be was now on a slab in the morgue. The most obvious next move was to sweat the other HCU members, but maybe there was another card to play. My original assumption was Saxton and Boyce were being paid off by Norton, to allow HCU to sell drugs. So what were the two detectives doing at Pistol Pete's now that Norton had his ticket punched? Conclusion: maybe Norton was just a pawn, maybe the money trail really led to Pistol Pete's.

But it was a theory, nothing more, and besides, even if I was on the right track, would it lead to Loohan?

It was a Monday night and the card tables were slow. We stood near a Pai Gow poker table and watched the lady dealer flip cards to a young couple.

"Is Teresa Perez working tonight?" Cody asked her.

"Don't know," she said, never taking her eyes off the cards.

We began walking the perimeter of the area, scanning for lime-green cocktail outfits. But I was also looking for men who fit a certain mold, their dress and mannerisms out of sync with the tourist and local populations, their physical presence exuding a sense of threat that made passersby avoid them like the flow of a stream around dumped trash.

It only took a few minutes, and it was Teresa who found us.

"Cody, you're always so easy to spot," she said, coming around a bank of slots, an empty tray in her hand. "Your head of hair is the only thing taller than the slot machines."

"Hey, supergirl," Cody said.

"Hi, Teresa," I said, marveling at the impression she made every time I saw her. Was she blessed with a destiny reserved for only the fewest of individuals? Her physical attributes were undeniable, her provocative figure and lovely features enough to stop a man in his tracks. But it was more than her beauty. I felt an aura radiating from her, one that was far more potent than appearances alone. *Stardom,* I thought. At that moment, though I knew it was an impetuous notion, stardom is what I would have bet was in Teresa's future.

"What brings you two handsome men to Pistol Pete's tonight?" she said, her eyes twinkling.

"Teresa," I said, handing her a picture of Loohan. "Have you ever seen this man?"

The shine went out of her face when she looked at the picture, and for a moment I saw a girl from an impoverished rural town where the local authorities portended not only corruption, but also a cruelty only those who lived in a third world country would understand.

"Yes," she said. "I think four days ago, he was in the common at my apartment complex."

"We saw Juan earlier today," Cody said. "He said this man was staring at you."

"It's true. Sometimes men stare at me. But when this one did, I couldn't wait to get out of his sight."

"Why?" I said.

She paused, and when she spoke, her voice was small, as if she was retreating from her words.

"He looked at me the way men sometimes used to when I was a child in Mexico. There is something rotten in his heart, I know it."

"Now, listen to me," Cody said, sitting on a stool, bringing himself to eye level with Teresa, his voice uncharacteristically quiet. "I don't mean to scare you, but this is a very dangerous man. I don't think he has any business being near your home. If you see him anywhere, you must call me right away."

"You are hunting him, for bounty?"

"That's right," I said. "He needs to be put in jail, where he belongs."

"The only time you saw him was four days ago?"

"Yes, Cody, only that once."

Cody exhaled, and I saw some of the tension drain from his face.

"Teresa," I said, "When you finish your shift, please don't walk through the dark parking lot alone. Have someone escort you."

"Okay."

Cody held his phone next to his face. "If you see anything makes you uncomfortable, call right away. It doesn't matter what time it is. I'll have my cell with me."

"I will," she said.

"Good." Cody's face brightened. "Hey, are you working tomorrow night?"

"It's my night off."

"Well, would you like to join us for a barbeque at Dan's place? Dan's an excellent cook."

"I am?"

"Oh, hell, yes. Quit being so modest. We'll have a fiesta on the patio!"

"Is Juan invited too?" Teresa asked.

"Of course he is," I said.

She paused, looking back and forth at each of us. "I think he'd enjoy it. And I will, too. Six o'clock?"

"Perfect," Cody said.

Teresa left to take drink orders after that. I watched her walk away, then looked past her toward the sports book on the other side of the floor.

"A great cook?" I said, my eyebrows raised.

"How hard is it to barbeque chicken and steak? I'll pick up everything we need at the supermarket."

"Let's take a walk." I pointed toward the far side of the casino.

We made our way around the tables, past an overpriced jewelry store and an expensive Italian restaurant. Next to the restaurant was the sports book, a large room that could seat at least a couple hundred bettors. A horse race was under way on a six-foot screen, and basketball and baseball games played on numerous smaller displays.

"NBA playoffs," Cody said. "The Jazz are still alive."

A few men were scattered among rows of chairs fitted with small writing tables. The only other people in the area were a pair of fellows at the bar watching baseball. I recognized one of them.

"The bodybuilder with the shaved head works here," I said.

"Doesn't look like he's working."

"Working on a buzz, maybe. Let's go say hello."

"Who's the blimp?" Cody asked, referring to an obese male sitting next to the bald man.

"No idea."

We pulled up stools at the bar.

"Yankees look good so far, huh?" I said to the bald man.

He grunted, his eyes not leaving the screen.

"All the money they spend, they better be good," I said.

He glanced at me, just trying to be civil, I thought, and said, "They're the class of the league." Then he looked again, his eyes clicking on mine.

"You were here the other night," he said. "You're the investigator, looking for the guy with the gook eyes."

"That's right."

"You find him yet?"

"No, can't say I have."

"Hmm." He turned his eyes back to the game, his pupils shining under the creases on his forehead.

"What did you say he's wanted for?" he asked. His profile was lit by the light of the television, the skin on his face tanned and tight against the bone.

"Rape, robbery, murder."

He turned on his stool, facing me. "Murder? Who'd he kill?"

"He's suspected of killing at least a dozen men."

"You shittin' me?"

"Why would I lie?"

His expression turned contemplative. He was quiet for a moment, then said, "You got any good leads on him?"

"Hard to say."

"I got your card in my office."

"Yeah, I know. I gave it to you."

"Hey," said the fat man, leaning forward, his girth wedged over the bar top. "You crackin' wise?"

"Not me, pal."

"Tell you what," said the weightlifter. "My name's Carlo. I run security here. I got a favor to ask you."

"Yeah?"

"Yeah. Give me a call if you find Loohan. That's his name, right?"

"Yes, it is. Why you interested in him?"

He smiled, his teeth perfectly even and movie star white against the pitted grain of his bronze skin. "Like I said, I run security here. A bad guy like Loohan, he shows up at my casino, who knows what trouble he can cause?"

He wrote his first name and phone number on a square of paper and handed it to me.

"Hey, Nickie," he said, raising his voice to get the attention of a black-haired bartender who was chatting up a slender cocktail waitress at the other end of the bar. "Get these two a round on the house, would you?"

"That's all right, Carlo," I said, standing. "We got to boogie." I slipped his number into my pocket. "I'll keep you posted."

Carlo gave me a long look before nodding, while his fat friend stared at Cody and me as if we were standing between him and his next meal.

"Have a good one, fellas," Cody said.

We walked straight out of the place, past Saxton and Boyce's car, through the dark parking lot to my truck. I started the motor and drove around to the side of the building.

"I want to try something," I said, parking in a stall with a view of an unmarked door.

"Employee's exit?" Cody said.

"Right. I'll bet you five bucks Saxton and Boyce come out here."

"Who do you think they're in there talking to?"

"Whoever's running the show, old buddy."

"And who's that? You're not talking about Sal Tuma? I thought he was long gone."

"That's right. He was forced to sell out."

"Who, then?"

"I don't know. I'm sure the ownership of Pistol Pete's is a matter of public record. Maybe I can access it on the Internet."

"Those two goombahs at the bar looked like a couple extras from *The Sopranos*."

"My guess is Tuma probably sold the casino to parties of a like persuasion."

"Huh?"

"Mobsters."

"And Saxton and Boyce are getting paid off by them, to allow HCU to deal drugs?"

"It's possible," I said, just as the door we were watching swung open. Saxton and Boyce stepped from the building onto the asphalt, holding the door open and speaking to a figure hidden inside.

I reached in my glove box for my camera, switched it to full zoom, and began snapping photos. But whoever the cops were talking to remained in the shadow of the doorway.

"Come on, show your face, greaseball," Cody said.

Saxton pushed the door open wider, and at that moment, I thought I might have got a decent shot of a lean man in a dark suit. Then the door swung shut, and Saxton and Boyce began trudging back toward the front of Pistol Pete's.

"You know what, Dirt? Screw the crooked cops and these dickweed Mafiosos. Seems to me they're both searching for Loohan, and maybe hoping we do the leg work."

"They think Loohan killed Norton."

"Yeah, I get that, but the problem is, none of this is getting us any closer to finding him."

I drummed my fingers on the steering wheel and started the engine.

"Let's take a spin by Zeke's," I said.

• • •

Monday night, nine P.M., and as we drove down 50, I wondered if Zeke's would even be open. After a long weekend of head banging, I imagined the death metal brigade might take a night off, to nurse their hangovers and lick their wounds. But the parking lot was half full, the windows glowing with neon light, and I could hear the bass thumping even before we got out of my truck.

As we walked to the entrance, our boots crunching over gravel and broken glass, I felt a pang of nostalgic regret. A year ago, I would have been walking this path into a friendly neighborhood saloon, the floor covered in peanut shells, country music playing on the jukebox, the air smoky and fragrant with barbeque. It had been a joint where locals and tourists alike relaxed in an ambiance that seemed a throwback to a simpler time. I remember getting drunk here one night, shortly after Sal Tuma's drug business got shit-canned. I should have been celebrating, but my girlfriend had just left me, and my drunk was a remorseful one. At the end of the blurry night, I somehow ended up at the home of the bartender, a braless twenty-five year-old thing with long brown hair, a belly button ring, and nipples that seemed permanently erect.

When we went through the doors, we were greeted with a wall of sound, the chugging assault of guitar and drums almost incomprehensible as music. But there was no band; the noise was pumping out of the house PA system. A few metal heads reeled around the mosh pit, but their gyrations lacked conviction. At the bar sat a motley collection of skinheads, long hairs, a couple bikers, and two tattooed young ladies I doubted were of legal drinking age.

None inside were dressed in HCU colors. More out of a desire to get away from the noise level than anything else, I pointed toward a door in the back, which led to a beer garden.

A half dozen picnic benches were arranged under lamps mounted on the pine trees surrounding the fenced-in clearing. From electric cords strung between the trees, a variety of banners advertised beer and liquor. A large barbeque on a trailer was parked off to the side, its black hulk beginning to rust.

Perched on a middle table were two dudes, cigarettes in their mouths and beer bottles dangling from their fingers. They wore black shorts and white T-shirts and glared at us as if we were intruding on a private moment. Cody apparently took this as an invitation and strode toward them without a moment's hesitation.

"How's it hangin', boys?" Cody said, a grin on his face, his eyes crinkled with good humor. They stared back at him without responding.

"Say, Joe Norton told me I should come lick y'all up to score some nose candy. I'm just looking for a half gram. Can you take care of me?"

The expressions on their faces went from incredulous to suspicious.

"Who are you guys, cops?" said one, a bony man of average height. He was tapping his skate shoe on the picnic bench rapidly, as if he possessed a wiry energy that needed constant release.

"Are you kidding?" I said. "Do we look like cops?"

"How do you know Joe Norton?" said the other guy, a stocky fellow with small, blunt eyes.

"I know how he knows him," said the wiry man, hopping off the bench and pointing at me. "He's the one who freaking shot Billy."

The other man stared at me hard. "You got a lot of balls to show your face around here."

"I'll take that as a compliment," I said, smiling. "Say, can I bum a smoke from you?"

The two HCU boys looked at each other, then the stocky one said, "What the fuck do you want?"

Cody took a step forward, his grin gone.

"We want to know who killed your boss," he said.

"Well, join the crowd."

"We think it was Jason Loohan. You know where he's at?" I said.

"Whoa, hold it," said the wiry man, his throat framed by tattoos crawling up from his shirt collar. "We never even met Loohan. He does his own thing, man. He ain't a part of us."

"What was he doing with Norton, then?" Cody said.

"Maybe they—"

"Shut up, Jimmy," the stocky one said.

"Hey," Cody said. "We think Loohan killed your boss, and we want to find him. You got a problem with that?"

The stocky man puffed out his chest and stared at Cody with half-lidded eyes.

"No," he said. "I got a problem with you."

"You do, huh? Tell you what, prick. Take your best shot, hit me as hard as you can. If you knock me out, you win. But if I'm still standing, I'm gonna snap your neck. I'm not kidding with that. If you survive, you'll go through the rest of your life in a wheelchair. Your hands probably won't work too good, so you'll have a nurse following you around to wipe your ass."

The man held his expression for a long moment, then turned his head and spat. "Fuck this," he said, and walked between the picnic benches and into Zeke's.

I sat on top of the table. "Take a seat, Jimmy."

He fumbled another cigarette from his pack and lit it with his last one, then licked his lips and gnashed his jaw as if he was chewing on his tongue. No doubt he was blasted on speed. He remained standing, trying to think, but I could tell his decision-making capability was short-circuiting.

"You're not cops, then?"

"Private investigators," I said.

"All right, look, man, Norton didn't tell anyone what he was doing with Loohan. But we all thought it had to do with a run Norton was making."

"A run?"

"Yeah. They were heading down south to the border, get it?"

"So Loohan went with Norton down south?"

"Don't know for sure, but I think so."

"What happened then?"

"Nothing. I mean, Norton came back with what he'd gone for."

"What about Loohan?"

"What about him?"

"You think he had reason to shoot Norton?"

"Hell, I don't know. I doubt it. Everything went smooth, far as I could tell."

"Fine," Cody said. "Where can we find Loohan?"

"I got no idea, man."

Cody put his hand on the man's shoulder and sat him down, hard, on the picnic bench.

"Where would you look for him?"

"That's a good question. Sometimes he stays in hotels, but I think mostly he's camping."

"Outdoors?"

"Yeah. Norton said he liked to follow a stream into the mountains on his dirt bike and make camp wherever the land is flat."

"What stream?"

"How would I know? Any damned stream."

"When do you expect to see him next?" I said.

He laughed. "I've never seen him in person, and now I probably never will. And I got no problem with that."

"You've never met him?"

"Nope. And I'm on the early flight out of town tomorrow. I'm done with this crazy shit."

"You know what, Jimmy?" Cody said. "That's the first intelligent thing I've heard you say. But we're not done here yet."

I hiked my boot up on the bench next to Jimmy and leaned into his face. "Who's next in command at HCU, now that Norton's dead?"

Jimmy snickered. "My guess would be Tom." Then he started laughing harder.

"I get the joke," Cody said. "Where does Tom live?"

"Don't know the exact address. Some dump he's renting near where Norton lived."

I looked at Cody, and he shrugged.

"Let's get out of here," I sighed.

·   ·   ·

As we drove off, I tried to make some sense of all the scraps of information we'd picked up. Every stone we turned over revealed something, but the problem was, none of it gave me any decent idea how to track down Loohan. Probably the most solid clue was Jimmy's remark that Loohan sometimes stayed outdoors. How the hell do you follow up on a lead like that?

I thought back to our last conversation with Joe Norton. I could still see the smirk on his face when he suggested Loohan would find us when he was ready. Maybe the best tactic at this point would be to wait Loohan out. It was a weak, defensive position, but we were running out of options.

Another thing was nagging at me. It seemed both the cops and the man in charge of security at Pistol Pete's were interested in Loohan, probably because he was a suspect in the murder of Norton. But the bullet that ripped a trench in Cody's shoulder was a small caliber round—I could tell by its relatively light report—while the rounds that blew Norton to hell were definitely large caliber. If Loohan owned anything more than a small firearm, he would have chosen the larger piece when he shot at us, given the distance. My guess was Loohan carried a small weapon, a .25 cal pistol, or maybe even a .22.

So if Loohan didn't kill Norton, who did? Who'd have motivation? At least that answer was pretty obvious—the Diablos Sierra gang. Would they be pissed enough to send a professional hitter after Norton? Given that HCU was moving in on the Mexican's territory, it was fathomable.

But did it really matter? The turf war between the Mexicans and the white trash gang, the involvement of the crooked cops and maybe even casino-based mobsters, none of it was my concern unless it led to Loohan. And so far, I saw no indication any of it did. Loohan seemed to be a lone wolf, a free agent, his affiliations temporary, his motivations unknown and perhaps unattached to any of the troubles brewing in South Lake Tahoe.

Or maybe, I thought wistfully, maybe he was just gone.

• • •

The white Switton house looked like an alien ship when we drove by, the industrial lighting so strong I had to squint against the glare. No cars were out front, aside from John Switton's Lincoln, parked in the driveway.

"Looks like no one's home but that tough old bird," Cody said. "What do you think?"

"If the band was rehearsing we'd see a car or two. Let's go. I have no desire to roust John Switton."

"What do you think of him?"

"You mean, do I think he's part of the goombahs at Pistol Pete's? I don't know. He's definitely not from around here."

"Did you like how he threw Tom around?"

"Yeah, not bad."

"He ain't no ordinary working stiff, I'll tell you that."

I hung a U-turn at the end of the street and drove back out to 50. Part of me wanted a drink, but I had a headache and really just wanted to lie down and turn my brain off. The strain of the last week was beginning to wear on me. I felt like I was in a boxing match with an invisible man.

When we pulled into my driveway and my headlights flashed across the front yard, I thought my eyes must have been playing tricks on me.

"What the...?" I said, and backed up my truck, pointing the headlights more directly at the broad L-shaped lawn that reached from my back fence to the front of my lot. I turned off the ignition, and Cody and I walked to the edge of the grass.

"Good god," Cody said, as we stood staring. Something, most likely a spinning off-road motorcycle tire, had carved a pentagram into the lawn, the points of the star reaching from my porch to the opposite fence. Chunks of sod were littered about, and the siding next to my front door was streaked with a muddy spray. I bent down and examined a particularly deep section of the damage. The imprint of a knobby dirt bike tire was unmistakable.

I went back to my truck and returned with a flashlight. The waist-high post and rail fence separating my yard from the sidewalk along the street ended about two feet shy of a taller fence marking the adjacent boundary of my property. A trail of soil and grass led from my lawn and out the passage between the two fences, across the sidewalk and down the street.

"You know," I said, "When I bought this place, I always wondered why the fence stopped short here."

"Probably so the owners could walk around it."

I looked at Cody, a pained smile on my face. "We need to find this rat bastard and exterminate him," he said. "I'm serious."

When I didn't respond, Cody said, "You surprised at this?"

"Not really. Stunned, yeah, but not surprised." I stared back at my ruined lawn, and felt like a fool for clinging to the hope that Loohan had fled town.

"Let's go inside," Cody said.

"You need coffee?" I asked.

"Why?"

"I want to take a walk."

"Where?"

"Along the stream out there," I said, pointing toward the meadow behind my house.

Cody raised his eyebrows. "Let's suit up and go hunting."

· · ·

A nearly full moon lit the creek and the thick grasslands sweeping out toward the snowcapped peaks a mile away. We crept along a trail that ran aside the stream, stopping every ten paces to listen for sounds that didn't belong. Did it make sense for Loohan to camp close to where I lived? No, but I'd given up trying to assign logic to his behavior. I was still trying to assimilate that not only was Loohan still around, but now he was taunting me, letting me know he was here and apparently not at all concerned about the threat I posed. But it was more than that. Within the blatant desecration of my property, his message was clear. He wanted me to know he had the ability to take me out at will.

I suppose he could have left some campy, threatening note taped to my door, telling me I better be looking over my shoulder. He could have written out his intention to do me harm, to settle the score for both my ongoing efforts to arrest him and my apprehension of his best friend. But that wasn't Loohan's way. He let his actions speak instead. In doing so, he remained less tangible and more ominous.

We came to a marshy section of the path and veered away from the creek, into the scrub where the ground was more firm. The rushing water should have obscured the sound of our boots crunching over the underlying dry grass, but I cringed with every step. I crouched as we moved forward, head low, my Beretta trained on a cluster of trees thirty feet ahead. The straps of my body armor dug into the tops of my shoulders, distracting me momentarily. I stopped, and Cody came up from behind, my sawed-off scattergun in his hands. We paused, staring into the trees. Then we heard a faint ticking sound.

Cody circled to the left, and I continued toward the trees, which I could now see were four large aspens, one which had fallen and rested at a sharp angle against another. Beneath them was a dense clump of deadfall. Whether there was a clearing inside the thicket was impossible to say. I moved one step at a time, lifting my knees high and bringing them down slowly.

The ticking sound again, definitely metallic. Cody had reached the tangle of branches and raised the shotgun to his shoulder, aiming into the brush. He nodded at me and I kept moving until I saw a trail of flattened grass. My automatic clenched in both hands, I inched my way along, until I could see the edge of a clearing.

In two running steps I burst forward, my arms locked, my finger poised on the trigger. In the sights of my firearm was the forehead of a skinny man sitting cross-legged, a fork in one hand, a tin can in the other, his food half-chewed in his open mouth. A small, battery powered lamp rested between his legs. He had light-colored hair and was perhaps twenty-five years old.

"Shit," I said. "Who are you?"

"My name's Darrel." His eyes were bulbous, like two eggs with pupils. A forty-ounce bottle of malt liquor was propped against his side.

"Clear, Cody," I said.

"Right," he said, and I heard him coming around the thicket.

"How long have you been here tonight, Darrel?"

"Since sundown," he stammered. I put my piece back in my shoulder holster.

"Have you heard a motorcycle out on the trail?"

"No, sir."

"You got a cell phone?"

"I do. But it ain't always charged."

"If you see a man on a dirt bike camping out here, call me. If it's who I'm looking for, I'll buy you enough beer to keep you drunk through the summer."

The thought was enough to put a wide smile on his face. I gave him my business card, then Cody and I hiked back to the creek.

"Haven't seen any motorcycle tracks," Cody said.

"The trail turns too narrow for a dirt bike in about a half mile," I said. "Let's keep going."

We crossed the stream when we reached that point, a steep, rocky section, the fast water glinted with silver in the moonlight. Then we doubled back on the opposite side, slipping in and out of the shadows wordlessly, smelling the air for traces of exhaust, scanning the dirt for tread marks. Nothing.

It was midnight when we got back to my house. Before we went in, I checked the windows and back door. Satisfied nothing had been tampered with, we went inside. We stood in the dark interior, looking out the front window at the damage done to my lawn

"I'd say fifty-fifty we'll see the cocksucker before sun up," Cody said.

"He's unpredictable, but at least we know he's still in town."

Cody tapped the barrel of my shotgun against the window glass.

"Here's my prediction," he said. "Jason Loohan's got a death wish—his own."

I shrugged out of my shoulder holster and made sure the safety on the Beretta was clicked off.

"I'm going to sleep out here," I said, setting my piece on the coffee table.

Cody pulled down the shades on the front window. "Tomorrow," he said, and ambled off to the guest room.

Boots on, Kevlar vest heavy on my chest, I lay on the couch. I dozed for a while, more in a state of semi-slumber than deep sleep. At around two I checked the house and walked out to my porch. I peered down the street and then out to the meadow, and after a minute, I came back in. Loohan was probably sleeping soundly in a hotel room somewhere, I thought.

I lay down again, closed my eyes, and hoped for some degree of rest. I rose once more at five and double-checked the doors and windows, then sat on my couch with my pistol in hand. The dawn came slowly.

18

A T FIRST LIGHT THAT morning, Pete Saxton took a cup of coffee to the cedar table on his deck, and watched the sun rise over a granite cliff layered with shelves of snow. Beneath the rock face, mist rose from the trees. The green mountainside stretched for miles along the horizon.

He lit his first Camel of the day, coughed up a wad of phlegm, and hawked it onto his lawn. It was two in the morning when he'd got home last night, after a visit to a woman in Truckee he sometimes dated. The horny bitch, he thought, snickering as he remembered how she begged for it up the ass. He'd planned on being on the road by midnight at the outside, but she was insatiable. God, he was tired. But he'd been waking at 6:00 A.M. for so many years he couldn't sleep later no matter how hard he tried.

Exhaling a stream of smoke, Saxton's thoughts returned to the murder of Joe Norton. The fingerprint and ballistics results would be in by the afternoon. Hopefully they would provide some direction. Saxton stared out into the sky, which had already turned a tranquil baby blue, soft puffs of clouds dispersing as the sun came full over the ridgeline. The scene looked like something from a postcard, but it did nothing to ease the trepidation idling in Saxton's gut.

When Saxton and Boyce had gone to Pistol Pete's to tell Severino his main man at HCU was dead, it had not gone well. Not that Saxton expected it to, but Severino's reaction was worse than anticipated, especially from a man who seemed almost incapable of emotion.

"*What?*" he'd hissed, when Saxton relayed the news. Severino's normally dead eyes came alive as if jolted by electric shock.

"We think it happened around two in the morning," Saxton said. "Someone shot him while he slept."

"Unloaded a magazine into him," Boyce added.

Severino rose from his desk, his face taught, as if the skin was stretched over an axe blade. He came around and walked behind the chairs where Saxton and Boyce sat. The office became silent. Severino faced the door and pressed his hands together, like he was performing an isometric exercise. After a minute he released his breath and turned to the two detectives he was paying off.

"Who do you think did it?" he said.

"I think we're looking at two possibilities," Saxton said, swiveling in his chair to meet Severino's dark stare. "First, the guy you said Norton had taken down south, Jason Loohan. From what I gather, he's a treacherous son of a bitch."

"What would be his motivation?" Severino said.

"I'm not sure, yet, but I consider him a person of interest."

Severino curled his upper lip, his nostrils twitching as if the air was fouled.

"What else?" he said.

"I think we have to consider the possibility this is retaliation from the Mexicans."

"I thought you said they were a bunch of pissant spics."

"That's still what I think," Saxton said. "But they'd definitely have motive."

"Who's gonna take over for Norton?" Boyce said.

Severino ignored the question. He walked back behind his desk and sat, leaning forward on his elbows.

"Your weekly envelopes are on hold for now."

"On hold?" Boyce said. "For what?"

"Norton was running the show," Severino said, addressing Saxton. "Without him, it creates problems. I need time to come up with a solution."

"What do you want us to do in the meantime?"

"I suggest you go find who killed Joe Norton," Severino said, his eyes boring into the cops. "We need to eliminate the threat, don't you think?"

. . .

Saxton finished his coffee and went inside to eat breakfast. He didn't quite know what to make of Severino's claim that Norton's death prevented the gang's ability to do business, and the payoffs would be on hold. Maybe it was Severino's way of asserting the money was not automatic, that the pay was based on the gang's performance. Saxton shook his head at the notion. He and Boyce were being paid to allow the gang to do business, and on the side, discourage the competition. They'd done their job.

Oh well, as long as the payments resumed soon, it wasn't really a problem. Especially since Saxton had searched Norton's room and found nearly twenty grand in cash. Split in two, it was enough money for Boyce to pull himself out of debt, and for Saxton to pay off a good chunk of his home upgrade bills. Not bad, for an unexpected bonus.

After eating, Saxton returned to his backyard and sat listening to the quiet gurgle of the hot tub. He kept on turning over the issues surrounding Norton's death, trying to reach conclusions. For the time being, none of the dots connected. What motivation would Jason Loohan have to kill Norton? None that Saxton could guess at. The more probable scenario involved the Diablos Sierra, but they were nothing but street punks, and Norton's death was no doubt done by a skilled hitter. He was almost positive none of the Mexicans who'd been hanging out at the Pine Mountain Apartments were capable of such a job.

Screw it, then. He stamped out his cigarette and went back inside. At least one thing was clear: Saxton's job was to find Norton's murderer. He was being paid by the Nevada PD, as well as Vic Severino, to do so. Time to quit chasing ghosts in his mind, and go to work.

Saxton showered and dressed in creased slacks and a beige sports coat. He spun the barrel of his .38 and snapped the revolver into the holster on his ribcage, and at eight sharp pulled up in front of Dave Boyce's doublewide trailer. He honked the horn twice and waited.

A minute later he honked again, and when Boyce didn't appear, Saxton shut off the ignition with a curse. An impatient frown taking hold on his face, he climbed from his car and walked to the front door. It was definitely time for Boyce to get himself a set of wheels, even if all he could afford was a freaking scooter, maybe like the kind they rented out to teenagers who zipped around South Lake Tahoe all summer long.

Saxton pounded on the aluminum frame of the screen door, the clattery thumps loud in the quiet morning. The neighboring units in the mobile home park were still, apparently inhabited by people who didn't wake and leave for their jobs at a normal hour.

"Come on, Dave," he said, knocking again, the sound reverberating against the metal siding. Saxton stood on the concrete porch, his thumbs hooked in his belt loops. Then he blew out his breath, swung open the screen door, and turned the knob of the front door. It was unlocked. As he pushed it open a few inches, a tiny current of concern pulsed in his chest.

"Dave!" he shouted. He reached in and flicked on the light switch. The doorway opened directly to the main room, the couch, coffee table, and easy chair nondescript and utilitarian. When Boyce didn't answer, Saxton stepped inside, the skin around his eyes tight as he slowly scanned the room. Down the hallway, the door to the bathroom was open, the light off and no sound from the shower. His fingers slid beneath his coat and released the holster snap holding his revolver. Gun in hand, he moved down the hallway. With each step his muscles grew tighter, until he finally stood at the door to the single bedroom. He banged on it with his fist.

"Goddammit, Dave," he said. He waited a long moment, then, standing aside the doorway with his back to the wall, he cracked opened the door and peeked into the room. What he saw made his breath catch in his throat, then alarm flooded his body. He opened the door fully and stood transfixed.

The damage to Dave Boyce's body was horrific. He lay face down across the bed, his nude corpse torn with entrance wounds the size of nickels, blood everywhere, the sheets soaked, the walls splattered and trails of red running downward. His head was turned to reveal his profile, his face blank, one eye shot out, a fist-sized piece of skull hanging from his scalp to reveal the gray maw of his brains.

Saxton backed out of the room. He closed his eyes and leaned against the hallway wall and tried to control his breathing. A creeping surge of nausea rose in his throat, and he hurriedly walked outside into the sunlight. He went to his car and leaned against it. His fingers felt thick and insensate as he dialed 911.

"911 Emergency, who's calling, please?"

"Cheryl, this is Pete Saxton. I'm at Dave Boyce's place. He's been shot to death."

The woman began asking questions, just doing her job, and Saxton stayed on the line with her until the black and whites showed up.

"Jesus, Pete, what happened?" said one of the uniforms, a craggy, older cop who spoke incessantly about his grandkids and his plans to retire.

"Detectives on the way?" Saxton said.

"Yeah. Galanis and McMann."

"Great." Saxton studied the tops of his shoes. The only two cops in the department as corrupt as he was. Self-serving, without loyalty to anything but their bank accounts.

Within a minute an ambulance wailed down the street, followed by the Douglas County medical examiner and an unmarked sedan. Nick Galanis and his partner, McMann, whose first name Saxton couldn't remember, climbed out of their car and ducked under the crime scene tape the uniforms had strung from one large pine to another, effectively boxing off the sidewalk and the porch of Boyce's home. Galanis, six foot, one eighty, flashed a grin at Saxton. Totally inappropriate, but Galanis always grinned, regardless of the situation. Devastating, Saxton had once heard a female suspect describe his smile. The detective had a full head of curly black hair, never missed a day at the gym, and was campaigning for promotion to captain, the position still vacant after Old Cunningham had a heart attack and finally made official his retirement. For the time being, Galanis had been appointed as acting captain.

McMann, in contrast, was bald and squat and looked like a pig. He'd arrived in Nevada about a year ago, amid rumors of trouble with the Chicago PD. A recovering alcoholic, he attended meetings and often emitted a palpable aura of frustration and unhappiness with his sobriety. "Poor bastard's got it bad," Saxton once commented to Boyce, watching McMann suffer through a booze-soaked department party.

Saxton stood before the detectives. Galanis's grin dissolved, his dark eyes scrutinizing.

"You all right, Pete? Why don't you take a seat in your car while we go inside?"

"Okay," Saxton said, not interested in Galanis's disingenuous concern. He watched the two go into Boyce's trailer, along with the ME, then opened the passenger door to his Ford and sat facing out, elbows on his knees. "Think," he told himself. He closed his eyes and tried to calm his nerves, but the nausea he'd been fighting suddenly flooded his mouth, and he spewed a bilious froth into the gutter. Coughing and spitting, he waved away an officer who approached, leaned back, and pressed his palms to his eyes.

He allowed himself five minutes, then rinsed his mouth with bottled water and grabbed a handful of mints from a tin container. Did Pete Saxton feel any personal grief his partner was dead? Not much, he had to admit. Nor was he concerned Dave Boyce's absence would disrupt his arrangement with Severino. Instead, his angst was centered on one fact that was growing increasingly clear to him: Norton and Boyce were murdered by the same very competent killer, and Saxton was probably next on the list. If not for him being away from his home until two in the morning, he might well already be dead.

Shaking a cigarette from his pack, Saxton rose from the car and saw a crowd had begun to gather. A few trashy housewives, three teenagers with skateboards who should have been heading to school, and a man with a camera next to a woman writing on a notepad. Probably reporters from the *Tahoe Daily Tribune*. How'd they get here so goddamned fast? Some rubbernecking neighbor must have called them.

The reporter, a pudgy, thirtyish man, pointed the camera at Saxton. Blocking his face with his hand, Saxton ducked back into the Ford. In the rearview mirror, he saw the man snap a shot of the car, then begin walking up along the passenger side. The reporter grew larger as he neared the car door.

Saxton thrust the door open and jumped out, almost hitting the reporter, who stumbled back and raised his camera. The man's face recoiled in shock when Saxton grabbed his forearm and twisted, bringing him to his knees.

"Let go of me. You can't—"

"You're interfering with police work." Saxton pried the camera from the reporter's sweaty fingers. "This will be returned to you after it's been determined none of the photos will compromise our investigation."

"I have every right to—"

"Invade my privacy?" Saxton snarled, blood pumping in his temples. He waved over two uniforms who'd just come out of Boyce's place.

"This citizen needs to be detained until we're done here," Saxton said. "Cuff him and stick him in a squad car. And tell the bitch over there to keep her distance or she'll be joining him."

By that time, another half-dozen spectators had congregated on the sidewalk across the street, staring in rapt attention, as if they were virgins witnessing a live sex act.

"Fucking ghouls," Saxton said. "Tell Galanis I'll be at my desk. I'm out of here."

• • •

The squad room was empty and quiet. Saxton drank a can of soda and smoked and tried to anticipate what was to come. A cop killing was an event that would shake even the hardest veterans. The department's reaction would no doubt be fueled by emotion. Everything would come under scrutiny. Standard operating procedures that sufficed in day-to-day investigations would be considered woefully inadequate. Arresting the party responsible for the fallen officer would dominate the lives of all ten detectives working for Douglas County. The fact Dave Boyce was not well liked was irrelevant—he was part of a sworn brotherhood that watched one another's back. No one gets away with killing a cop. The intensity level would be cranked to full throttle.

If an arrest wasn't made promptly, it was likely the state police, or maybe even the FBI, would be brought in. That could prove disastrous. It didn't take much to imagine the Pandora's Box an outside police agency might crack open if they began poking around. At stake was not only Saxton's career, but also Severino's drug enterprise, which of course led right back to Saxton.

Saxton stood abruptly, cursing as his knee hit the desk. He needed to go alert Severino of the shit storm brewing. If Severino was smart, he'd hunker down, pull the HCU boys off the street, maybe go on a long vacation. Saxton climbed into his Ford and swung out to the highway toward Pistol Pete's, his foot mashed to the floorboard, the tires howling, the sedan pulling ahead like a racehorse out of the gate. As he neared the casino, he dialed Severino's untraceable cell.

"We need to talk," Saxton said, bouncing into the parking lot. The black glass of the casino hotel looked superheated in the sun. Beyond the building the lake was white, as if bleached of color.

"Make it around three," Severino said.

"Now. I'm outside the casino. Meet me at the back door."

"It better be important."

Saxton hung up and walked across the black asphalt to the Employees Only door. It opened, and he slipped inside, silently following Severino down the hallway to his office.

"What now?" Severino said, sitting behind his desk.

Saxton looked around the windowless room as if for the first time, and something about it seemed surreal to him. He blinked, then turned his eyes to Severino.

"My partner is dead. Dave Boyce was murdered last night. It looks like it was done by the same guy who killed Norton."

After a moment, Severino said, "Are you sure?"

"He was torn apart in his bedroom by multiple large caliber rounds. Same as Norton was. Ballistics will confirm it by the end of the day."

Severino cleared his throat and clicked his pen a few times before setting it down.

"How do you see it?" he said.

"The whole situation is a three-ring rat-fuck is how I see it," Saxton said. "I think someone's decided to shut HCU down. Someone who's not afraid to kill a cop. Guess who's probably next on the hit list? Me. After that, maybe you."

Severino pushed back his chair and crossed his legs. "Do you need a drink, Pete?"

"No. I've got to get back to the squad room. I've got a long day ahead of me."

"Do you think we underestimated the Mexicans?"

"It's possible. We're gonna be all over them like stink on shit, I can tell you that."

"Good."

"Now, listen to me," Saxton said. "If we don't make an arrest in a hurry, the state police or even the FBI might be brought in. If that happens, things could get out of control."

"Meaning?"

"Meaning they may find links back to you. Is that clear enough?"

"That would be unfortunate. For both of us."

"You're goddamned right it would be. If I were you, I'd say it would be a good time for a vacation. Like maybe something overseas, until this blows over."

Severino's fingers stroked his jaw, the dark grain of his skin shining in the florescent lighting.

"You make any progress on finding Jason Loohan?" he said.

"No. I don't see how he's a player in this—not as a suspect in Norton or Boyce's murder, anyway."

"Hmm." Severino stared at his desktop for a long moment, then raised his eyes.

"When you found Norton dead, did you find any money?"

"Yeah, a couple hundred bucks," Saxton said. He knew Severino would eventually ask this, and he wasn't surprised the question came at a time when Severino thought he could catch him off balance. But Saxton was too smart to fall into that trap.

"That's it, huh?" Severino's eyes probing the lie.

"Yeah, why?"

Severino dismissed the question with a brief shrug, then stood and opened the office door, signaling the meeting was over. When Saxton passed by him on the way out, Severino said, "I don't mean to insult your intelligence here, just a little reminder. You're a cop, and I work at a casino. We've never heard of each other."

• • •

Arriving back at Douglas County police headquarters, Saxton could feel the stress level as soon as he walked in the building. There were the murmured remarks, "Sorry about your partner," "How you holding up," "Boyce was a good cop," and so on, but once the obligatory sympathies were dispensed with, the somber mood was replaced with an angry tension. The squad room was now half-full with scowling detectives, pacing and hovering near Saxton's desk. Saxton sat stone-faced, waiting for Galanis and McMann to return from the crime scene. They arrived fifteen minutes later, Galanis shifty-eyed, and McMann looking like he wanted a drink. Galanis went into the office he'd moved into the week previous and motioned at Saxton. Saxton followed him, shutting the door and taking a seat.

"Pete, I need you to tell me what you and Dave were working on, who you think might have done this," Galanis said, his handsome face full of concern and empathy. Saxton stared back, knowing the face was full of shit. Behind his appearance, Galanis was a man who cared about only one thing—his own bottom line. He was a master chameleon, able to shift his personality instantly to manipulate situations in his favor. Around the squad his deceptive nature was tolerated, because over time, The Snake, as he was sometimes called, had proven himself a good detective.

Saxton measured his words carefully. He knew Galanis was aware he and Boyce had been taking drug money, in the same way Saxton knew Galanis was getting paid off by a prostitution ring, and was also involved in illegitimate building permits. He decided to play it upfront, for the moment.

"A gang of Mexicans have been ramping up their drug dealing. Boyce and I were discouraging them."

"So, you think they put a hit on Boyce?"

"It's possible."

"Kill a cop, just for doing his job?"

"Wouldn't be the first time."

Galanis turned and stared out the window, where a field had once been cleared for construction and was now overgrown with weeds. Beyond the field a car made its way up a road carved into the pine-covered mountainside that overlooked the police complex.

"You know what this reminds me of?" Galanis said, turning back to Saxton. "A drug cartel assassination. You familiar with the cartel killings in Mexico?"

"Not in detail."

"It's an unholy mess down there. Whole families in their bedrooms, waxed with automatic weapons. The unlucky ones are tortured first, sometimes to death. You live in Juarez or Tijuana, and you don't cooperate with the cartels, you go to sleep and maybe you never wake up."

"Yeah, I heard it's bad."

"We're assuming at this point the same man killed Joe Norton and Dave Boyce. What's the connection, Pete?"

"Norton was a drug runner," Saxton said.

"Was he doing business with the Mexicans?"

"No."

"Maybe he pissed them off."

"I think it's likely."

"Why?"

Saxton shrugged. "It's a dirty business."

A small smile began on Galanis's face. "Okay, Pete, I understand. But the main priority here is catching the killer of your partner. Regardless of anything else, we must do that, and do it quick."

Saxton forced a smile in return. "I think we're on the same page, Nick."

"Good. Here's what I want to do. I'm going to send three SWAT men to your house today. One will take position in the vacant house across the street from yours. The other two will wait in your house. As for you, I want you out on the street, do what you always do, business as usual. Go home at a typical hour. Keep your curtains drawn, and turn out the lights when you'd usually go to bed."

"You think he's coming for me tonight?"

"Boyce last night, Norton the night before. I'd say you're next on the list."

Saxton fought the urge to jump up and backhand the snide smile off Galanis's face. So cavalier, the way Galanis concluded Saxton was marked for death. And so quickly The Snake seemed to have decided on a plan that, if it worked, would assure his permanent promotion to captain. It would be the perfect political score for him, orchestrating the capture of the cop killer within twenty-four hours. Of course, it didn't concern him in the least that Saxton would be used as bait. Galanis seemed to know Saxton had no other options, unless he wanted to resign and flee out of town.

"Hey, look," Galanis said, "we're going to get this scumbag. If he doesn't come tonight, we'll find another angle. One way or another, we'll get him. No one kills one of us and walks. No way. And after it's over, I'll help you sort out this drug dealing problem."

Of course you will, Saxton thought bitterly. Dave Boyce's body was barely cold, and Galanis was already angling to move in on the action.

19

"Yes," Stuart Gold said, rising from his desk and clapping his hands. The scene he'd just written was perfect. For the last three days, he'd been in a state of creative bliss, the thoughts coming so rapidly he could hardly type them before even more tantalizing ideas occurred to him. The theatrical storyline he'd nearly finished was one that would appeal across all cultures, to the old and young, the rich and the poor. Everyone would love the story of a humble girl from an impoverished background hitting the big time. But the story was not simply about a poor Latina becoming a star. It was much bigger than that. Stuart Gold's masterpiece spoke of the magical essence of talent, how its power could transcend the most dire circumstances and bring joy to the world. His passionate presentation of this theme would touch the very core of humanity.

This would be the vehicle to launch him back to the forefront of the Las Vegas entertainment world, and then beyond, to New York and London. And of course, Teresa Perez was the centerpiece.

Stuart paced around the study of the home he'd rented, a three-bedroom ski-in/ski-out chalet. From his back deck, a gentle slope led to a shutdown chairlift that rose over two thousand feet into the Sierras. During the winter, the area would be crowded with skiers and snowboarders, but for now it was deserted. Most of the snowpack near the base of the lift was gone, revealing glades of grass and dirt. Up higher, below the towers and steel cables, wide fields of melting snow sparkled under a sun high in the pastel sky.

Two days ago he'd proposed to Teresa she record a demo disk, a simple compilation of pop songs. It was required at this early stage of her career. She'd responded enthusiastically, but was concerned that rehearsing the numbers at her paper-walled apartment would disturb the neighbors. He told her she could use the theatre at Pistol Pete's, and she seemed grateful. But when he woke the following morning, sipping a nonfat caramel latte and enjoying the view of the lake from his second-story balcony, he recalled overhearing her cell phone conversation earlier in the week. Something about some people causing trouble at her apartments. Though he wasn't prone to snoopiness, Stuart decided to check out the Pine Mountain complex. Just a quick drive-by, to get a sense of where his prized client lived.

When he saw the graffiti, junker cars, and barred windows, he felt the beginnings of a mild panic attack. What would it be like here when darkness fell and predators roamed the street? As if they had heard his thoughts, three young gangbangers emerged from an apartment, their jeans baggy, bandanas low on their foreheads. They stared at the spectacled white man in his maroon Mercedes, the undisguised hostility in their eyes sending stabs of anxiety through Stuart's heart. He cranked his steering wheel and turned out of the cul-de-sac and pushed the gas pedal to the floor.

When he'd arrived back at the safety of his chalet, he mixed himself a gin fizz. He almost never drank in the morning, but he needed something to calm his nerves. The thought of Teresa coming home at night to that nasty and squalid neighborhood was no more acceptable than the concept of an infant playing on the freeway. Every night she stayed there posed unacceptable risk. He was surprised she'd not yet been raped. Or worse. Something must be done about her living situation, and immediately.

Stuart adjusted his glasses and called Teresa, his fingers nervously tapping his knee. When she didn't pick up after three redials, he left her a message. By the time she called him back, around noon, he worked himself into somewhat of a dither.

"Young lady, as your manager and agent, I insist you take my calls. I've been worried sick about you."

"I'm just fine, Stuart. What are you worried about?"

"Listen, darling, please don't be offended by this, but the apartments where you live, they are atrocious. I am not at all comfortable with you living in such a dangerous place."

"I live there with my younger brother," Teresa said. "It is what we can afford."

"Well, if money's the issue, then I will help you. At a minimum, you need a safe, comfortable home."

Teresa hesitated. All her life she had lived with the threat of violence. In the remote village where she was born, she'd leaned how to deal with unwanted attention. Once she had sliced open the face of a would-be suitor who got drunk and demanded sex. She was fifteen at the time. A year later an older man tried to rape her, and she'd grabbed his testicles and pulled so hard she heard something pop. She learned to identify trouble with a glance and was proactive in steering away from it. When that was not enough, she was quite willing to fight. Living in this manner had become second nature to her.

Moving forward, might it no longer be necessary to stay constantly on guard? Teresa knew stars lived in opulent settings, where the greatest threats were their own egos. She envisioned nothing as grandiose for herself. A safe, comfortable home, as Stuart put it, would be paradise enough. Some place away from the desperation and violence and cruelty that had always been present in her life. Perhaps this was a privilege that came with the recognition of her talent. If so, wouldn't it make sense to embrace it?

Though the answer seemed obvious, Teresa felt a tugging reluctance. Maybe it was because she believed accepting charity would create an obligation on her part. Or maybe it was just a fundamental, subconscious mistrust of a lifestyle different from what she had always known. Change is scary, she admitted to herself. But she also recognized she must continue moving forward, away from her past.

"Stuart, if I were to move, Juan must come with me."

"Of course, of course I realize that. You are his legal guardian."

"Any financial help you give me, we must keep track. I consider it a loan, and I'll repay you once I can."

"And I would expect nothing less from you. For now, though, I suggest you move into my home. I think you'll find it splendid, and I will not accept a penny from you."

"Your home? Oh, we couldn't do that."

"Why not? I have more room here than I could ever use. You and Juan can have the upstairs bedrooms, each with its own bathroom. You'll have plenty of privacy, I assure you."

"But we wouldn't want to impose."

"Teresa, the most important thing is your safety. If you're not comfortable here, we'll find you another place. But you should not spend another night in your apartment. You have far too much to lose."

"I'll have to think about it, Stuart."

"Why don't you come on over and take a look around? I'm only five minutes away."

Teresa was in her bedroom, where her brother couldn't hear the conversation.

"Okay," she said. "Give me directions. I'll get Juan and come over."

• • •

Juan was suspicious when Teresa said she wanted him to meet her manager.

"Right now?" he said, looking up from his homework. It had been a short day at school, and he was looking forward to finishing his assignments and relaxing before the evening shift at the restaurant.

"Yes," Teresa said.

"What for?"

"He said he has a surprise for us." It was a truthful comment, in a way. She could never lie to her brother.

Juan knew in an instant Teresa was hiding something. He considered himself a good judge of people, and Teresa was especially easy to read. But he also trusted her, so he decided to play along. He clicked shut his binder and set it aside.

"Okay, let's go."

They drove off in Teresa's pickup, crossing over Pioneer Trail and then onto the road bordering South Lake Tahoe's massive ski resort. A steep, well-paved street led into a neighborhood adjacent to the slopes, where the homes were built on lots that had been carved into the mountainside. As they climbed the grade, Juan noticed most of the structures were recently built, some still in the final phases of construction. He looked at the stone and natural wood facades, the huge windows over redwood balconies, and he wondered at the mysterious forces that allowed some to reside in such splendor, while others were relegated to the cheapest and most run-down living quarters.

When Juan first arrived in the United States, he didn't see the Pine Mountain complex that way. The modern plumbing and electrical appliances were all remarkable improvements over his modest dwelling in rural Mexico. He felt like he'd stepped through a time warp, into an advanced civilization he'd only seen in magazines. For the first six months in his new environment, every day seemed like a miracle.

And then the novelty of the new lifestyle began to wear off. No one around him was amazed by a microwave or a cell phone, and he realized these things were taken for granted here, to the point that discussing how cool they were made one sound like an idiot. Soon it became clear everything he marveled at was not only less than magnificent, but was considered basic and mundane. His wide-eyed naivety fading, he began to understand there was far more he could strive for in this county. True, he currently existed at a low rung on the social ladder, but that left only one direction to go. After all, this was the land of opportunity.

At sixteen, Juan knew his entire life lay ahead of him. He was determined to graduate from high school, and then the next big step, on to a college degree. Who knows where his path might lead after that? Maybe to one of these spectacular homes. Perhaps the world wasn't so mysterious after all.

Teresa stopped in front of a multilevel spread, its front highlighted with decorative stonework. A column of river rock rose from the foundation up one side, the chimney reaching a few feet above the peak of the shingled roofline. From the street Juan could see to the rear of the property, where thick wooden pillars supported a redwood deck that overlooked the snowcapped peaks beyond.

"This is where Stuart lives?"

Teresa double-checked the address. "Yes, this is it." She looked at Juan with an odd smile he couldn't quite read.

They followed a flagstone walkway to the front door and rang the chimes.

"Teresa, gracious, you're here. Come in, please. And you must be Juan."

The man wore sandals, loose-fitting corduroy pants, and a lavender T-shirt with a yellow smiley face in the center.

After a moment Teresa nudged him, and Juan realized he was staring. Embarrassed, he said, "Yes, hello."

"Well, come in, let me show you around. I got a great deal here on a six-month lease. The rent is astronomical during the winter season, but surprisingly affordable until then."

As Stuart led them from room to room, then outside to the back deck, Juan kept shooting glances at Teresa, confused as to the purpose of the tour. What did this strange man wish to do, make them jealous of his fancy home?

When they got to the bedrooms upstairs, Stuart said, "So, what do you think?"

"Would you give us a minute, Stuart?"

"Of course." Stuart left and Teresa sat on the queen-size bed. She looked up at Juan.

"Stuart says he's worried our apartments are not safe. He wants us to move in here."

"What? In this house? With him?"

"Well, yes. Juan, Stuart is a very nice man, and he has nothing but our best interest in mind."

"But, we could never afford a place like this!"

"He's offering us free rent."

Juan paused and blinked. Outside the bedroom window, a tall pine partially obscured the sun, the light splintering through the needles. A bluebird landed on a branch and added a twig to the nest it was building.

"Nothing is free, Teresa," he said, feeling foolish as it occurred to him he was repeating words often uttered by his father.

"You're right. Stuart will let me pay him back once my career takes off. And," she added, "with the money we save, think how much sooner we can bring Mama and Papa here."

Juan peered into the spacious bathroom, where polished fixtures gleamed against granite tile.

"We've always paid our way. This doesn't seem right."

"Things are changing for us, Juan, for the better." Teresa stood and placed her hands on her brother's shoulders. "Can't you see that?"

Juan looked into Teresa's gold-flecked eyes. The opportunities she'd dreamt of were now becoming real, and Juan knew he must support her.

But things were happening so suddenly—moving was a major event, and they'd never even discussed it! The fact that it was being thrust upon him made him feel like he had no control over the path of his life. Was this how things would be, now that Teresa's career was gaining traction? If so, he would need to tolerate it, at least until he was old enough to forge his own way.

But one thing Juan would not tolerate is walking into a bad situation. The offer of free rent at a resort-like home would almost certainly come with obligations. Stuart might have other motivations. But he seemed harmless enough. No doubt Stuart wasn't interested in Teresa sexually; Teresa had said he was a *puta,* and Juan saw this was true from the moment he saw him. Maybe Stuart really was a kind soul who wanted to help them. Time would tell.

Despite his reservations, he couldn't deny the lure of moving from his low-rent apartment to a place palatial compared to anywhere he'd lived. Juan sighed, as a fresh storm of colliding issues and emotions swarmed into his head. The prospect of moving from the environment of poor Mexicans and the Diablos Sierra losers both excited him and made him feel a creeping sense of shame. Living at Stuart's place would be a guilty indulgence, a lifestyle unearned by a lowly teenage busboy. It also allowed him a convenient escape from the gangbangers, who had not only humiliated him, but had also insulted Teresa. The sense of relief he felt over this made him grit his teeth in frustration.

For a moment, Juan felt the weight of his life bearing down, and he longed for the guiding hand of his parents. It wasn't right he'd been forced into adult situations at such an early age. He'd never had a chance to experience being a kid. He was sure he must have been a carefree child once, but it was too long ago to remember. Now, all that pertained to his life, his decisions, his actions, seemed to have an unfair gravity.

Juan set his jaw. It was weakness that birthed thoughts like these. The weakness was always lurking, continually challenging him to be strong, to become a man. He had his whole life in front of him to be cautious, if he chose. But opportunity had knocked *today*, and it was the time to stop being a coward.

"We'd be crazy to turn this down," he said to Teresa. "Which bedroom is mine?"

20

I T WAS PAST EIGHT when Cody finally ambled out of the guest room. "Good morning," I said. I'd already drunk a pot of coffee and my eyes were bloodshot from staring at my computer screen.

Cody stretched and ripped an explosive fart. "What's for breakfast?"

"We're out of grub. Let's go out."

He went to dress, and I turned back to my computer. My search for the ownership of Pistol Pete's had been fruitless. If I wanted the information, I'd have to drive to Carson City and inquire at the state office.

I went outside and leaned on the deck railing, surveying the damage to my lawn. After breakfast I'd stop at the local nursery and pick up some rolls of sod. Repairing Loohan's work would require at least a couple hours of hard labor. The pentagram would still be visible no matter how meticulous I was. I was sure Candi would ask about it when she came into town tomorrow.

Other than that, it was a splendid morning. Birds chirping, sunlight scattered over the deck, the sky a peaceful blue. The air was crisp when a light breeze stirred the pine needles. It would have been a good day to straighten up my place, lift some weights, and prepare for Candi's visit.

I said as much to Cody as we drove out to the restaurant a few minutes later.

"So, instead, you're working. That's life. Why complain?" he said.

"Just in a bitchy mood, I guess."

"I think you need to get laid."

"Who doesn't?"

"Pull up your panties and let's concentrate on finding Loohan."

I parked, and we walked into the local diner. A noisy clatter of activity, every table full.

"We need to find where Tom lives," I said. "Rabbit the drummer probably knows." A waitress sat us and cleared the dirty plates and glasses from our table.

"Or we could spin on by the Pine Mountains, check to see if HCU is hanging out."

"So you can check on Teresa?" I said.

"Why not?"

"Let's try the Switton house first."

"Fine. You should order the works. You're looking a little gaunt."

"I feel all right. Just tired, maybe."

The waitress took our order, then Cody told her to double it. She returned with an impossible amount of food. I didn't think I was that hungry, but once I started eating, I couldn't stop. Scrambled eggs, bacon, hash browns, flapjacks, toast, sausage links, orange juice. When the plates were empty, I should have felt like a stuffed bear heading for hibernation. Instead I was surprisingly refreshed.

"Now you look ready to work," Cody said once we were outside, his face ruddy in the glittery sunshine.

"I guess I was low on fuel."

Cody drove us toward the house where John and Robert Switton lived, his elbow propped out his window as he steered through the light traffic. He tried a few different radio stations until he found a song he liked, an old number by George Thorogood. Watching him tap his fingers to the music, I was struck with a sense that Cody was at his most content when facing adversity. Actually, it was more than that. He was happiest when he sensed direct conflict. Violent conflict.

But in this case, I didn't know why he was in such a good mood. The week we'd spent hunting Jason Loohan had got us next to nowhere. Last night I was certain he would soon show his face, but doubt was already creeping around the edge of my mind. Loohan could have already left town, leaving us to flounder in a futile search. He could already be in Canada or Mexico, smiling as he imagined me endlessly looking over my shoulder.

I was hesitant to ask Cody what he was thinking. We had no real leads, and I wasn't in the mood to hear his gut instinct or intuitions.

Nonetheless: "Why the happy face?"

Cody smiled, his eyes bright and clear. "I had a dream last night."

"And?"

"I pissed on Loohan's corpse. Call it a premonition."

I burst out laughing. Served me right for asking.

We turned off 50 and drove to the white house where the Swittons lived. No cars out front, or in the driveway. We knocked on the door.

"Nobody home," Cody said.

"Listen. You hear that?"

"No."

We stood silently, and I could make out a faint thumping. At times random, then falling into a pattern.

"I think Rabbit's playing the drums," I said.

"I don't hear anything."

"There's a cinder block building in the backyard. It's probably where they jam."

"You want to go back there?"

I didn't answer, straining my ears, but the thumping had stopped. I rang the doorbell again.

We stood on the porch for the next few minutes, knocking and ringing the bell, until the door swung open. Rabbit was wearing cut-off jeans, jogging shoes, and a sleeveless shirt wet with perspiration. A yellow sweatband, the kind NBA players wore in the seventies, was plastered to his forehead.

"Hi, Rabbit," I said. "How's it going?"

He looked at me, his expression blank, one eye roving. Then he smiled. "Oh, hi guys."

"Pounding the skins?" Cody asked.

"Huh?"

"Were you playing the drums?" I said.

"Yeah! I just made a new solo. Want to check it out?"

"Sure," Cody said.

"How about your dad, Rabbit? Is he home?"

"Nooo. He went to Sac-a-tomatoes."

"Sacramento?"

Rabbit didn't answer, instead waving for us to follow him inside. We went through the house, out a sliding glass door, and across the backyard to the building in the rear of the property. He opened the double doors to reveal a room dominated by a huge black drum set. Against the walls were guitar amps, mic stands, and racks of electronic gear.

Hopping lithely onto a platform that elevated his drums a foot off the floor, Rabbit sat behind the kit. He closed his eyes and after a pause began playing a light cadence on the snare drum. He alternated buzz rolls with rim shots and off-time accents, creating something I thought had a jazzy feel. But then he went into a simpler pattern, increasing in speed and volume on the snare until his hands flew upward to the cymbals and his feet went crazy on the bass drums. He started mixing bass drum blasts with patterns on the tom toms, his hands a blur as they went from the smallest drums to the deep floor toms. He finally fell into a syncopated rhythm, blasting away on the double bass pedals while his sticks whipped from drum to drum and crashed away at his cymbals.

When he stopped he was breathing hard. He wiped his face with a towel and stared out in our direction.

"Bravo!" Cody said, shaking his fist. "That was hot!"

I clapped my hands and said, "Rabbit, that was incredible. I've never seen anybody play like that."

"Did you like it?"

"Yes, man, it was great."

"Outstanding," Cody said.

"Oh, thanks," Rabbit said, and I think he might have blushed, or maybe his face was red from the exertion.

"Rabbit," I said as he climbed down from the drum riser, "the reason we came by is because we need to talk to Tom."

"Tom is my guitar player."

"I know."

He didn't reply, his face contorting, perhaps in confusion, or maybe in an effort to make a decision.

"Do you want to hurt him?" he said.

"No. No, I promise we don't."

"Will your dad be home soon?" Cody asked.

"No."

"Maybe we should go, Dirt."

"Tom's probably at home. You want his address?"

Cody and I stared at Rabbit, our mouths open in surprise.

"I don't need my dad's permission for everything," Rabbit said. "I'm a man." He pulled a card out of his wallet and read slowly: "Tom lives at two, three, seven, two Callow Avenue."

• • •

The address Rabbit gave us was for a street a block away from Joe Norton's ex-residence. The powder-blue paint on the duplex was peeling, and the driveway was stained with years of dirty motor oil. We idled by, my eyes straining for motorcycle tracks.

"See anything?" Cody said

"No. But park down the street. We should gear up."

Five minutes later we approached Tom's home. Cody took the near side and I came from the opposite direction. I wrapped my fingers around the grips of my automatic but left it holstered as I peeked over a fence along-side the property. Garbage cans, a rusted snow shovel, a stack of yellowed newspapers.

We came to the front door, and I tried without success to peer around the curtains behind the street-facing window. I heard the murmur of a television, then a loud laugh. I rang the doorbell.

"We don't want any!" A male voice, more laughter. I rang again.

"Man, what part of 'no soliciting' don't you understand?" a voice said as the door opened. It was the weak-chinned, bearded guitarist I'd first seen at the Switton's house. Sitting on a couch inside I could see Tom and another dude I didn't recognize. A bong smoldered on the coffee table, and the room was hazy with pot smoke.

"Sorry to interrupt your wake and bake, boys. Tom, could I talk to you for a sec?"

Tom hauled himself off the couch. "What are you gonna do, kick my ass?"

"Don't tempt me. You going to invite me in?"

"Hell, no. You got something to say, say it here." He stood in the door-way. "You got your eight hundred-pound gorilla with you?"

Cody came up behind me, shotgun over his shoulder. "Good morning, America," he said.

"Looking for Jason Loohan, Tom. Seen him around?"

"You know what? No, I haven't. I haven't seen one hair on his asshole, man. As a matter of fact, I only saw him once, for about two minutes, since I moved to freaking Lake Tahoe. I ain't spoke with him, I ain't seen him since then."

"How long ago was that?"

"Probably a week ago."

"I heard he'd gone with Joe Norton down south to make a buy. Some people think maybe Loohan was involved in Norton's murder."

"Yeah, well, some people dig circle jerks."

"Hey, wiseass," Cody said. "We don't give a shit if you guys are dealing. It doesn't concern us. What you should be thinking is, if Loohan had reason to kill Norton, maybe that same reason might apply to you."

Tom's expression turned serious for a second, then he grinned crookedly and gave an exaggerated roll of his eyes.

"And you guys are supposed to be *professional investigators*?" He barked out a short laugh and slammed the door in my face. I braced myself, ready for Cody to push me aside and body slam the door open. But instead he laughed to himself and began walking toward his truck.

"Just like that?" I said.

"He's right, Dan. We're pissing in the wind. If anyone in HCU knew where to find Loohan, we'd know by now."

"So where does that leave us?"

"Loohan was seen at the Pine Mountains recently. Let's swing by and have a look-see."

I threw up my arms. "I got no better ideas," I said.

•   •   •

The Pine Mountain complex could have been written off as a typical slum, a decrepit, low rent habitat for those who had no better options. But for every graffiti-covered wall and cardboard-taped window, there was a neatly trimmed plot of grass, or a colorful collection of hanging plants spilling over an iron balcony rail. It was as if the place was at war with itself. Or maybe the war was between those who aspired for something better, and those who viewed their residence as temporary and simply didn't give a shit.

Just as we pulled up, my cell rang. Marcus Grier.

"I hope you're sitting down," he said, his voice quiet and solemn. "Dave Boyce was found shot to death this morning."

"Oh, my."

"Looks to be by the same person who killed Joe Norton."

"Is South Lake Tahoe PD investigating?"

"No, not yet anyway. It happened in Nevada, and we've been instructed to lay low for now."

"What do you make of it, Marcus?"

I heard him take a deep breath. "I think Boyce was involved in things for his own personal interest."

"That's putting it diplomatically."

"It was the work of a professional," Grier said. "Probably someone hired by the Diablos Sierra gang."

"That's as good a theory as any. But here's another angle—I heard Loohan had gone with Norton to score some drugs down near the border recently."

"So?"

"I don't know. Maybe he's involved somehow."

"I'd love to interrogate him, but our APB turned up nothing. We ran a complete electronic scan—no ATM activity, credit card charges, nothing. Not even a blip."

"Tell you what—if I catch him, you'll be the first I call."

"Do me a favor, would you, Dan? Try to keep him alive."

Grier hung up, and I told Cody of Boyce's murder as we walked into the common.

He listened with his head cocked at an angle. "I didn't like that guy anyway," was his only comment.

The picnic bench in the center was unoccupied. We stood against a wall and surveyed the area. A pair of bandana-wearing *cholos* appeared at the far corner of the common and eyed us sullenly.

"Shall we interview them?" Cody said.

"Sounds like a good way to get shot."

"Looks like they're playing it low key to me. What have we got to lose?"

"What do you want to say to them? Sorry for stomping your ass the other day, can you help us find this guy we're looking for?"

"Let's tell them Loohan is part of HCU."

"Do me a favor, would you?"

"Yeah?"

"Go easy. I've got enough problems."

"Don't worry, I'll turn on the old Gibbons charm."

"Oh, that's a relief."

We walked toward the two gangbangers. I smiled and waved as we approached.

"We ain't breakin' no laws. What chu want?" said *Cholo* number one, leaning with his foot against the stucco wall, his eyes like knives against his brown skin.

"We're cool here," Cody said. "We ain't cops."

"Maybe you're dead, homes," said the second gangbanger, younger, his body like a whip. "You just don't know it yet."

"No one lives forever," I said, trying to maintain my casual smile. "I heard you've been having trouble with some bad cops and white trash gangbangers. We're trying to put them out of business. So maybe we got some common interest here."

They exchanged glances, then one said smirked and said, "You think we need *your* help?"

"You never know," I said. I pulled a picture of Loohan from my pocket. "This dude is with the white boys. We want to take him off the street."

They studied the picture, then the younger one said, "We see him, *we'll* take him off."

"Have you ever seen him?"

"Yeah," said the older one. "He's been around."

"Really? When?"

"Yesterday." He handed the sheet of paper back to me.

"We think he might have been involved in two murders," Cody said. "Just happened. Couple guys, pumped full of lead in their bedrooms. One was one of the cops giving you a bad time."

The older one didn't change expression, but his buddy grinned, his mouth full of silver caps.

"He had nothin' to do with *that* shit, homes."

"Who did?"

They shrugged, both now smiling. Cody lit a cigarette and blew a stream of smoke from the shade into the sunlight.

"Keep it real, boys," he said, and we turned and walked away.

"You know what I'm tempted to do?" Cody said as we strode out to the street. "Camp out at this joint and wait for Loohan. I can't believe he was here yesterday. Come on," he said, pacing toward the Perez unit. But the apartment was dark and nobody answered when Cody knocked.

"I'm gonna call her. Hang loose."

"Let's scout the perimeter," I said. I took off toward the alley leading to the parking stalls, Cody following with his phone to his ear.

Sometimes you just look around, not knowing what you're looking for, not knowing what you'll find. A discarded receipt, a comment from a passerby, maybe the emergence of an idea hiding in the shadows of the mind. If Loohan was here, I wanted to retrace his steps and hope for a light bulb to click on. I wandered along the row of covered parking spots, looking at every car, searching for something that didn't belong.

Never in my career had I failed to find a subject. Someone would always talk, or failing that, the subject would do something to reveal himself. Living off the grid was a bitch, and very few criminals had the discipline to do so.

I pulled myself up and peered into a Dumpster against a chain link fence. I scanned the bags of garbage, hoping for a vision. It didn't come.

"Screw this," I said. I jumped down and saw Cody had stopped near the entrance to the alley. He snapped his cell shut and I waited for him to come to where I kicked at the gravel.

"Teresa and Juan are moving today," he said.

"What? Where to?"

"Her manager is leasing a fancy vacation pad near the ski resort. He told them they could move in rent-free. He was paranoid about Teresa living in this slum."

"This manager, you think he's legit?"

"Seems to be. At least he's not trying to get into her pants. His shoes are the long-lasting variety.

"Huh?"

"He's a little light in the loafers. Guy could give you change for a ten, all in threes."

"Are they still coming over to barbeque tonight?"

"Yeah. Some of the theatre people are helping them move. They rented a U-Haul. They don't have that much stuff—Teresa said she and Juan would be at your place by six."

"Fine. Let's go door to door. I want to see if anybody else here has seen Loohan."

"I think it's a good thing she's getting out of here."

"No doubt."

We spent the next hour canvassing the residents like a couple of vacuum cleaner salesmen. Two people recognized Loohan's picture. Neither could provide any insight into why he was here, or where he might be.

It was getting toward midafternoon when we left. I drove across town to the south side and picked up four rolls of sod and a narrow shovel I thought would make the job easier. I could feel the calories from the huge breakfast waiting to be burned.

At my house I changed into work jeans and my old tennis shoes and began cutting the sod into strips to fit the ruined portions of my lawn. I stripped off my shirt and let the sun beat on my back, sweat dripping off my nose and into the soil. Cody offered to help, but after a few minutes, he moved into the shade of the porch.

"You know, I think you want to do this on your own."

"Why don't you head out to the supermarket, pick up what we need for tonight?"

"Okay. See you in a bit."

After he left I fell into a rhythm, measuring, cutting, stomping the new lawn in place. Muscles taut, dirt and sweat smeared across my skin, my mind went blank within the physical labor, my motions trance-like. At some point Cody returned, but I barely noticed. Finally, past five o'clock, I finished up, then swept the driveway. Not bad, I thought, checking out the results. Despite the exertion I felt relaxed and well rested.

As it turns out, being well rested was a good thing. Because when I came out of the shower a little after six, Cody was pacing.

"They're late. It's not like Teresa. And she's not answering her cell."

21

Vic Severino was a man of habit, and apparently did not partake in hobbies or activities other than work. He spent most of every day in his office, in at nine and never leaving before eight P.M. He usually ate lunch and dinner alone, often a solitary figure at a restaurant. When Severino went home to his upscale condominium in a development off the lake, John Switton didn't know what he did other than watch TV. Maybe pull the wings off flies.

Irish John had spent the last few days watching Severino, timing his routines. John would have preferred more time, at least seven days of careful surveillance. But Vinnie Tuma had now been missing for almost a week, and with each passing day, the probability of retaliatory action against John increased. If he had any doubt, it was erased yesterday when Severino told him he had nothing to worry about, there were others believed responsible for Vinnie's disappearance. It was the kiss of death. In the moments leading to a whack, you always told your target everything was fine, all forgiven, no problem. Then the bullet.

At six P.M. John locked his office and left through the casino, waving good-bye to Carlo and Fat Denny, who were parked at the sports bar as usual. He drove home, had dinner with Robert, and sat staring out his back window. A slow hour passed. When the last hint of light faded from the skies, John got in his car and returned to Pistol Pete's. Wearing coveralls and a cap, as if working for a utility company or perhaps a janitorial service, he parked near a steel door at the back of the building. The door, inconveniently located for most of the employees and locked to the general public, opened to a hallway, the nearest office being Vic Severino's.

During the weekend the surrounding parking lot might have been crowded, but on a Tuesday evening in the slow season, it was free of cars. The black asphalt was unlit, marked sporadically by a handful of old growth pines protected by the forest service.

From the deep trunk of his Lincoln, John removed a large cardboard box, nearly big enough to hold a household dishwasher. He put the box on a dolly, backed through the door, and wheeled it down the hallway until he reached Severino's office.

A quick glance up and down the hall, then John parked the dolly and twisted the doorknob. He stepped into the office and shut the door behind him.

Severino's eyes snapped up from his computer screen, and he froze for a second and stared at John's attire, at the latex gloves on his hands. Then he yanked open his desk drawer and ducked in a surprisingly fluid motion. But John was already in position, his feet planted firmly, his arms outstretched, both hands pointing a silenced .22 pistol. The first shot hit Severino in the shoulder, and as he twisted away, the second slammed into his ear, straight into the brain.

John hurried to where Severino lay collapsed in his chair and stuffed cotton into the wounds, then sealed the bloody holes with duct tape. The hollow-point .22 bullets had performed just as John planned. They flattened as they entered the body, losing velocity and lodging inside. The .22 was the perfect weapon for the job. Lethal and tidy. Not a speck of blood on the furniture or walls.

A couple deep breaths, then John went back to the office door. He put his hand on the knob, knowing if he was spotted now, his entire plan would collapse. This was a moment of great risk. He eased the door open and pulled the dolly inside, then locked the door. The hallway had been empty. His breathing steadied, but sweat was now threatening to soak through his armpits. Always the sweat.

John removed an acetylene-fueled cutting torch from the box and began searching for the safe he knew Severino used as a holding store for the money the casino laundered. He shut the desk drawer, seeing the .38 pistol his victim had futilely reached for. No safe under the desk. How about behind one of the framed posters hanging from the walls? John pushed on the one directly behind the desk. COURAGE—THE WILLINGNESS TO OVERCOME YOUR FEARS, it said. Bingo. A wall safe, combination dial, a polished steel handle. John pulled on the handle, knowing it would not open.

But it did. He experienced a brief moment of flooding elation. Opening the safe with the torch would have taken at least ten minutes—John had bought a safe and practiced. Severino must have been in the process of moving money. A stroke of luck.

A green plastic bag was crammed into the interior. John pulled it out and quickly checked the contents. Bundles of cash. C-notes, twenties. Well over a hundred grand. Maybe a million. Hard to say. Five hundred grand, at least. More than he had hoped for. More luck. He'd celebrate later, if all went well.

Severino's body had slid off the chair and lay crumpled on the floor. John dragged it by the arm, hoisted the corpse upright, and lowered it into the cardboard box. Severino settled to the bottom in the fetal position, his sightless eyes staring. The luster of the black marbles no more.

A knock on the door made John jump.

"Vic?" Vic, you in there?" Christ, it was Carlo.

Silent as a cat, John moved to the doorway. Carlo would have a key. If the door opened, John would have no choice but to shoot him.

Five seconds, John's heart thumping like his son's bass drums, sweat stinging his eyes. Then an envelope slid beneath the door, and John heard Carlo's footfalls, and then silence.

John exhaled and put the .22 back in his pocket. He dropped the money and the torch in the box, on top of the body. Then he sealed the box with tape, pushed the swivel chair neatly under the desk, closed the safe, and made sure the framed poster was straight.

Sixty seconds. Sixty more lucky seconds was what he needed. He turned the lights off and eased the door open, then pushed the dolly out into the hall. Empty. Twenty feet of brightly lit hallway to the exit. Like swimming in mud.

But no one came, and the parking lot was dark, welcoming dark, and he curled his fingers under the box and effortlessly lifted it into his trunk. It wasn't until later he marveled at how easy it was. Close to two hundred pounds, like it was nothing.

Irish John pulled away from Pistol Pete's Casino for the last time, the cool lake air blowing in his open windows. He felt outside himself, as if in a different time and place. His life, Robert's life, at stake. He'd done what he had to do, but it seemed surreal. So far, everything had gone like clockwork, so maybe he could pull it off. But he wasn't done yet.

Ten minutes later he parked at the marina out on the keys and wheeled the box over fifty yards of tire-lined planks to a twenty-five-foot cabin cruiser he'd rented. He stepped onto the boat and dropped an aluminum ramp from the gangway to the dock. Then he pulled the box aboard and eased out of the harbor. Except for the Tahoe Queen, visible miles to the north, there wasn't another vessel on the water.

Heading for the middle of the lake, John listened to the deep hum of the motor and the water slapping rhythmically against the hull. This was the home stretch. Soon all the evidence would be gone, buried forever in the depths of Lake Tahoe.

If Irish John the Hammer felt a tinge of regret, it was for Sal Tuma, a man who had been there when John was desperate. Tuma would probably be stunned John betrayed him. A funny thing, the Mafia. All based on loyalty and a blood oath of silence. Allegiances sworn for life. But for what? The right to not work a steady job, to not earn an honest living. The right to steal, rob, cheat, and kill. All in the name of supporting your family. Nothing more important than family.

But in the end, it was always every man for himself. The list of traitors in recent years could fill a book. Thirty years in a federal pen, or testify and get witness protection. More and more were choosing the latter. Every mobster knew eventually it would come down to this, if they lived long enough.

John had quit the mob because he knew all the professed loyalty in the world meant nothing if he were dead or imprisoned. He had forged his own way, legitimately. Until fate stepped up and drew him back in. No denying fate. His actions today were his destiny, irrevocable and inevitable. He stared out over the bow, unblinking, his hands gripping the wheel. His life was the culmination of all he had done, and there was no escaping his past.

Thirty minutes out John shut off the throttles. The boat rocked gently in the swell, the lake like black ink. John dumped Severino's limp body from the box and shoved it into a steel drum he'd bought a hundred miles away, at a yard in Sacramento. Guaranteed rust-free for thirty years. He dropped three thirty-five-pound steel plates on top of the body, then cut up the box and wedged the pieces in. Next, his coveralls, hat, and gloves. And the torch cutter, unused. Finally, he pounded the lid on and clamped it shut with vice grips. Lights twinkled on the distant shorelines. He looked back the way he'd come and saw the glitter of the casinos in Stateline rising above the black expanse.

He pushed the drum to the edge of the cruiser, and it took everything he had to tip it over the gunwale. It teetered for an instant, then fell into the water with a brief splash and vanished. John had read Lake Tahoe was one of the deepest lakes in the world.

Clutching the dark plastic bag full of cash, he started the motor and began back toward the south shore. After a minute he slowed, disassembled his pistol, and tossed the pieces in the water. That should be the last of it, he thought. No one would miss him or Vic Severino until the morning. By that time he and Robert would be on a plane under assumed names, heading for Europe to start anew. The Tumas and the police would be left grasping at thin air.

22

"MAYBE THEY'RE STILL MOVING," I said, pulling a clean shirt over my head.

"No, she said it wouldn't take long, and she always takes my calls." Cody paced back and forth in my family room, his phone clenched in his fist.

"I'll try Juan's number," I said, flicking open my cell. It went to voice mail.

"Put your shoes on and let's go," Cody said.

"To the apartments?"

"Yeah. And if she's not there, we can try her new pad. She gave me the address."

"Sure you're not being paranoid?"

"With Loohan spotted there yesterday? Come on, we're wasting time. I'm low on gas, let's take your rig."

In two minutes we were hitting it down the street, Cody leaning forward in the passenger seat like a bent spring, his lips a tight, colorless line.

"Step on it," he said. I hit the gas around a corner, the tires howling as they fought for traction. We turned onto 50 and sped through a couple greens and then blew a red before turning off and careening down a series of side streets. I almost ran over a cat, then power slid through a corner and bounced to a stop in front of the Pine Mountain complex. Cody was out the door before the springs stopped rocking. I followed him, my Beretta tucked in the back of my jeans.

We knocked on the front door of the Perez's apartment, and when nobody answered, we jogged around and into the common, to their back patio. The screen was shut, but the sliding glass door was open. Inside it was dark, and when Cody slid open the screen, I could see the furniture was gone.

"Teresa!" Cody yelled, walking inside.

It took us five seconds to see nobody was home and the unit was vacant.

"Let's see if her pickup is here," I said. When we walked out to the parking stalls, I saw the small, rust-colored truck in a covered spot.

I put my hand on the hood. "Still hot."

Cody reached in an open window and picked up a cell phone from the seat. He held it in his palm, and I could see his ears turning red, the way they did when he was either under intense pressure, or on the verge of losing his temper.

"No wonder she hasn't returned my calls."

We walked to the end of the row and turned the corner to a back street that was seldom used. A U-Haul truck was parked at the curb. Cody opened the door to the cab. The keys lay on the seat.

"What the hell?" he said. I went around to the rear and pushed up the unlocked gate. It was empty.

We circled the truck, staring up and down a street bordered by stucco walls on one side and an open field on the other.

"Shit. Try Juan's cell again, would you?"

I did, with no success. As I hung up, a young woman came from the alley, pushing a baby stroller. Behind her an elderly Mexican couple shuffled along.

"Excuse me, ma'am," I said. "We're supposed to meet Teresa Perez. Have you seen her by any chance?"

"Who are you?" She looked at us beneath thick eyelashes, seeing two white men she had no reason to trust.

Cody bent down, bringing his eye level to hers. "We're her friends, ma'am. We think she may be in trouble. If you've seen her, please tell me. We're here to protect her from someone we think wants to hurt her."

After a long moment, she shrugged. "I saw her about half an hour ago. She was sitting in a purple car. I waved, but I think she might have been asleep."

"A purple car?"

"Yes, parked right here."

"What kind of car?"

"It was the car your president was assassinated in," said the old man, stepping forward with a glint in his eye. "Before you were born. But I remember."

"Which president?" I said, but before he could respond, I knew the answer.

"Kennedy. In a Lincoln Continental with suicide doors."

Cody and I locked eyes. "Luther Conway," we said simultaneously.

•   •   •

We barreled over Spooner Pass toward Carson, Cody driving like a fiend, while I tried to reach DeHart at Carson City PD. I left a message, asking that they send units to Luther Conway's house to investigate a potential kidnapping. Then I called Marcus Grier, who said he'd put out an APB for Conway.

"We can't help Teresa if we wreck," I said, bracing myself as Cody pushed my truck through a downhill corner at almost double the speed limit.

"You think Loohan is with Conway?" he said. His straw-colored hair was damp with sweat and pulled back from his forehead, his eyebrows knotted in a V.

"I think we're going to find out."

"If they've laid a hand on her, I'll kill them both."

"Easy now," I said, the words foolish as soon as they left my mouth. Like telling a stampeding herd of buffalo to slow down.

I assembled my gear as we drove: body armor, stun baton, pistol loaded, extra clip, my sawed-off shotgun, a dozen shells. When we reached Carson City, we switched seats at a stop light so Cody could gear up.

Thirty minutes from when we left Teresa's apartments, we parked a few houses down from Luther Conway's Victorian-style home. There was no sign of Carson City PD. The sun was going down, dusk settling over the high-desert valley. The sky was laced with orange and pink streaks along the distant ridges.

The purple Lincoln we'd seen when we were last here was not in the driveway or on the street. I eyed the detached garage at the end of the driveway.

"Garage first, then house," I said.

We moved silently toward the garage, a flat-roofed structure almost wide enough for three cars. The roll-up door was closed. Next to it was a side door, one that looked less than stout.

I rattled the handle of the door. Locked.

"Kick it in," Cody said, shotgun pointing at the lock.

Beretta in hand, I reared back my leg and slammed my heel into the jamb, which gave way in a burst of splinters. I jumped into the garage, finger poised on the trigger, Cody following with the twelve-gauge. The interior was lit by dim red lights. There were no vehicles, just a bed and a desk on the far side.

On the bed sat a teenage boy, 150 pounds of lanky bones, his face hidden by a hairstyle as long in the front as the back. With a flip of his head, he shook his hair from his eyes, and stared at us with his best bad boy expression.

"Whoever you are, get out," he said.

"Where's Luther?" Cody crossed the room in long strides.

"Who knows? He doesn't share his schedule with me."

"Oh, yeah?" Cody grabbed him by the neck and slammed him against the wall. I watched Cody's thumb seek out the nerve below the chin. The kid gasped and struggled.

"Hail Satan," he cried.

"You think you're tough, huh?" I said. "Is Luther with Jason Loohan?"

A few straggled sounds, then Cody moved his thumb off the nerve, dropped the kid onto the bed, and grabbed his wrist. He held it at an angle that forced the kid's shoulder to twist awkwardly.

"You're gonna answer our questions, or I'm gonna cause you agony you won't believe."

Tolerating pain can be learned, to a degree. Survivalists and cage fighters develop the ability to endure extreme discomfort for limited lengths of time. But for the uninitiated, relatively small doses causes complete mental shutdown. The brain can only focus on one thing: make the pain go away.

"Stop it, stop!" the boy screamed.

"Where are they?" Cody snarled.

"You're going to break it!"

"Where are they?"

"I'll tell you! I'll tell you! Luther and Loohan have a virgin for a black mass!"

"Where?" Cody barked.

"I'll show you," the boy whimpered. "Just please let go."

· · ·

The minutes ticked by as we bombed back over Spooner Pass toward the lake, Cody at the wheel, the kid between us in the cab. Jesus Christ, somebody's son. Maybe the product of bad parents, or maybe just a bad seed. One thing I noticed, his teeth were straight and white. Likely had braces and regular cleanings. He also wore a pair of black designer skate shoes, the expensive kind. Could have got them anywhere, I suppose, but I didn't think this punk was a tough-luck case from the streets. More likely a failed product of middle class suburbia.

"When we get there, you're gonna do exactly as we say," I said. "You mess up, I will personally break your bones." He tried to look away, but I grabbed his hair and made him look in my eyes. "Whatever is going on in your pea brain, make sure you remember what I just said."

He swallowed and nodded. Cody screeched around the final sweeping corner leading to Lake Tahoe and floored the gas. We drove in silence, hitting close to a hundred on the straight sections along the lake, until we turned left on Kingsbury Grade. About a mile up the winding road, the kid said, "Turn here."

It was a paved street, probably private, built to access a few old cabins we passed. The road narrowed to a single lane, then turned to dirt. We followed it around a steep bend onto a long straight above a deep gorge, the dirt crumbling beneath my tires. The road turned away from the gorge and into the forest. The last of the twilight was fading fast when we reached a small turnaround.

The purple Continental was facing us, parked for a quick exit. Cody skidded to a stop, blocking it in. When we got out, I heard a muted thumping coming from the Continental's trunk.

I grabbed a crowbar, while Cody secured the kid's hands behind him with a plastic tie, then strung a rope through the tie. Cody wrapped the rope around his hand, creating a leash—if the kid tried to run, Cody could yank the punk's shoulders out of their sockets.

The thumping again, louder. I jammed the crowbar under the lock, but the old Detroit steel held fast. I shoved it in deeper and gave it a sharp jerk.

The latch popped and the lid rose up on its springs. Juan Perez lay in the trunk, his hands tied and his mouth duct-taped, his eyes wide and bulging.

I slit the ropes binding his wrists and tore the tape from his mouth. He scrambled out of the trunk like a feral cat.

"They've got my sister," he said, and before I could speak, he took off like a mad squirrel down a path heading into the forest.

"Shit," I whispered.

"Keep your mouth shut and lead us to them," Cody told the kid. "Move it."

We set out at a jog. In the woods it was almost full dark, spires of pine and fir surrounding us, the air cool with nightfall. The footing was uneven, rocks protruding from the trail every few steps. A tiny glow of moonlight penetrated the trees, not much to go by. We maintained our pace, stumbling at times.

"There's a clearing right up there," the kid said after a long minute. "That's where they are."

We crept forward, smelling smoke. Flickering shadows became visible. I could feel the textured grips of the Beretta digging into my palm. Then, as I peered from around a huge pine, a scene emerged unlike any I'd witnessed.

Three granite slabs towered over a clearing perhaps fifty feet square. Torches and candles burned on rock ledges. A large, red pentagram had been painted on the cleanly swept dirt. Presiding over it, resting on an upended kettle, was the bloody head of a goat, its eyes glazed in death. Beyond that, propped up against a stone face, was a black cross made with lengths of two by six. Tied to the cross as if for crucifixion was a naked Teresa Perez. Her head was tipped forward, her lustrous hair covering her face.

Unconscious, I thought. But then she raised her chin and saw me. A range of emotions flashed through her eyes—fear, rage, hope, shame, despair. My consideration of her mental state was brief, however, because Jason Loohan casually stepped from the shadows behind the cross. He stroked Teresa's breast then dropped to a knee, bringing his face to the triangle of black hair between her legs.

"Freeze!" I shouted, leaping forward, my sites trained on Loohan's back. I would have shot him, but if my bullet passed through his body, it might have hit Teresa. A frozen moment, then like a lizard, Loohan darted behind the cross and disappeared into an opening in the rocks.

Dropping the rope tied to the kid, Cody rushed into the clearing. To his left I caught a quick glimpse of a startled Luther Conway, then he was gone in a flicker of light.

"Loohan," I said, pointing. I ran forward and slid into the narrow crevice into which Loohan had vanished.

Cody pulled a knife and began cutting the ropes binding Teresa. "I'll come around the other way," he said.

I shimmied deeper into the crack, my boots wedged beneath me, the rough granite catching the straps of my bulletproof vest. It was a tight fit, but soon I hopped out on the other side, my feet crunching into thick brush. I looked out at a rock-strewn patch of forest lit by the moon. There were dozens of places Loohan could be hiding.

Staying low, I moved along the rocks looking for a trail. Freshly broken sticks marked a deer track leading away. I paused and strained my ears. I heard the crackle of brush, but it could have been Cody. I crouched, inching forward.

It was a bad situation. Loohan could be watching me from any number of spots, waiting for my head to pop into the moonlight, and I'd be dead before I heard the shot. The only advantage I had was Cody. But I had no idea where he was.

I kept moving and reached a low rock ledge. I lay on my chest and pushed my head over it, looking to the right and left. The ledge was the top of a face that dropped down farther than I could see. I saw anchors cemented into the rock. Probably a popular climbing wall. There were plenty of handholds, but I doubted Loohan was on the face. I didn't see anywhere he could hide.

Then, from unexpectedly close, a voice.

"Help! Help me, please!"

It was Luther Conway.

I crab-walked along the top of the ledge to where it angled away. Peering over, I saw Conway clinging to the side of the face, about twenty feet below, his silver hair shining against the gray stone.

"I'm stuck! I have nowhere to go!"

"Who is it?" Cody said, stepping from the trees behind me.

"Conway. You still got that rope?" I said.

"Fuck him," Cody whispered, looking over the cliff. I could see the Satanist's white fingers trembling where he gripped the rock. "Let's go find Loohan."

"Just give me the rope. And cover me."

He pulled the ball of clothesline from his pocket. "This is nuts," he hissed. "Loohan could double back and find Teresa."

I tossed the line down to Conway. It stopped just beyond his fingers.

"Grab the rope," I said.

"I can't—I can't, I'll lose my grip!"

"Then you're on your own, asshole!" Cody yelled.

"Take a deep breath, Luther. You can do this," I said.

Conway raised his head, staring up at us, his face stark and colorless in the moonlight. He took two breaths, his cheeks puffing out like a balloon. Then he shot his left hand up and snatched the end of the rope. I stiffened my back, expecting to feel his weight. But his hand must have been slick with sweat, because it slid off the thin line, then his feet scuffled and he clawed like mad to find purchase.

"No," he cried, and in an instant he was air born, falling back, arms and legs outstretched, his eyes round with terror, his howling white face illuminated by the moon. His final scream faded until we heard him crash into the trees hundreds of feet below.

"Fuckin' A," Cody said.

I stared down into the void for a couple of seconds, blinking.

"Come on," Cody said. "Let's get back to the clearing."

We followed a path, moving quick and silent. If I saw the slightest movement, I was ready to blast away. But all was still at the clearing, the torches flickering garishly against the black cross where Teresa had been tied.

"Teresa!" Cody yelled.

"I'm here." She was crouched behind a rock on the edge of the clearing. She stood partially so we could see her. I looked around for something to cover her nakedness, but neither of us had our coats. As spectacular as the sight was, I averted my eyes. And so did Cody.

It was silent for a second, then another voice rang out, from the direction of the rocks behind the cross.

"I got him, I got him!"

I ran over and began forcing myself through the narrow fissure again, rubbing skin off my palms. Cody followed behind me, but I didn't know if he'd fit through. When I dropped into the scrub on the other side, he was still grunting and swearing.

Not five feet from where I stood, Juan Perez lay in the brush holding Jason Loohan in a chokehold. Juan's arm was buried deep, his left hand grasping the right wrist in classic form. Loohan looked out cold.

"Just like you taught me, Dan," Juan said. Twigs and leaves were wound in his hair, and his face was scratched and bleeding.

I trained my automatic between Loohan's eyes. "Juan, you better let him go. You could kill him," I said.

Juan released his grip and scrambled to his feet, deadfall cracking under his shoes.

"Almost there," I heard Cody grunt. I looked over and saw him shoving himself from the crack. In that fraction of a second, I sensed rather than saw Loohan move, and I didn't have time to realize I'd blown it before his hand came up, holding an ugly little .25 cal. pistol. His first shot slammed against my vest, knocking me back into the rock. I got off a wild shot as I staggered, but it missed and Loohan was pointing his gun at my head.

I had an instant to regret every wrong decision I'd ever made, then I heard a deep blast from behind. Loohan's body jolted, his stomach tore open, his entrails falling out on his shirt. Cody stepped past me, the shotgun smoking in his hands, and brought his heel down on Loohan's gun hand.

"Any last words, shit bag?" Cody said.

"Call an ambulance. You can't kill me." The calm, even tone of Loohan's voice was startling.

"I think you've misinterpreted your situation."

"You can't kill me," Loohan said again.

"Wrong," Cody replied. The shotgun roared, and Loohan's face dissolved into a bloody maw of bone and gristle.

My eyes rose from Loohan's corpse to Cody Gibbons. He flipped the twelve-gauge to his shoulder and frowned at some blood that had splattered on his pants. Juan stood with his mouth open, staring down at Loohan's dead body. He stared with such intensity that I wondered if he expected Loohan to continue insisting he couldn't be killed.

Cody stepped back and looked at me, his eyes flat and without expression, as if awaiting my judgment. The best I could do was a nod and an attempt at a smile. Cody had done as he saw fit, because that's how he did things. Being that Loohan was probably planning the rape and murder of both Teresa and Juan as a final statement before coming after us, I would not question my partner's actions. If it came to it, I'd support Cody's contention of self-defense 100 percent. I had the flattened slug in my flak jacket to prove it.

Outside the law, living by his own rules, judge, jury, and executioner. At least Cody made no pretense of it. He had deemed the world would be better off without Jason Loohan, and so be it.

Juan, Cody, and I stood there, stars twinkling above in the black sky. For a moment I experienced a sense of joyful relief. An evil man who attempted to kill me and those close to me was dead. The threat removed, I could move on with my life. I could tend to my home and make a living and try again to have a steady relationship with a woman. I could try to lead a normal existence.

But I knew the death of an amoral person is always a hollow victory. I'd long ago conceded the population of lowlife sadists is inexhaustible. Their kind is replenished continually from an aberrant gene pool no science or law can remedy. In a world where violent criminality is woven into the fabric of every society, salvation is at best a temporary state.

"He would have died anyway from the gut shot," Cody said, walking past me. "Besides, I was just tired of messing with the guy." I smiled despite myself. I could always count on Cody to simplify things and bring my philosophical musings to an end. Good-bye, Loohan. Rot in hell. God love Cody Gibbons.

•   •   •

We never saw the kid from Luther Conrad's garage again. I imagine he'd scampered off into the woods somewhere, but I didn't care. I'd dealt with enough grief for the day.

Cody stripped off his pants and shirt so Teresa could cover herself. He carried her on his back to save her bare feet from the rough terrain while we walked down the trail. Cody, in his boxers, carrying Teresa piggyback. Quite a sight.

I fell back to where Juan walked behind us.

"You okay, partner?"

"I feel fine."

"How'd you manage to get behind Loohan?"

"I saw him coming my way, but I hid behind a tree before he saw me. When he went by, I jumped on his back."

"You're one brave kid."

"He said he would kill me. I'm happy Cody shot him."

"I'm sorry you had to see that."

"Sorry for what? Those men would have murdered us."

"I'm glad that didn't happen."

"*Si*. So am I."

I patted him on the shoulder and we continued without further conversation.

"Are we in California or Nevada?" Cody said when we got to my truck. He lowered Teresa into the cab.

I thought about it for a second. "I don't know exactly. Right on the border."

"Why don't you call Grier, then? I don't feel like dealing with any of those dildos from Nevada."

"First things first," I said, pulling a flashlight from my gearbox.

I pointed the light at Luther's Continental and went through it, careful not to leave prints. On the floor of the rear seat was a bottle of ether and a couple of rags, no doubt used in the kidnapping of Juan and Teresa. Aside from that, the interior and trunk were empty. When I swung the light around on the way back to my truck, it flashed across something metallic in the trees. An off-road motorcycle, covered with pine branches.

A pair of leather saddlebags was attached to the rear fender. "Jason Loohan's worldly possessions," I said.

"Who cares?" Cody said.

"The guy was a bitch to hunt down. Maybe I can learn something about him."

"Whatever floats your boat, Dirt."

• • •

Marcus Grier wasn't too happy to hear from me, being well past his quitting time, but he seemed pleased to learn Jason Loohan was no longer among the cast of troublesome characters running around Lake Tahoe. Not pleased enough to come out in person, though—instead a couple patrolmen and two detectives showed up, followed by the meat wagon.

They managed to haul Loohan's body out, but picking Luther Conway out of the trees would have to wait until daylight. Grier must have put in a good word for us, because the cops let us go after a single round of questioning, apparently seeing no indication of criminal wrongdoing on our part. They seemed more fascinated by the demonic symbols in the clearing. "Pretty weird shit for a place like South Lake Tahoe," one said.

We packed into my truck, Teresa sitting on Cody's lap, and Juan crushed in the middle. I drove us to the Stateline Emergency Center, where Cody insisted a physician confirm the ether would have no residual effects. We left Juan and Teresa after arranging for Teresa's agent to drive them home upon the doctor's release. It was getting on to eleven when we finally headed toward my place.

"I'm ready for whiskey and I'm starving," I said.

"You always get drunk after a case, don't you?"

I thought about it for a second. "If it involves death, yeah."

"Why?"

"I don't know. Probably because I just want to forget about it."

"Well, in this case, I'd say we have reason to celebrate. So, cheer up. Let's go mix some highballs and barbeque those steaks in your fridge."

I sighed, knowing a boisterous drunk would not happen. Oblivion was probably the best I could hope for.

23

WHEN WE GOT TO my house, I wheeled the barbeque from the garage onto the deck, while Cody mixed the drinks. I powered down a whiskey-seven and took a cigarette from his pack and leaned on my deck railing and watched the smoke twirl off into the darkness. I felt insentient, like I was in a dazed stupor. I always felt that way in the hours after a shooting.

I walked back inside, where Cody was clattering about in the kitchen.

"Grill hot yet?" he said, holding a plate of raw meat.

"Should be."

"You okay? You got that thousand-yard stare."

"Hold on," I said, and walked out to my truck and unlocked the box welded to the bed. Loohan's saddlebags lay atop my gear. I held the bags in my hands. It felt a little eerie possessing the property of a man who died trying to kill me.

I went back inside and dropped the bags onto the kitchen table. They were stuffed full, probably packed with clothes, I thought. I popped the snaps on one bag and pulled out two pairs of rolled-up jeans, socks, and a couple T-shirts. I opened the second bag, and beneath some more shirts was a cellophane-encased block about the size of a brick. Within the plastic, the contents were a dull green.

Outside, Cody was cooking the hell out of the steaks, smoke billowing from the barbeque like the house was on fire. I hustled over and turned the propane to low.

"Christ, come inside before someone calls the fire department," I said. "I got something to show you."

He followed me to the kitchen table, and I peeled away the plastic wrap. Bundles of money started falling out. Thick bundles, all hundreds.

"Cowabunga!" Cody opened a packet and began counting.

"Five grand," he said.

"Times sixteen," I said, the cash spread across the table.

"Yo ho ho and a bucket of piss!"

"Drug money," I said.

"Who gives a shit? It all spends the same."

I stared at bills, briefly wondering what Loohan might have done to come into possession of eighty grand. Something bloody, I assumed. Whatever it was, I hoped the knowledge of it died with him.

"Probably only cost five thousand or so to get Juan and Teresa's parents into the US," I said.

"I'm having lunch with her tomorrow, before I head back to San Jose. I'll make the arrangements."

"Maybe put a chunk in a college fund for Juan, huh?"

"I'd say the brave little dude deserves it. Did you really teach him that sleeper hold?"

"Never thought he'd use it."

"Here's to him. He may have saved our asses."

I took a big slug from my glass, and a grin took hold on my face. It felt like a long since I smiled like that, and it felt good, damn good. Some days, the world *did* seem like a better place.

Cody laughed and backhanded my shoulder. "Come on, man, let's drink."

• • •

And drink we did. When I crawled out of bed the next morning, my head was aching and my pad was littered with beer cans and an empty whiskey bottle lay shattered against the fireplace. I staggered to the refrigerator and drained a Budweiser, the can clicking against my teeth. Nothing like an ice-cold beer to start the day. Just one, I told myself, while a quiet little nudge in my chest said, just a few more, why not? When I was younger, I might have stayed on a roll for days. But now I knew better. Eventually you learn. That's how age and experience works, I guess.

After guzzling water, vitamins, and aspirin, I went to work straightening up the place, hoping to make it presentable for Candi's arrival in the afternoon. Then I fell onto the couch and slept for a while, until Cody woke me.

"Time for me to hit the road, Dirt."

I rubbed my eyes. "Thanks for your help, buddy."

He waved me off, and I walked outside with him.

"You got any plans for your share of the loot?" I asked.

He squinted out toward the lake, where the sun cast a shimmering brilliance over the water.

"Something tells me I'll spend it," he said. "Listen, I'll drive back up next week so we can watch Teresa's debut."

"Wouldn't miss it."

He started his oversize diesel rig, winked and gave me the thumbs up, then drove off, his tires humming on the pavement until he turned the corner and was gone.

When I walked back inside, my cell was ringing. Marcus Grier.

"Sleep well last night?" he asked.

"Like a goddamned baby."

"So did I, to be honest," he said, as if he was perplexed by the fact. Then he cleared his throat. "I've got an update for you, Mr. Reno. They caught the man suspected of murdering Dave Boyce and Joe Norton."

"Really?"

"Yes. Actually, caught is the wrong word. Douglas County SWAT set up a stake-out last night at Pete Saxton's house, and at two A.M. they killed an intruder. Probably the most violent shootout ever in this area. Over fifty rounds fired."

"Crazy, man. Who was the guy?"

"They think a cartel assassin from south of the border. DEA in El Paso is working on an identification."

"Is he linked to Diablos Sierra?"

"Don't know yet, but immigration agents are already heading here to look into it."

"Sounds like the local drug trade is in trouble."

"Hell, I'd settle for a quiet month or two."

"Amen to that, Sheriff."

"Is Gibbons still at your place?"

"No, he left for San Jose this morning."

"Well, there may be hope for us yet," he said, and I chuckled along with him.

24

C ANDI'S TWO-NIGHT STAY TURNED into a week, a series of lazy afternoons in bed and breezy nights out on the town. The week felt like a vacation of sorts, a stark contrast to my solitary home life. I finally conceded it was more than just sex and good company—her casual nature and quirky sense of humor brought a lightness to my life I had long been without. She made me feel like a different person, a better person. When she took off back to Elko, I offered she move in if she got the job she interviewed for at the community college.

The day after she left, Marcus Grier told me the members of the Diablos Sierra gang had been rounded up and deported, based on alleged ties to the same drug cartel believed to have sent Dave Boyce's and Joe Norton's assassin to South Lake Tahoe. All were deported, except for their leader, Rodrigo, who contacted a staph infection and died in the local hospital.

But that news was soon eclipsed by the reported disappearance of three high-ranking executives from Pistol Pete's Casino. My eyes bugged at two of the names: Vinnie Tuma, nephew to mobster Salvatore Tuma, and John Switton, who was named as legal owner of the casino. The FBI came to town to investigate and two young agents interrogated me three times at my home. *Yes, I know who Salvatore Tuma is. Yes, I know he used to own Pistol Pete's. No, never met Vinnie Tuma. Never met Vic Severino, either. Met*

John Switton twice. Seemed like somebody you wouldn't want to mess with. What else? He had a mentally disabled son who played the hell out of the drums.

And that was it. Because what else could I tell them? I had no idea what happened to the missing men. No bodies, no evidence of foul play, their homes intact as if they might show up at any moment.

The resulting void of ownership at Pistol Pete's created a huge headache for the Nevada gaming commission, as John Switton had no known heirs, other than Robert, who was also missing. Eventually, to save the casino and the jobs it provided, the operation was put up at state auction and acquired by a casino management company out of Las Vegas.

As an afterthought, I drove to Zeke's one night after the agents left my house, curious if members of HCU were still hanging around. Not only were they not there, but a white sign on the door said CLOSED UNTIL FURTHER NOTICE. A half-dozen times I called the number I had for Zak Papas, and each call went straight to voice mail.

On the same day Cody rolled back into town for Teresa's performance, Candi called to tell me she got the job and would take me up on my offer to move in.

"What's next, a couple kids?" Cody asked.

"Like the woman in Reno said, I'm not complex enough to handle parenthood."

"Who said that?"

"The one with the big fake melons, remember?"

"Oh, yeah. She's probably right. I don't think you're complex enough to handle a steady woman, either."

"Thanks for the analysis, Doctor Freud."

"Anytime."

And so on, over slow beers at Whiskey Dick's and a light dinner before heading to Pistol Pete's show hall.

The production was what I would call casual entertainment, some singing and dancing, a bit of hokey humor, the plot more a satire on spies than anything else. Then the lights went dim and Teresa came from behind the curtain, dressed in black and gold. The spotlight followed her to center stage, where she began to sing.

The hundred or so people in the audience, many who had been chatting sporadically, went dead silent. Teresa's voice filled the air with presence, the notes soaring with a clarity and fullness unlike anything I'd heard. I wanted to laugh and cry at the same time, a strange sensation.

She finished the song, and the small crowd erupted in applause.

"Damn, look at the goose bumps on my arm," Cody said.

When the show ended, we met Teresa and her manager at the casino coffee shop. Juan showed up a few minutes later, having missed his sister's performance because he was working the dinner shift at the Redwood Tavern.

"You'll have plenty more opportunities to see Teresa perform, I assure you," the manager said. A gay, clean-cut Woody Allen. "Give me a few months, I'll have this girl on stage in Vegas. And that's just the beginning."

"Teresa, you need a bodyguard to keep the paparazzi away, you know who to call," Cody said. Teresa laughed and leaned into Cody's arm, her eyes delighted.

"I want to thank you men from saving her from those horrible, devil-worshipping perverts," the manager said with a shudder.

"Give Juan credit, too," I said.

"Dan, don't forget, tomorrow nine A.M., at my school."

"Shit, is that tomorrow?"

"And he's supposed to be Mr. Organized," Cody said. "Dirt, maybe I better come along to make sure you don't stick your foot in your mouth."

"No," I said automatically, then I said it again.

"I don't think it's that bad of an idea," Juan said. "Cody, it would be great if you would come."

Oh boy.

. . .

First period, Thursday morning, South Lake High School, looking out at thirty teenagers in skinny jeans, baggy jeans, black concert Ts, braces, wristbands, various degrees of acne.

"Uh, good morning, kids. My name's Dan Reno, and this is my partner and good friend, Cody Gibbons. We're licensed private investigators and fugitive recovery agents, or bounty hunters. A career in this field could mean working for a firm, or working for yourself, as Cody and I do. If you work for yourself, in many ways it's like running a small business. You need to have an accounting system so you can bill clients and keep track, and—"

"Dan, hold on a sec," Cody interrupted. "How many of you guys out there know what a sleeper hold is? Some of you? Good. I'm not going to demonstrate because it's a very dangerous move, but it's a darn good thing Juan Perez knew how to pull it off, because just last week we had some trouble with a murderous degenerate, who Juan wrestled and knocked out cold. That's right, he did, and if not for that, I might not be here talking to you today."

"Juan did that?" said a girl, dark hair streaked with blond, blue mascara, testing the school dress code with her tanned cleavage and short jean skirt.

"That's right, hot stuff," Cody said. "The man was armed, too."

"Wow." She looked at Juan in a way that made me think he would probably soon be dealing with a new type of challenge in his life.

"Hey, Perez, way to go, dude," said another student, a big white kid. Juan smiled and blushed.

I started again. "As I was saying, from a business point of view—"

"Do you carry a gun?" a student asked.

"Yes, at times."

"Often is more like it," Cody interjected. "Let me tell you, the ability to use a firearm can mean the difference between life and death. I remember once...."

And that's the way it went. Forty-five minutes later, and the students were still clamoring for more of Cody's stories. I managed to slip in a few sentences here and there, trying to provide a little perspective on the realities of the job. But I was just boring them. Besides, Cody was a natural in front of a group, so I finally sat back and enjoyed the show. What else could I do?

EPILOUGUE

EARLY JUNE, AND I was keeping busy with a few routine jobs, a rash of shoplifting at a local supermarket, and a missing person case that resolved itself when an eighteen-year-old girl resurfaced after a week shacked up with a rock musician in a San Francisco hotel.

And, Candi had moved in.

We had just finished reorganizing a closet to accommodate her vast wardrobe (at least compared to mine), when my phone rang. It was Zak Pappas.

"I see you called me umpteen times," he said.

"It took you a month to figure that out?"

"I've been in rehab," he sighed. "No phone for thirty days."

"Oh. Sorry to hear that. Look, I was calling for a couple reasons. First, I wanted to ask you if the Hard Core United gang is still around."

"Beats me. I haven't heard from them, but I wouldn't expect to."

"All right. The other reason is I see Zeke's is closed. Is that permanent?"

"Why would you care?"

"Because it was one of the best joints in town, at least until you shut down the kitchen."

The line went quiet, and when he spoke, his voice was small with humility.

"Yeah, I screwed the pooch, okay? The shrinks tell me I wanted to get back at my old man for some shit from my childhood."

"We've all got our baggage, Zak. What are your plans now?"

"I don't know. I blew all my money, and my brother from Dallas footed the bill for my rehab. I figure I need at least twenty grand to reinstall the flooring I tore out for the mosh pit and get the dining room in shape."

"That's what you want to do? Restore Zeke's Pit to how it was before?"

"I want to get my life back on track. If I had the money, I would."

"Why not apply for a small business loan?"

"Dude, I was packing an eight-ball a day up my beak. I just about flushed my life down the crapper. No sane person would give me a loan."

"Sanity was never one of my strengths."

"What?"

"You know how to run the kitchen?"

"Hell, yes. I ran it for years. The beef brisket? That's my recipe."

"If I front you the money, are you confident you can make Zeke's like it was before the death metal bullshit?"

"If I stay clean, and I will, you bet."

"Then let's meet there and shake on it."

"Wow. You sure?"

"Why not?" I said. I needed a place to hide Jason Loohan's cash from the IRS, and the restaurant had been thriving when Zak's old man was alive. Maybe a partial ownership would even be a profitable thing over time. Sometimes you got to go with your gut. And my gut said that beef brisket was the best I'd ever had.

•   •   •

The first snow came early that fall. One day it was seventy and sunny and the next morning the sky was dark with clouds and by noon heavy flakes swirled down from the sky. Only one thing predictable about weather in the mountains—it's unpredictable. When I drove to Zeke's to work the bar for the lunch shift, two inches lay on the streets, and the pines were coated in white.

Candi came by after her last class and walked up to the bar, her high heels stepping on the peanut shells scattered over the wooden floor planks.

"Those shoes will never do for winter," I said.

"Maybe I'll just wear them in the bedroom, then."

I made her a coffee drink and we sat at the table I liked, one I'd moved onto the stage next to the front window looking out over Highway 50. Cars crunched over the snow, chains rattling, headlights on, wipers trying to keep up with the steady fall from above. We watched in silence, cozy in the heat from the wood-burning stove in the corner.

"You know what?" I said. "Time to turn on the Christmas lights."

"In October?"

I got up and hit the switches, and the bulbs laced around the trees outside came alive, the colors flashing and reflecting off the snow-covered ground.

"It's just beautiful, isn't it?" Candy said, her green eyes dancing in a kaleidoscope of red and blue. The jukebox kicked into Hank Williams Jr.'s "Family Tradition," and the twang of the fiddle brought a smile to my face.

"Hey, look at this," she said, handing me an alternative culture magazine she liked to read. "This reminds me of the guy you were describing." Her fingernail tapped on a picture of four men standing on a canted bridge over a waterway.

"Swiss Metal Band Redefines Boundaries of Genre," the caption read. I skimmed the short piece, until pausing at a comment on their drummer, a musician of "extraordinary talent and creativity" named Ernst VanHinkel.

Except the man in the picture was Rabbit Switton.

• • •

I never drew any conclusions as to the fate of the missing mobsters from Pistol Pete's, other than a fair certainty they were dead. I also never gained any insight regarding the role of John Switton, other than to assume he had fled the country and was living incognito overseas. I did find out, though, that Salvatore Tuma's New Jersey home had been raided by the Feds, and he was under incitement for a number of RICO charges.

As for my own life, I stay happy on a daily basis, and why the hell not? My house among the tall pines and granite faces is cheerful with a woman's touch, and I'm thankful every day for that. Damn thankful, because change is as inevitable as the turning of the season. That evil might again invade my life I have little doubt, but I never invest myself in that thought. That keeps me sane I suppose, or as close as I'll get.

ABOUT THE AUTHOR

Born in Detroit, Michigan, in 1960, Dave Stanton moved to Northern California in 1961. He attended San Jose State University and received a BA in journalism in 1983. Over the years, he worked as a bartender, newspaper advertising salesman, furniture mover, pizza cook, debt collector, and technology salesman. He has two children, Austin and Haley. He and his wife, Heidi, live in San Jose, California.

Stanton is the author of five novels, all featuring private investigator Dan Reno and his ex-cop buddy, Cody Gibbons.

To learn more, visit the author's website at

http://danrenonovels.com/

If you enjoyed *Speed Metal Blues*, please don't hesitate to leave a review at

http://amzn.to/YHsimN

To contact Dave Stanton or subscribe to his newsletter, go to:

http://danrenonovels.com/contact/

More Dan Reno Novels:

STATELINE

Cancel the wedding–the groom is dead.

When a tycoon's son is murdered the night before his wedding, the enraged and grief-stricken father offers investigator Dan Reno (that's *Reno*, as in *no problemo)*, a life-changing bounty to find the killer. Reno, nearly broke, figures he's finally landed in the right place at the right time. It's a nice thought, but when a band of crooked cops get involved, Reno finds himself not only earning every penny of his paycheck, but also fighting for his life.

Who committed the murder, and why? And what of the dark sexual deviations that keep surfacing? Haunted by his murdered father and a violent, hard drinking past, Reno wants no more blood on his hands. But a man's got to make a living, and backing off is not in his DNA. Traversing the snowy alpine winter in the Sierras and the lonely deserts of Nevada, Reno must revert to his old ways to survive. Because the fat bounty won't do him much good if he's dead…

Dying for the Highlife

Jimmy Homestead's glory days as a high school stud were a distant memory. His adulthood had amounted to little more than temporary jobs, cheap boarding houses, and discount whiskey. But he always felt he was special, and winning a $43 million lottery proved it.

With all that money, everything is great for Jimmy—until people from his past start coming out of the woodwork. First, his sexy stepmother, who seduced him as a teenager. Then his uncle, just released from Folsom after a five-year jolt for securities fraud, a crime that bankrupted Jimmy's father. Mix in a broke ex-stripper and a down-on-his luck drug dealer, both seeking payback over transgressions Jimmy thought were long forgotten.

Caught in the middle are investigator Dan Reno and his good buddy Cody Gibbons, two guys just trying to make an honest paycheck. Reno, straining to keep his home out of foreclosure, thinks that's his biggest problem. But his priorities change when Gibbons and Jimmy are kidnapped by a gang of cartel thugs out for a big score. Fighting to save his friend's life, Reno is drawn into a mess that leaves dead bodies scattered all over northern Nevada.

Coming in 2015:

DARK ICE

HARD PREJUDICE

Made in the USA
San Bernardino, CA
07 September 2016